SUPERHUMAN ENEMIES

"You have not found the three missing air carriers?" the Elder asked the two Young Ones as the Irish Sea crashed against their tiny rock island.

One replied, "No, sir. Perhaps Foster and the other meddlers who projected into this time from their own backward era have taken the carriers."

The Elder thundered, "Don't be foolish, Young One. The meddlers lack the brain capacity to understand our weapons." Then the ancient being considered for a moment. "But if you are right, we will have to take action against them."

"What sort of action, sir?" asked the other Younger One.

"Termination . . ."

Ø **SIGNET**
(0451)

ROBERT ADAMS' CASTAWAYS IN TIME

☐ **CASTAWAYS IN TIME by Robert Adams.** It was a storm to end all storms, but when the clouds finally cleared, Bass Foster and his five unexpected house guests find they are no longer in twentieth-century America. Instead, they are thrust into a bloody English past never written about in any history books. . . . (140990—$2.95)

☐ **CASTAWAYS IN TIME #2. THE SEVEN MAGICAL JEWELS OF IRELAND by Robert Adams.** Drawn through a hole in time, twentieth-century American Bass Foster finds himself hailed as a noble warrior and chosen to command King Arthur's army. Now Bass must face the menace of an unknown enemy that seeks, not only to overthrow Arthur's kingdom, but to conquer and enslave the whole world. (133404—$2.95)

☐ **CASTAWAYS IN TIME #5. OF MYTHS AND MONSTERS by Robert Adams.** As Bass Foster's fellow castaways in time struggled to save Indian tribes from Spanish invaders, it was only natural that they use the advance technology that had been left by travelers from a future beyond their own, but what awaited them was a horror even modern weapons of war might not be able to defeat. . . . (157222—$3.95)

☐ **CASTAWAYS IN TIME #6: OF BEGINNINGS AND ENDINGS by Robert Adams.** This time Bass Foster and his fellow castaways have attracted the attention of mysterious, awesomely powerful beings who might bring the world tremendous benefit—or destroy it with terrifying force. Hidden enemies are tracking their every move, scheming unspeakable dangers to lay in their path. . . . (159721—$3.95)

Buy them at your local bookstore or use this convenient coupon for ordering.

NEW AMERICAN LIBRARY
P.O. Box 999, Bergenfield, New Jersey 07621

Please send me the books I have checked above. I am enclosing $_____
(please add $1.00 to this order to cover postage and handling). Send check or money order—no cash or C.O.D.'s. Prices and numbers are subject to change without notice.

Name_____

Address_____

City _____ State _____ Zip Code _____
Allow 4-6 weeks for delivery.
This offer, prices and numbers are subject to change without notice.

CASTAWAYS IN TIME #6

ROBERT ADAMS
OF
BEGINNINGS AND ENDINGS

A SIGNET BOOK

NEW AMERICAN LIBRARY

PUBLISHED BY
PENGUIN BOOKS CANADA LIMITED

NAL BOOKS ARE AVAILABLE AT QUANTITY DISCOUNTS WHEN USED TO
PROMOTE PRODUCTS OR SERVICES. FOR INFORMATION PLEASE WRITE
TO PREMIUM MARKETING DIVISION, NEW AMERICAN LIBRARY, 1633
BROADWAY, NEW YORK, NEW YORK 10019.

Copyright © 1989 by Robert Adams

All rights reserved

First Printing, May, 1989

2 3 4 5 6 7 8 9
SIGNET TRADEMARK REG U.S PAT OFF AND FOREIGN COUNTRIES
REGISTERED TRADEMARK   MARCA REGISTRADA
HECHO EN WINNIPEG. CANADA

SIGNET, SIGNET CLASSIC, MENTOR, ONYX, PLUME,
MERIDIAN and NAL BOOKS are published in Canada by Penguin
Books Canada Limited, 2801 John Street, Markham, Ontario,
L3R 1B4
PRINTED IN CANADA
COVER PRINTED IN U S A

Dedicated to the memory of the late Fritz Goetz, rifleman and friend.

Wind howled and wailed about the stone walls and lofty spires of ancient Eboracum—once called Jorvik, now called York. The day preceding had been as bright and sunny and balmy as a summer's day might be, but in the night this toothed storm had blown in from Thule by way of the North Sea, temperatures in the environs of the episcopal city had dropped precipitately, and so much water had been dumped, that the streets had begun, by wan daybreak, to run as swiftly if not as deep as the current of the river.

Within the complex of buildings which constituted Yorkminster, in a sizable chamber which still seemed cramped and cluttered due to the high shelves packed with jars, caskets, boxes, amphorae, vials, flasks, bowls, trays, kettles, small caldrons, bags and cases of a plethora of sizes, shapes and descriptions, a cowled and robed man sat before a heavy, slate-topped table. Deep in thought, he occasionally roused himself sufficiently to scribble notes and reminders to himself with a quill on a sheet of fine vellum.

Wool clothing lined with silk, old-fashioned trunkhose, and ankle-high shoon of quilted doeskin were not enough to keep the chill from his old bones this dank, dismal day, so he had had a fire laid and lit on the hearth and also had fired a small brass brazier nearby on the tabletop over which to warm his hands from time to time.

And old his bones truly were, this man now called His Grace Harold, Archbishop of York. A new-come stranger, knowing nothing of him, would have seen the high-ranking churchman and probably have guessed his age to be about late sixties or early seventies—venerable enough for these times in which most men, even those of noble and exalted rank, considered themselves fortunate, lucky, and blessed by God to see fifty winters—and that stranger would have been wrong, very, very wrong. In the natural, the expected order of things, creatures are born in their present and live on into a future until their demise; this old man, however, was come into this world he presently occupied not only full-grown but more than a half-century old—although, due to an artificially produced longevity drug he had, he then looked no more than thirty to forty years of age.

Born in A.D. 1968, Harold Kenmore had been employed as a research scientist in a government-sponsored and -operated project in a facility called Gamebird by the middle of the third decade of the twenty-first century. More than a decade earlier, he had been one of the members of the team of scientists which had at last developed a means to retard the effects of aging of the human body. Therefore he ranked quite high in his profession and even owned the grudging respect and regard of the military bureaucrats in charge of the Gamebird Facility.

Part of the work of the Gamebird Project was the attempt to find or develop a means of time travel; previous generations had so far depleted that world of fuels and raw materials that even the vast expenses of the possibly impossible would be considered justified if said expenditures would only result in an avenue whereby the virgin resources of past times might be plundered to the benefit of the impoverished present.*

A decade and a half of work resulted in a device that, while expending horrendous amounts of precious energy, would project inanimate objects somewhere out of sight and retrieve most of them undamaged. However, living animals all seemed to come back dead, many of them terribly mutilated and/or decomposing as well. Even so, so critical were the needs for fossil fuels and certain ores become that the government brought inexorable pressure to bear on the project directors so that, against their better and more informed judgment, a series of human experiments were then commenced.

The first man projected was dead when retrieved, but thorough examination of his corpse and clothing established that he had been in thirteenth-century France or, possibly, Savoy. Therefore, the second human volunteer had been steeped in mediaeval Romance languages, garbed in recreated thirteenth-century European attire, and projected. His body, hideously maimed and dead, had been near-naked when retrieved, with a piece of parchment nailed to its forehead with a legend stating in Low Latin, "I am a dead spy."

For all that a tight lid of secrecy had existed from the very beginning and had been screwed down even more tightly as the human experiments had progressed, still word of the disasters had gotten out somehow, and volunteers of the proper calibers had become virtually nonexistent. But the governmental pressure had not slacked off at all, and so, when one of the most promising of the younger scientists, Dr. Lenny Vincenzo, had volunteered to be the third projectee, the project directors had felt that they had

* Read *Castaways in Time* #1, Signet Books, 1982

to accept him, had to use him, had to make the sacrifice and send him to his virtually certain death.

A real prodigy, holding, despite his youth, several advanced degrees, Dr. Vincenzo had not required as much preliminary hypno-education as had either of his ill-fated predecessors, which fact had allowed them to move faster—though not nearly so fast as the impatient government might have wished.

After a retrieval device had been surgically implanted under the skin of one thigh, Vincenzo had been, at his request, dressed in late-fifteenth-century clothing, provided with reproductions of period coins in copper, brass, silver, and gold, then projected. He had never been retrieved. *A* rotting cadaver, the retrieval nodule properly placed under the sloughing skin of one thigh, had indeed arrived back at Gamebird, lacking head, hands, feet, and external sexual organs . . . but it had not been the body of Dr. Lenny Vincenzo; the blood type and a host of other tests had proved that. And since, without the nodule on which the equipment in the lab could home in, there was no way of trying again to retrieve the young man, he was completely lost somewhere in past time.

The project director, still under unbearable pressure from the increasingly threatening government, realizing the young man's irretrievable loss and suffering deep pangs of guilt over his part in so dooming him, had suicided, publicly and very messily. He had been replaced by a Dr. Jane Stone, who, in addition to holding scientific degrees commensurate to the position, was a lieutenant colonel in the government security service.

Within his own lifetime, Dr. Harold Kenmore had seen his country of birth change from a republic ruled over by popularly elected representatives to a dictatorship in all but name—tightly regimented, savagely policed; even the most intimate aspects of

every citizen's life were spied upon, lest the unhappy, deprived, and brutally downtrodden people
rise in revolt against the family dynasty which had
stolen away their freedoms and the country. Therefore, despite his relatively privileged status, Kenmore was not at all happy with his present life, there
and then . . . nor had he been the only such man on
the project.

Dr. Emmett O'Malley had been another such.
Younger than Kenmore and so not really remember-
ing the United States of America that once had been,
he still knew of the experiences of friends and even
relatives who had suffered cruelly at the callous
hands of the dictatorship's minions and therefore had
become willing to risk as much as his life to escape.

A third of this water had been Dr. Lenny Vincenzo, and no matter what others in the project or
the government might wonder or guess or suppose
or suspect, Kenmore and O'Malley *knew*. Their true,
though short-term, friend and colleague Leonard
David Vincenzo had not only escaped, he had used
the Gamebird Project and the dwindling energy supplies of the hellish government itself to speed him
on his way to freedom. Even thinking of what the
brave, desperate young scientist had done was a
heady experience for Kenmore and O'Malley.

However, subsequent to the loss of Vincenzo and
the suicide of the responsible director, his successor
had suspended human-type projections, though still
sporadically experimenting with certain attempts to
reverse the activity of the equipment and bring things
from past to present, skipping from year to year,
century to century, geographical location to geographical location; the success of her experiments
had been spotty at best.

But hope springs eternal in the human breast. Des-
perately certain that somehow, someway, sometime
they could and would find or make a way to gain

access to the locked and guarded facility, learn how to operate the requisite devices, and thus project themselves to a somewhere, sometime that they could not imagine could possibly be worse than life under the existing regime, the two conspirators took up the study of history. After some time, they at length agreed upon northwestern Europe in the second half of the fifteenth century. This done, they began studying books, tapes, and period maps and began to use the easily available hypnostudy system to acquire languages and skills of various archaic sorts, passing off their interests and courses of study as just harmless hobbies.

Meanwhile, being very careful, fully realizing the deadly danger of it all, Dr. Emmett O'Malley—young-looking (the longevity process having more or less frozen his age at mid-twenties), handsome, with a well-developed gift of the blarney—entered into a sexual liaison with Colonel Dr. Jane Stone, thereby eventually gaining access to the projection labs and knowledge of the equipment therein contained.

In addition to using his own lab to surreptitiously compound longevity booster capsules disguised as headache remedy and taken a few at the time back to his quarters, there to be hidden away, Harold Kenmore had hypnotrained himself in antique jewelry-making methods, signed out on loan a quantity of bulk gold, silver, and copper, and set up a small workshop in a corner of his bedroom. There he actually had made some jewelry, and those who saw it had praised his skills, but he had also cast the precious metals into coin shapes and into plain finger rings of varying weights. He also had hypnoed a course in costume design and had fabricated complete sets of clothing to his and Emmett's measures in fashions of the times they were contemplating.

One of Emmett's degrees was in the field of ferrous metallurgy, and to this he added hypnocourses in depth and breadth, seeking and at last developing a way to fabricate superior steel from crude pig iron and certain common elements under very primitive conditions. He had proved this theory by fashioning two broadswords and a brace of daggers, plus several smaller knives.

From the very outset of the preparations for their private scheme, their forlorn hope of escape from the hateful, hate-filled madhouse of their world, the two men had seemingly become fanatics in the category of physical exercises of all sorts, and so few if any of their peers and keepers considered it odd that they at last took up fencing, too, proceeding— aided, of course, by hypnostudy—from footwork to foil, then épée, then saber. At length, they began to fence with the broadswords; in the beginning of this, they used these weapons alone, and as they became more adept at handling the heavy, ill-balanced blades, they began to try fencing Florentine, with a dagger in the left hand.

All these disciplines, manufactures, and studies took time, of course, sandwiched in as they perforce were between the necessities of work, the Gamebird routines of endless meetings, conferences, evaluations, and the like, not to mention the time necessarily consumed by Emmett's torrid affair with Colonel Dr. Jane Stone. It took time, years passed, but then Harold and Emmett had the time, for their longevity-treated bodies aged only minutes while those not so treated aged days and weeks. Lenny Vincenzo had been gone from their world for almost five years before the two men decided that the time at last was ripe for their escape to they knew not what.

Over the years of increasingly harsh and regimented dictatorship, most once-honored holidays of all natures had been abolished and the average worker labored six-day, seventy-two-hour weeks, week after week, for twelve months of every year, paid less and ever less real income, the purchasing power of which at the best proved never enough to buy the needed amounts of the increasingly scarce and dear necessities of life. Not even the slightest surcease was available. Use of tobacco was illegal. Though rigorously discouraged and under constant surveillance, religious practice was allowed on one day each work week. Uses of alcohol, hallucinogenics, or narcotics invariably brought lengthy stays in government labor and reeducation camps if used other than under a physician's orders or, preferably, his direct supervision. Those adjudged insane or unable to work due to injury or physical impairment were killed. Only the elite—bureaucrats, military, higher echelons of police and overlapping internal intelligence departments, valued people sequestered away in certain government research projects such as Gamebird, or a very few others—were allowed to lead lives of anything save endless drudgery, malnourishment if not outright starvation, hopelessness, and unceasing terror.

However, within a five-day period—the last two days of an outgoing year and the first three days of the incoming one—designated the President's Birthday Celebration, most if not all strictures were eased nationwide. Government outlets gave away not only free foodstuffs to all comers, but tobacco, spirits of many sorts, items of footwear and clothing, and even supplies of hallucinogens. During these wild Days, public appearances in chemically altered states not only went unpunished but were aggressively encouraged. Travel, normally very much restricted, not only was eased during these Days but was free to those with proof of family elsewhere in the country if the round trip could be accomplished before the Days had ended. Many, drunk or spacey, went forth and about in odd attire or none at all, unnoticed and

unremarked by any. There were always some killings
and other violence during the Days, but usually the
then-short-handed police ignored the smaller in-
stances of violence—though they were always quick
to put down mobs by deadly methods. The bodies,
however slain, were just collected and delivered to
the nearest rendering plant.

At the Gamebird Project, on the banks of the Po-
tomac River, as at all the other projects run by the
government, the resident workers were, though comparatively lavishly provided for and kept in luxury,
sequestered, not allowed to leave the complex and
grounds save in supervised groups for very necessary field trips or visits to their superiors elsewhere.
Their families, if they had them, were supported and
housed, but their only contacts with them through
the year long were in the forms of letters (always
and thoroughly censored, incoming and outgoing),
videotapes (ditto) and the exceedingly rare vision-
phone call. The Days represented the only chance
available to the sequestered men and women for
physical contact with their loved ones, and those with
families invariably took advantage of the opportunity, knowing that their transportation would be assured and first-class. For this reason, the population
of Gamebird during the Days dropped drastically;
and for most who did stay on at the Project, there
was no work and almost unlimited license. Travel
about the various sectors of the vast complex, usually strictly forbidden without necessity and author-
ization from some lofty source, was permitted, while
obvious drunkenness and odd behavior was expected.

For these many reasons, Harold Kenmore and
Emmett O'Malley had felt that their best, indeed
their only decent, chance to carry out their escape
scheme would be upon one of the Days. Over their
shirts and trunkhose, they had donned the coveralls

issued them for outside work in cold or wet weather, filling the cargo pockets of these with precious metals, longevity-booster capsules, food concentrates, and other small items. Their parka pockets were likewise crammed full, then they slung on their baldrics, buckled their dagger-belts and slung their cloaks over all. They slipped their sheathed broadswords into place in the baldrics, rinsed out their mouths with grain alcohol, and splashed the rest of the stuff over their clothing before setting out from their quarters—arm in arm, singing a lewd song, and clutching a half-empty liquor bottle.

Descending to the lowest level of their part of the complex, they found the guard cubicle completely untenanted, so they just boarded one of the small electric rail cars and let it take them through the tunnel under the width of the river and into the lowest level of the southern segment of the Gamebird Project, wherein was located the experimental time-travel facility.

In the southern terminal, the guard cubicle was tenanted, but all three of the guards therein were snoring—one in a chair, two on the floor. Bottles in various stages of emptiness were scattered about the cubicle, and a pungent smell of burning rope hung thickly in the air. Emmett casually helped himself to the key to the lift, and the two scientists ascended swiftly to the level they sought, a little shocked at the ease of it all.

But that had all ended at the door to the facility itself. The guard on duty there had not been asleep or drunk or other than fully awake and alert. However, he had known Emmett by sight, had been aware of the man's relationship with the director, and had stayed unsuspicious long enough for Emmett to get in sufficiently close to deprive him quietly of consciousness.

Using the entry card his high-ranking sometime

lover had given him, Emmett had let them into the huge room and, after positioning Harold on a silvery, circular plate set in the floor, he had raced about the room, going from one bulky device to the next one, pushing buttons, pulling levers, turning dials, and scrutinizing displays. At length, he had wheeled over a metal-covered console about four feet high by two feet or so square, centered it on the silvery disk, and begun to plug its thick cable into a larger device nearby, while Harold gazed blankly at the jungle of dials, knobs, buttons, gauges, and small levers of varying colors and sizes which covered the top surface.

Dr. Emmett O'Malley returned to stand beside Kenmore on the disk, and his big, freckled hands moved quickly and surely over the controls. A deep hum that seemed to come from everywhere and from nowhere had begun sometime while O'Malley had been back among the banks of devices and was increasing swiftly in loudness, even as a blue-green glow that did not seem to have a visible source became brighter and greener all about the chamber.

At almost the last moment in that world, Col. Dr. Jane Stone had appeared from out of the shadows, leveling at them a sonic weapon which could have been their deaths save that Emmett had preset the device to project them immediately, sufficient power had been achieved, and they had winked out of the furious woman's world even as her finger had tightened on the trigger.

The two escapees had arrived not in the past of their own world but in that of a parallel one, or so Harold Kenmore had come to believe after much study and the passing of many years. They had come to earth literally, arriving on the packed-earth floor of the lowest level of a stone defensive tower near to the bloody border between the kingdoms of England and Scotland. They had come early in the reign of

King Henry VII Tudor, A.D. 1486 or 1487, in winter as in their own world, and soon after a party of Lowland Scot rievers had captured the first floor of that tower. A party of these ruffians were even at the moment of the scientists' coming in the process of brutally torturing and maiming an already wounded man in hopes that his screams of agony would bring down the remainder of the garrison from the floors above.

Infuriated by what they witnessed being done to the captive by the savage captors, Harold and Kenmore had used twenty-first-century weapons—heat-stunners, projectors which made use of sonics to cause conflagration or bring unconsciousness, depending entirely on the setting—to not only eliminate the torturers, but send the entire force of rievers spurring hard back toward Scotland, screaming mindlessly or praying, terrified at the sight of the two green-glowing man-shaped demons who had appeared from nowhere.

The tortured man, who had been lord of this place called Whyffler Hall—then an old-fashioned motte-and-bailey residence-fortification, though with a stone tower and a stockaded bailey—had died under his torture, and his widow, heirs, and retainers had assumed the two fortuitously arrived newcomers to be at least gentlemen due to the richness of their attire and the fine swords they bore and could use so well. And in those times it was well to have the strong arms and sharp blades of any fighters available, for the Lowlands to the north were all aboil and the border was all aflame from end to end.

In some hidden glen of the Highlands, a dark religion had been born, and had grown horrifically among the wild clansmen. Although its practitioners presumably had once been good, decent Christian folk and, indeed, still carried some of the hallmarks of the Faith—most notably, the Celtic Cross—their new and savage beliefs bore no relation to the worship of Christ or to that of any of the old pagan gods, either; for all that they called themselves Balderites, they did not reverence that pagan Norse deity, but rather a One who was female, had no name, and was referred to as Mother of All or, simply, the Mother.

And a singularly bloodthirsty mother she was, demanding of her followers no less than every drop of the blood of every man, woman, and child who did not immediately rush to join her minions when first they heard of her. In her name, declared her priests and her priestesses, all previous allegiances, all oaths and bonds of service and fealty were declared void; not even ties of kinship were or could be stronger than obedience to her murderous dictates. In her name, not even matricide, parricide, fratricide, sororicide, filicide, mariticide, or other murders of near and distant kindred were wrong so long as these victims did not revere her.

Worse, the gory, lunatic religion had spread like wildfire even among the close-knit, interrelated Highland clans, tearing many apart and almost exterminating others in the fierce internecine fighting. Though many a Highland chief was slain, few of them or their immediate families became Balderites, but a few did, and under their wily, war-wise leadership, the hordes of blood-mad, ill-armed, but murderously determined men and women of the new religion swept over the hills and through the glens, killing, killing, ceaselessly killing. They slew the low and the high, male and female, withered ancients and suckling babes. The terrifying word of them flew before them, and the strong and able either fled or took to their keeps or mottes or fortified steadings with all their retainers, kindred, and kine, while the weak and helpless rushed to join immediately they came in proximity to the red-handed worshipers of the Mother.

Despite their numbers, few of these Highland Balderites were in any way well armed, and they lacked cannon or even more primitive siege-engines of any description, so if any keep, hold, motte, or steading could withstand their initial attack, could beat back the horde with casualties, the Balderites were as likely as not to move on in search of more helpless prey. Those Highland folk who survived their furious rush southward did so in one of three ways: by being swift, by being strong and determined, or by joining them. All others died, their lifeblood going to soak the ground and help to appease the insatiable bloodthirst of the Mother of All.

By then in their thousands, the horde of fanatics swept against, lapped about the walls of Edinburgh itself, but fewer left than had arrived, so they did not long remain. However, their numbers were swelled in the Lowlands. The Chief of Grant brought all his kin and clansfolk to become Balderites; so too did the chiefs of Kerr, Hay, MacAdam, Kennedy, and not a few smaller clans and septs.

From behind the stout walls of Edinburgh, the King of Scotland called upon his earls to raise an army, sent words of warning to the English border lords, and prayed speedy assistance against this heathen menace from everyone of whom he and his council could think—King Henry of England and Wales, *Ard-Righ* Brian VI of Ireland and all the other *righs* of that island, the Regulus of the Isles (which domain was just then in one of its phases of not being an actual part of the Kingdom of Scotland), the King of France, the King of Burgundy, the Holy Roman Emperor, the King of Aragon and Leon, the Caliph of Granada, the Grand Duke of Portugal, and the King of Denmark and Norway. He even dispatched a letter to Rome beseeching that a Crusade be preached against the Balderites. Then he hunkered down to await developments and troops.

While he crouched there, powerless to do aught but hold the walled capital without the aid of the earls and other magnates of the feudal kingdom, the Kennedy Clan and its septs, all fiery with the zeal of new converts, not only sent boatloads of slavering Balderites to carry the message of the Mother to the folk of Northern Ireland, but made so bold as to launch seaborne attacks against the islands and coastal lands held by the Clan MacLean and the Regulus of the Isles and that virtual if unnamed king's many dependent clans.

In the Irish Kingdom of Ulaid, already racked by civil war, the Balderites were able to establish at least a foothold, but the grim Northern Ui Neills to the west of them lined their rocky coastline with poles bearing Balderite heads, stakes on which rotted impaled Balderite bodies, and frames whereon were stretched flayed skins of Balderites.

The Regulus, Iain, already in cold fury against the Balderites because of the losses they had cost him in his mainland holdings, especially in the Inverness country, called upon his vassals at Lewis, Skye, and Uist for their famous, infamous, dreaded Scots-Dane axemen—those professional mankillers known in Ireland as *galloglaiches*—and remorselessly held his own at Islay against the Kennedys and the rest while he awaited the arrival of enough force to counterattack.

Meanwhile, guided by veteran rievers of Clans Grant, Armstrong, Kerr, and Hay, mobs of Balderites were religiously butchering both across the length and width of the Scottish Lowlands and pressing over the border into England. It had been one such group, that one just then being led by the very Chief of Grant, which had been sent off in shrieking terror by Drs. Harold Kenmore and Emmett O'Malley.

That had not been the first Balderite incursion

against Whyffler Hall, nor was it the last. Occasionally reinforced by trickles of harried survivors of other Balderite raids, the two twenty-first-century men and the Whyffler family and their retainers continued to hold the hall and its nearer environs for almost two more years before the new king, Henry VII Tudor, led his host north to the beleaguered border lands, scoured them clean of the Celtic hordes, then crossed the border to join with the combined forces of the Scottish earls near Edinburgh.

The pleas of the King of Scotland had been heeded. In Rome, the then-Pope had sent word to his bishops to preach a holy crusade against these savage pagans in Scotland, and even as King Henry's English-Welsh-Norman-Breton-Angevin host marched toward Edinburgh, ships were landing parties of crusaders along the east coast—descendants of Vikings from the Kingdom of Denmark-Norway, Goths from Sweden, Frisians and Flemings, Burgundians, French, Leonese, Portuguese, Granadans, fighting men representing most of the small states that made up the Holy Roman Empire, a few Switzers, some Italians of various kinds, Castilians, Navarrese, Moors, and even a few scarred, black-skinned noble knights of the Kingdom of Ghana.

For all the awesome forces at their command, nonetheless, the two royal allies did not anticipate either a quick or an easily won victory, for they now faced an aggregation of fanatics who, while they might retreat before superior force, had never been known to yield or surrender under even pain of instant death for themselves or loved ones. By that point in time, the survivors of the rampage down from the Highlands—birthplace of the murderous heresy—now were not only well armed but were become veteran warriors—younger and elder, men and women. They were well supplied in all save gunpowder and the priests' powder necessary to its fabrication, and, thanks principally to the conversions of some of the Lowlander chiefs, they now held some castles and strongpoints around which they could rally in the face of attack.

When the king sent word galloping through all England and Wales, through too all his royal possessions on the continent, for more men, more supplies and sinews of warfare, the Widow of Whyffler Hall designated her stalwarts, her two most trusted and provenly courageous gentlemen, to lead her small contingent to answer the summons of her sovereign; and so did Harold Kenmore and Emmett O'Malley find themselves riding at the head of a force of some sixty-odd men—fourteen lances, as the folk figured in those days—all of them wearing white surplices over their clothing, to join the royal crusading armies gathering just southwest of Edinburgh.

A particularly powerful gust of the icy-toothed arctic wind sent big drops of rain rattling against the leaded-glass panes of window of the archbishop's alchemical laboratory with a sound almost as loud as that of arquebus balls showering in volleys upon stoneworks. Lifting his quill for a moment, the old man turned his head to look at the dull-grey nothingness beyond those panes, then resumed his scribbling of notes on the sheet of vellum. He well knew that his memory was not all that it once had been, and he wanted to be certain that every thought and nuance would be adequately covered in the letter that he shortly must begin to compose—compose personally, not leave to the offices of even his most trusty secretary or clerk—to be sent to Cardinals Sicola and D'Este of the Italian Faction in Rome.

Although their physical appearances had changed very little, of course, the two men who led the Whyffler Hall retainers across the border and north into Lowland Scotland in the damp of late-spring A.D. 1489 were drastically changed by their two years of life in a sporadically embattled fortified residence. They had been deadly swordsmen to begin, but now they were become as well accomplished horsemen and more than accomplished also in the uses of spear, axe, mace, crossbow, and various primitive firearms, along with the proper laying of bombards and other engines of defensive siegecraft.

Both now went bearded and wore clothing but little better than that of those who followed them, the clothing in which they had arrived having finally fallen apart of long and strenuous usage. Knowing full well the incipient dangers into which they rode, the peril that might lie between them and the royal camp to the northeast, all rode at least partially armed, weapons ready and slow-matches all lit and smoking, only the heavier pieces of defensive armor left off . . . though slung within easy reach at all times. True, they had no fear of ordinary bandits, for none such silly enough to attack a force of fourteen lances existed alive, but stray bands of Balderites had been known to do or try some very irrational things, like all fanatics who own little or no fear of death.

They had not been able to plan any sort of direct route to the gathering of hosts, for across any such they had contemplated there always lay the lands of one of the Balderite clans—Armstrong, Kerr, Hay, the southeastern Gordons, and eke some of the Murrays. Finally, after the intercession of Lowland Scots relatives of the Widow of Whyffler Hall, it had been arranged for the Whyffler Hall lancers to cross into Eliott lands, join the smaller Eliott contingent of clansmen, then proceed to the town of Hawick-on-Tweed, where they would fall in with the forces of Clans Douglas, Scott, Stuart and Johnstone; then the combined force would march or fight their way to Edinburgh.

As the basically peace-loving Harold Kenmore had feared and the increasingly fire-eating Emmett O'Malley had hoped, the procession of the combined force from Hawick was one skirmish or fight or small battle after another for most of the way, but they were to find in the end that, hard and bloody as had been their hotly contested passage, other English, Welsh, and Lowland contingents as had come by land routes had suffered as much or more, shed as much or more blood in reaching Edinburgh. But reach that great gathering the most of them at last did.

Artair Dubh, Tanist of Douglas, who had been chosen overall leader of the contingent, had commended both of the English gentlemen from Whyffler Hall in most glowing terms when he had turned them and their force over to their erstwhile overlord, His Grace Sir Humbert Howard, Duke of Northumbria. His Grace had well known just what the lavish praise of so famous and ferocious a fighter as Sir Artair Dubh of Douglas meant and had mentally marked both men as types who would bear watching in the coming campaign. True, he was unfamiliar with any family called Kenmoor and what of it, but both were patently gentlemen, and any Irish gentleman, such as this Ui Maille, could be nothing if not a fighter or a priest; the gentry of that island produced only the two kinds.

Less than a week after their party's arrival, there had been a stir in camp, great rejoicing and feasting, when, down from the Highlands, the great host of the Clan Chattan Confederation had come, their Captain, the Mackintosh, bearing in his baggage a cask of brine containing the heads of the Balderite Chief of Grant and his three sons.

The kings shortly announced that between the earls and the most powerful clans—MacKay, Sutherland, and MacKensie to the north, Cameron, Campbell, Chattan, Gordon, and Drummond to the south—the brutalized Highlands now had been scoured virtually clean of the bloodthirsty heretics who called themselves Balderites. Now God's will must be done as thoroughly in the Lowlands and wherever else the bestial pagan killers might be found by the fine, God-fearing, Christian fighting men here gathered.

And done it was, messily, very bloodily, exceedingly brutally, and very thoroughly. Those who had killed so mercilessly could not hope for quarter or mercy of any kind; they knew it and fought to the very death in most cases. Those few unfortunates so very unlucky as to be taken alive invariably were, after interrogations by clerics and laity, subjected to deaths by exquisite and inhumanly prolonged torments, these exercises performed publicly, that as many Crusaders as possible might see, hear, enjoy, and exult in the entertainments.

The continuing arrivals of Crusaders from oversea and trickles of Highlanders from the north gave the two kings more men than they really had need for, so at any strongpoint the Balderites chose to hold, they were simply invested by sufficient force while the bulk of the army marched on westward, deliberately herding their mobile foes in the direction of the Clan Kennedy lands and the sea.

Although the Regulus of the Isles had contributed no forces to the host of the two kings directly, he had given aid to both the Campbells and the MacLeans in their Highland battlings against the Balderites, then commenced to prowl the islands and the sea, up firths and rivers, his galleys packed with grim axemen out of Lewes, Uist, and Barra, with equally grim and unforgiving MacLeods, MacDonnells, Mackinnons, MacFies, MacDonalds, and eke a few Appin Stewarts.

The galleys and ships landed enough men on Arran to raise two sieges, then joined with the formerly besieged Hamiltons to drive into the sea or slay every Balderite on that island. The galleys nibbled hard at the coasts of Kennedy lands, raiding, looting, burning, killing, raping, destroying standing crops, and slaying all kine they did not bear away. All communication between the Balderites now established in the northerly portions of the Irish Kingdom of Ulaid ceased as ships and boats from Kennedy, if not taken or sunk in very sight of land, just never returned, nor did so much as one friendly curragh, boat, ship, or galley land anywhere upon their interdicted coastline.

At last, Eideard Kennedy, chief of that ilk, had dispatched a small boat bearing a herald and a message for the Regulus. Two days later, a galley towed that boat close enough that the tide might bear it into shore. The severed and mutilated heads of its crew of oarsmen were stuck or hung to the gunwales of the blood-smeared craft and the naked, incomplete body of the herald stood impaled upon the sharpened stump of the mast, its flesh still warm to the touch; a *cour bouilli* tube hung from the herald's neck had contained a brusque message: "The Regulus of the Isles, Sheriff of Inverness, and always a most pious Servant of Our Lord Jesus Christ, will have no dealings with honorless, foresworn pagan heretics who delight in the butchery of women and children. There can be no terms, no hope of quarter. If the hellspawn who styles himself Eideard Ceannaideach of that sorry ilk cravenly renders up his sword to the Regulus, he will be afforded the protracted dog's death his infamy has earned him, and if the Regulus has not the joy of hearing the death-screams of this heretical thing, then most assuredly the King of Scots will."

Even while the host of the two kings moved inexorably westward, their outriders having already come within sight of Loch Doon on the eastern border of Clan Kennedy lands, a coalition of smaller, individually weaker neighboring clans who had never succumbed despite all their sufferings to the Balderites assaulted and conquered first Park Castle, in the lands of the Western Hays, then formidable Castle Kennedy itself. As they began to push up northward into the heart of Kennedy lands, driving before them any and all Balderites they could not catch and slay, the Regulus mounted assaults upon all five of the coastal castles with a fleet now augmented by bottoms out of Campbell, Mackensie, MacKay, and Ross. And then another coalition of the warbands of smaller clans fought their way across the River Ayr, slaughtered several hundred Balderites on the banks of the River Doon, then pushed on south into Kennedy.

In the end, a very few Balderites managed to somehow run the grim gantlet of galleys, ships, and boats and win to the temporary safety of Ulaid, in Ireland; all the rest died in Clan Kennedy lands, and not one, of any age, sex, or condition, was left alive in all Scotland by the time the Crusaders and clansmen were done.

The two scientists saw it through to the sanguineous end. In one of the last real battles of the Scottish part of the crusade, Emmett O'Malley, separated from his own men in the hurly-burly of combat, chanced to be in the right place at just the right time to save the life of a Scottish earl, standing back to back with the magnate among the well-hacked corpses of his bodyguards and the pagan foes until clansmen could hew their way to a rescue. The earl had knighted O'Malley on the spot, delivering the buffet with his nicked, blood-clotted battlebrand. Later, when things were become less hectic, the earl had summoned his freckled battle companion to his camp, gifted him with a fine destrier and a heavy purse, and insisted that Sir Emmett accompany him and his when they pursued the crusade against the Balderites into Ireland. Emmett had duly set sail for Ulaid with the multinational force of holy warriors, but then he had stayed in Ireland and had not set foot again in England for many a long year. On the eve of the day he was to leave the Northumbrian camp, he and Harold Kenmore had evenly divided between them the thousand or so longevity-booster capsules they still owned and needed to swallow at lengthy intervals of time lest they begin to age.

O'Malley had adapted quickly and thoroughly to the rough, very primitive, and often cruel world into which they had been projected, and Harold had thought that he had too . . . until the long-drawn-out slaughter of the march from Edinburgh and the crowning horrors of man's inhumanity that had been that march's culmination in Kennedy. He had done all that had been required of him, true, but dutifully, not with the marked enthusiasm of his companion. He had fought bravely enough and well, for all his steadily increasing soul-sickness, and when the last of the unspeakable things had been done, he had led the triumphant march of his loot-laden lances back to Whyffler Hall.

There, the Widow—a fine figure of a woman, really, of less then thirty winters, still in firm possession of all her teeth and with not a trace of grey hair—had made it clear that the hall needed an adult man as master, that she needed a husband and would favorably receive importunings from Squire Harold, who already owned the high regard of everyone he had aided and sustained before the king had come north, the men he had so well led and captained on the recent crusade, the nearer Scots chiefs, and eke the mighty Duke of Northumbria.

But poor Dr. Harold Kenmore, haunted waking and sleeping by horrible memories of events which he had felt duty-bound to take part in or at least witness in the commission, could not then think of, contemplate, the seeking of happiness, wedding, begetting of children into a callous, brutal world wherein such hideous enormities could be wrought upon the tender, quaking flesh of not only men and women but children and even helpless infants, these very deeds being committed in the holy name of God.

And so he had taken leave of Whyffler Hall and the folk he had come to know and love, those with whom he had shared privations, hardships, and danger for so long. He had set out with no real destination in mind, and when he chanced to fall in with a large party of knights, gentlemen, and their retainers bound for York and points south of that city, he had accompanied them, the roads and tracks across mountains and moors being far too dangerous then to afford safe passage to lone riders or even smaller parties. As the most of these men were also vassals of His Grace Sir Humbert Howard or of that man's near-relatives, the Percys, Squire Harold was well known to them and more than welcomed as traveling companion through lands still infested with robbers of all kinds, outlaws, and wild beasts.

It proved a lengthy trip with so large and slow-moving a party, but for the same reason, it was a peaceful journey; there were just too many bannerets and pennons borne above too many well-armed men to suit the bandits resident in the areas through which they passed. The only deaths and injuries which occurred were caused by pure accidents or resulted from hunting, and these could have as easily happened anywhere and anytime.

For all the companionship and hearty camaraderie of the men with whom he rode—few of them other than outgoing, gregarious, and very generous—Harold still found much time to think along the way, and he came to one rock-bound decision: However he chose to sustain himself in future, it would have, must have, nothing whatsoever to do with war, with fighting, with killing. After quite seriously considering, weighing out all aspects of retiring to one of the numerous monasteries and taking holy orders, he decided instead to carefully explore the possibilities of entering a trade of some nature, such a course as was being followed by not a few younger sons of noble houses and landless gentlemen.

In York, therefore, owning goodly patience and not lacking for time or the patronage of friends and acquaintances from out the royal host that had gone up to Scotland and extirpated the pagan Balderites, he bided his time and, eventually, found himself first interviewed, then stringently tested, and, at long last, accepted by the Goldsmiths' Guild as a True Master. Although some of his gently born acquaintances sniffed at and frowned upon his entry into this "common tradesmanship," even they had to admit that a man must find or make a way to keep body and soul together; and, too, it was not as if precedent had not been long since established, for Squire Harold was in no wise breaking new ground in becoming a legal goldsmith. And, these acquaintances consoled themselves, as a gentleman born, he was naturally gifted in all the arts—why, it was said that his test-pieces submitted to the Guild Masters were even now displayed by them as examples for all to try to emulate, first-quality work; besides, there never seemed to be enough honest, reputable craftsmen of that water about.

Harold had been established for some years at his new trade, had produced many a fine piece of work, and was, indeed, becoming renowned beyond Yorkshire, with apprentices, servants, a complete bachelor's household, in fact. Then one day, while he was locked in his tiny personal workshop, rapt in the exacting task of carving the final embellishments into the wax of a commissioned piece of jewelry, a hesitant but insistent pounding upon the closed and locked and bolted door of his cranny distracted him.

All members of his household were aware that the

one sure way to provoke true rage from the usually gentle and mild-mannered Magister Harold was to disturb him whilst he created in his little sanctum sanctorum, and the curds-white face of the journeyman whom the goldsmith confronted when he flung open the door testified to that man's unmistakable terror.

Harold was stammeringly informed that a masked nobleman—a patent foreigner to judge on the grounds of his attire, manner, and atrociously accented English—even then stalked the reception chamber of the shop-residence, most impatiently, and had threatened to use his jeweled dagger to notch the nostrils and ears of the journeyman was his master not immediately summoned to wait upon his noble caller, personally.

Ever gentle and caring, Harold first had taken time to assure the shaken young man that he had not incurred his master's wrath, then had doffed his work apron and stalked toward the stairs that led downward, quite prepared to render harsh words to the alien jackanapes below. In the England of that era, artists of all sorts, especially those who worked in gems and precious metals, lived and worked under the protection of both king and church and were so legally immune to the caprices of the nobility and the gentry.

A glance through the window on the landing showed him a houseyard crowded with armed men, servants, and stamping horses, all of them babbling in a language that sounded much akin to Lowland Scots Gaelic. Harold took out his own twelve-year-old command of that tongue and used it to address his haughty visitor.

"My lord, I am Master Harold Kenmore, gentleman-goldsmith. Now, what was so urgent that it required a threat to disfigure my good journeyman? My lord must know that all in my household labor and abide under both royal and episcopal protections, unlike those in some less enlightened realms.''

The only immediate answer was a chuckle from beneath the samite travel mask, a sparkling of the green eyes above it, and a shaking of the Spanish-forked, brick-red beard below it.

So rich, lavish, and colorful was the attire of the foreigner as to almost cross the line to the gaudily pretentious. The high boots and the short cape were of soft doeskin and both dyed a brilliant green, as too were the elbow-length suede gloves under the fingers of which showed the bumps of several large gem-set rings. His trunkhose were of the finest wool, and all the rest of his clothing nothing less than rich silks and satins and velvets. Harold noted professionally that the huge brooch securing the plume to his cap of crushed samite was a true work of art—reddish gold set with first-water amethysts—and that that master or others of similar expertise had put much time, artistry, and effort into the gold-and-jeweled hilts and sheaths of his sword and belt-dagger, the clasp of his *cour bouilli* purse, and all his buckles; even the points securing his sleeves were tipped with gold set with tiny gemstones. The foreign nobleman was a footpad's or highwayman's dream come true. It was no wonder he went abroad with such a retinue of armed men and burly servants; a more prudent, less flamboyant man, if he wore such things at all other than at court, would have hidden the most of them under a voluminous travel cloak.

While still emitting a maddeningly familiar chuckle, the big, tall—tall as Harold, which was indeed tall for this malnourished age—lithe and muscular nobleman slowly had peeled off his gloves to reveal big, scarred, calloused hands with—a pure wonder for even a nobly born man or woman of the times—*clean,* square-cut nails; in addition to the earl's ransom in gold and gems that bedecked eight fingers and one thumb, those hands were covered in bricky-hued hair over a profusion of freckles.

And that last was for Harold the missing piece of the puzzle. Even as the bejeweled fingers untied and removed the mask to show the grinning face beneath it, Harold Kenmore exclaimed, "Emmett!"

Frantic that his eldest son, Prince Arthur of Wales, might die of the wasting disease that no physician of England, Wales, or France had seemed capable of curing or even ameliorating, King Henry VII Tudor had sent a plea to his cousin, Brian VIII, the High-King of Ireland, that some of his royal physickers be sent to try their wiles on the dying boy. With this medical party had come certain nobles of the Irish High Court, among them none other than Sir Emmett Ui Maille, son-in-law of the High King, court swordsmith, and secretly reputed by not a few, though never loudly, to be a sorcerer as well.

Over that day's dinner with his old friend, the Irishman had confided, "Och, Hal, for a' their oft-boasted expertise, it's I could see that nane o' Brian's physickers could do aught what hadnae been tried the many times o'er already by their English, Welsh, and Frenchified likes, and nae good out o' any o' it. So, be he left tae the artless arts of these blind fumblers who ca' themselfs physickers, the puir bouchal will nae see anither year, I trow."

Harold had sighed and laid down his knife, saying with true sadness, "Aye, Emmett, it's always bitter hard to see anyone die, especially a child or young person like Prince Arthur, but at least his death would not signal the end of this new dynasty, for His Majesty does have at least one other legitimate son, Prince Henry."

"And if aught should befall that bouchal, too, Hal?" demanded O'Malley. "And that is just what so preys on the puir, harried mind o' King Henry, that he'll come tae his death w'oot legal heirs and the realm he sae loves and cherishes wi' fa' agin intae sich as the Wars o' the Roses, nae tae lang past, that lang-lasting savagery that near sundered England. That be just why I come tae see ye, auld frind. While the sae-called physickers can do naught, I ken that ye and me, we can . . . I think.''

Dr. Harold Kenmore just stared blankly. ''But . . . but what, pray tell, Emmett, what can either of us do for Prince Arthur? I know nothing of the practice of medicine. I'm a goldsmith, and before that, I was a chemist. You've no medical degrees, either . . . have you?''

O'Malley shook his head of red hair. ''I dinna recall too clear, sae tell me: The longevity boosters, were they nae said to be firm proof agin a' ills and afflictions o' the human body?''

And so Harold Kenmore had departed York for the first time since he had arrived in that city years before. He had left his business under the care of his journeymen, they to be supervised by masters of the guild until his return. Little did he know then just how long a time that was to be.

The longevity-booster capsules, which did, indeed, contain such powerful antibiotics as to, in Emmett O'Malley's words, be firm proof against all afflictions of the human body, cured Prince Arthur of Wales of his near-deadly wasting illness. This miraculous feat delighted the near-distraught king, but when he who had done it told the royal physician and several of his furious colleagues that he could not explain to them how to formulate similar drugs, the spiteful crew saw him charged with witchcraft and borne away for interrogation, close confinement, and torture.

Physicians and churchmen alike, they reckoned without the gratitude of the young man's sire and the speed with which he could muster force and put that force to use. The church property wherein Harold was immured quickly found itself ringed round about by a powerful scratch force of nobles of the court, knights, sergeants, and pikemen. A herald courteously but firmly informed the senior cleric resident that his king desired that the prisoner, Magister Harold Ceanmoor of York, Gentleman, be immediately rendered up whole, hale, and in possession of all his goods. Any failure or delay of this order would force the men gathered outside to take whatever steps necessary to themselves free the gentleman and deliver him to the sovereign.

The senior churchmen tried to bluster of ecclesiastical rights, but when they saw an ironshod ram being readied for use, they acquiesced with the best faces possible under the circumstances.

But once in possession of Harold, King Henry, sagacious man that he was, realized that this would not be the end of the affair, not as matters just then stood. Vindictive and carping as a pack of unpaid whores, the physicians and chirurgeons were certain to not let the matter lie, to keep blathering of witchcraft and sorcery and such claptrap until they had gotten the object of their wrath onto first a rack, then a stake. And Arthur had ever been a sickly lad, too. What could be done should he again become so ill as he had this year if his savior was become scattered ashes around an iron stake?

Henry had been so worried and harried when first Harold had been brought to the summer court at Coventry by that Irish nobleman that he had scarcely learned more of the man than his name before he had ordered that he be allowed to try his physick on the nearly dead prince. Over the fortnight which had followed, as the raging fevers began to abate and the young man began to find it possible to hold down thin broths, syllabubs, watered porridge, and wines,

as the festering sores on his body began to scab over
and heal, as the hair which had fallen out began to
grow back again, the king had spoken a few times
briefly with the man of York who had wrought so
wonderful a thing for him, but had always found it
necessary to rush off to other matters.

Now, King Henry summoned this physicker of
York to his private audience chamber in the Coventry Palace and closeted with him for long hours. So
well pleased was he with what his probing questions'
answers told him of this savior he just had saved that
he summoned a trusted clerk and dictated, signed,
and sealed a letter to his friend His Grace Peter
Spears, Archbishop of Canterbury. Then he had
Harold Ceanmoor of York disguised, smuggled out
of the palace, and sent well guarded by provenly
loyal retainers to Archbishop Peter's seat, one of his
noble guardians bearing the letter.

By the time Harold Kenmore returned to court, it
being by then back in London and about to commence another round of travels about the realm, he
was become himself a cleric, styled Monsignor Harold Ceanmoor. Henry added a newer title: Physicker
to the King. He also made it abundantly clear to the
deposed holder of that title and to all other court
physickers and chirurgeons that further expressions
of animosity toward King's Physicker Monsignor
Harold would quickly and assuredly result in their
lives becoming most unpleasant and, possibly, even
coming to abrupt ends. Several of these practitioners
suddenly decided to leave court entirely; all of the
others took pains either to avoid any proximity to
the newmade royal physicker or to ingratiate themselves to him, fawningly.

After that, Harold moved with the court, which
seldom stayed in any one place for long, lest its huge
crowds eat a host out of house, home, and lands.
Having come to truly like and to trust the judgment

of Harold, King Henry kept him close by and often asked his advice on matters far weightier than those of his profession.

Harold came to feel a deep and true friendship for the man who was his patron and ruler, too, and to trust him enough to divulge to him just who and what he was and just how he had arrived years ago in the border country. At the king's express wish, a party of noblemen of the court, knights, and men-at-arms rode up to Whyffler Hall, and there Harold and Henry descended to the cellar of the old tower wherein the otherworldly device still squatted and glowed greenish through its coating of dust and cobwebs. Harold also showed the king a heat-stunner and demonstrated how it could set afire wood and render metals white-hot. Before the party left to return to the court, the king had the entrance to the ground level of the tower walled up solidly and saw a royal seal set in the new masonry. He ordered Sir James Whyffler that the tower should be incorporated into the new hall the knight was just then beginning to build, but that no one lacking royal writ was ever to be allowed to break the seal, tear down the wall, and enter to that which lay below. Inordinately flattered that his simple knight's fee holdings should be so honored as to be the secret repository of royal possessions, the knight had solemnly oathed himself and his heirs to honor the commands of his king.

Prince Arthur, unlike his robust younger brother, Prince Henry, never was well for long throughout the course of his life and his lengthy reign. Usually, one or two longevity-booster capsules were enough to put him to rights, however, and Harold began to let longer and longer periods elapse between the times when he took them himself, hoarding the irreplaceable things against the dread that Arthur's next illness might be worse and require more of the steadily dwindling supply.

In the spring of A.D. 1506, there came by sea routes word of a great and most terrible plague that even then was ravaging parts of the middle eastern lands. Although in some ways similar to the Black Death and causing numerous fatalities, it also was said to differ in divers ways from that other, centuries-old scourge. All that seemed to be known of its origin was that the pest had been moving westward out of Asia for some years. It had decimated the Syrias, then rampaged through Turkey and Armenia; all Outremer had been hard hit by it, and some declared that the Pope of the East lay dead and that Constantinople resembled a huge and reeking charnel house. In Alexandria, the Khalifah had closed every port in Egypt, Libia, and Tunisia, then set armed men to turn back any caravan bound from any direction other than south.

By late summer, word was that the newcome pest was rife in the Agean isles, Crete, Greece, and the countless little principalities that in Harold's world were the Balkans. By the following spring, all Italy was reeling from the shock of its onset, along with the kingdoms which lay along the mighty Danube River, from Kilia to Gran, the cities of Buda and Pesth being especially hard hit by it, it was rumored. In England, those who had hoped that the colder, wetter climate and the salt sea moat that lay on all quarters might protect the realm from these horrifying new pest ravages were disillusioned and thrown into despair when outbreaks were reported first in Sweden, then in the Empire Duchy of Pomern, and finally in Copenhagen; the pest appeared in Sweden and Denmark in seaports, but that in Pomern first burst out in a large and wealthy monastery.

As the relentless sweep of the plague neared English shores, more rumors and much wild speculation concerning it and its effects flew before it. In the East, it had earned the name of Priests' Plague because such an inordinate number of clergy had succumbed to it. But from what Harold had been able to get from numerous conversationalists from oversea he had deliberately sought out for just this purpose, folk in towns wherein there was much trade had seemed to suffer the ravages of the disease far and away more than had those scattered out in the countrysides. Also, a very high number of the nobility seemed to come down with it, and this dictum seemed to apply to all countries hit so far. At that time, he had been unable to make rhyme or reason out of the mass of information.

During the winter of A.D. 1507–08, when the pest was in full force in Burgundy, France, and Frisia, every man and woman possessed of any wit knew that England and Wales must surely be next, and an endless chanting proceeded from every church, chapel, cathedral, and monastic establishment, while the entire island seemed to be overlain by day and by night with a thickening pall of the smoke of frankincense. But undaunted by pious prayers or burning incense, the Priests' Plague came in its own time to unleash its countless horrors upon King Henry and his miserable subjects.

CHAPTER
THE SECOND

Within a period of fourteen months of the coming of the Priests' Plague, sixty percent of the nobility and nearly half the gentry of England and Wales were dead, along with most of their households. Nor had the court been spared. King Henry and his children, dosed lavishly with Harold's longevity-booster capsules, still lived in health, but his queen had declined in favor of a decoction compounded by her personal physicker and both she and said physicker had consequently died.

Well-to-do persons of all classes in country, towns, and cities—and most especially port cities situated on seacoasts and the navigable rivers and canals—had died like flies. But hardest hit of all walks in the land had been the clergy; not a single archbishop remained alive and precious few bishops or monsignors, Canterbury and Yorkminster being almost untenanted by any save wailing ghosts, as too were a large proportion of the great abbeys of the land.

But there the comparison to the Great Plagues or Black Death ceased, for while gentry and yeomanry out on the land had sickened and often died with their families and households, the bulk of the humbler sorts had been unaffected or not much affected or afflicted by the sweeping catastrophe. There had been few real halts to the production of food crops and kine husbandry, and such shortages of foodstuffs as had occurred in the land had been caused not by the lack but by the fully understandable reluctance of folk to transport it to or even near the stricken centers of population.

Also, despite the widespread extirpations of high-ranking or powerful churchmen and their retinues and households, and the virtual extinctions of large, ancient, and wealthy monastic communities, religion still flourished in all the land, especially on the humble parish level and in the form of smaller and poorer or more strictly ordered abbeys and monastic groups. Moreover, as often is the case under such awful circumstances, the advent of the hideous, death-dealing scourge upon the realm and its relentless movement among its helpless victims sparked a fresh flowering of religious zeal among the bulk of the survivors of all stations.

Despite a lack of general famine in most of England and Wales, things were quite bad enough for a while. Bands of now-masterless folk wandered the face of the land, looting castles, manors, and halls, savaging underpopulated towns, sometimes fighting with such similar bands as they encountered in their rovings; but over time, not a few of these came down with Priests' Plague themselves, and most of the thus-sobered or outright terrified folk either returned to the land or took to the woodlands and wastes to live by banditry and poaching of the unhunted and rapidly proliferating game beasts. The short sway of these lawless bands had wrought much terror, suffering, and harm upon the already stricken land, but they had, unknowing of it, also wrought not a little good in their depredations, Harold later concluded, in that they had wantonly fired numerous of the steadings, farms, halls, manors, castles, and abbeys after they had looted them, thus destroying and subjecting to direct-flame sterilization countless reservoirs of the plague.

Indeed, as the court and realm slowly, in fits and starts, began to recover to some extent, King Henry—at Harold's insistent urgings—had ordered the destruction by fire of the bodies and effects of plague victims and the use of fire, boiling water, and powerful caustics to thoroughly cleanse all nonflammable items once owned by those now dead of the pest and the interiors of all the now-untenanted buildings. All existing cesspits were filled in and new ones dug elsewhere. In numerous seaports, hulks were packed with flammables, stacked with the remains of victims, towed well out to sea, and set aflame. Harold was later convinced that it had been these stern measures by the king's order that had aided in preventing in England and Wales the sudden recurrences of plague that racked parts of Italy, France, the Spanish Peninsula, and other areas for two or three or more years after its initial onset.

Mainland Scotland had suffered about as badly as its southern neighbor, especially in the Lowlands, but not so the western isles or Ireland. The Irish ports, like those of Egypt, had been tightly closed long before the pest came to England, Wales, and Scotland; not even the routine coastal raidings had been practiced by the wild Irish on the western seaboards of the larger island during the course of the plague, a real blessing in the underpopulated, ill-defended time.

At the height of the ghastly resurgence of the plague in Italy, the Roman Pope, Saint Peter's Bishop of the West, had sickened and died and his successor, Cardinal Diego al-Ahbyahd de Málaga, had felt it imperative in the confused times to reempower Christian monarchs to reassume the filling of sees falling vacant within their realms.

While the various royal residences here and there

were being sterilized according to the king's dictates, he and what by then remained of his court and retinue journeyed about the country, meeting and reassuring all of any station with whom they came in contact, avoiding towns, castles, and abbeys and living in pavilions, mostly. Foods of most sorts and forage were found to be plentiful in the countryside and the hunting was superb.

Immediately upon discovering that Osbert Norton, Bishop of Durham, had lived through an attack of the Priests' Plague and fully recovered his health, King Henry had designated the middle-aged cleric to fill the vacant archbishopric at Canterbury, then, prior to his departure south, had seen the now-senior churchman of the realm consecrate his erstwhile chaplain-physicker, Harold Ceanmoor of York, archbishop of that city and archdiocese. That much accomplished, the monarch had provided the bemused Harold as complete a retinue as straitened circumstances would allow and sent him off around the realm to seek out worthy monsignors, abbots, priests, even lowly deacons, if necessary and that was all that still lived, to fill the plentitude of empty bishops' seats.

To Harold's protestations of unworthiness for such unearned rank, honors, and responsibilities, the scarred warrior-king had replied in private, "Pah! If any man deserves rank and honors, it's you, old friend. Man, you saved my life and the lives of my get in the plague and my chosen heir's twice over, now. Were you at all worldly and warlike, I'd see you knighted and then ennobled, but as you seem most comfortable in a cassock, then I bow humbly to the dictates of God and your conscience and name you a prince of the Church as now is my regal right, once more. I'd meant, in the beginning, to place you at Canterbury and then fight the Church, if necessary, to retain you there, but this way is going to be

much better, much easier, I think. You've been con-
secrated by a man who might well have succeeded
to his present, paramount place even without the
thorough winnowing of his peers by this plague, so
it will be up to *him* to fight any battles that might
loom on account of your elevation. Far better him
than me to fight any contentious clerics.'' The king
had chuckled.

''As regards your upcoming journeyings, old
friend, there lives no man, clerical or lay, of any
station, into whose judgment and loyalty I place
more trust. You own the wisdom of more years than
ever I or any man of whom I can think will ever live
to see, moreover. You know the kind of men I and
the realm need for bishops, and you own the God-
given wit to easily and quickly see though the charlatans and poseurs you will doubtless encounter,
hither and yon.

''Harold, I care not a fig for the birth or breeding
of the men you place in these vacant sees, only that
they be personally worthy and capable, relatively
honest and scrupulous, and at least outwardly pious,
with their loyalty being to king first, to Rome second.''

And that was how it had been. His Grace Harold
Kenmore, Archbishop of York, had set out upon his
way, following the orders of his king, his friend, and
performing those tasks set to him by his monarch to
the best of his abilities. And he had done well, as
Henry had known he would. Right many a humble
but honest, loyal, and capable English or Welsh parish priest had found himself abruptly departing his
peaceful country parish forever to wear the ring of
an office he never had so much as dreamed of filling.

Gradually, the realm began to show signs of re-
covery, and it was well that recover it did, for less
than three years after Harold's elevation, King Henry's horse chanced to fall whilst he and the hunt pur-

sued a fine stag in the New Forest and the monarch died instantly of a broken neck. Thanks to the meticulous groundwork laid by Henry, the succession was uncontested, peaceful, and orderly.

Arthur II Tudor was not yet twenty-six when crowned by Osbert, Archbishop of Canterbury; his wife and one infant had died, but he still had two young sons and a daughter. Very soon after he became king, a marriage was arranged for him with a daughter of the King of Denmark and Norway. Astrid of Denmark produced two more children to him before dying in childbirth. The next marriage arranged for him was with a daughter of his second cousin (once removed), the *Ard-Righ* of Ireland, Brigid of Tara; of the five births, two of the infants were stillborn, one died while still in the cradle, but the other two outlived their mother. On the twentieth anniversary of his coronation, King Arthur II was again a widower, and he and his councillors were seeking about for an advantageous marriage for both him and his widower-brother, His Grace Sir Henry Tudor, Duke of Aquitaine.

With maturity and succession, Arthur Tudor's general health had improved to the point that Harold had finally felt it safe to leave the court and remove to his see at Yorkminster, wherein in the years since his elevation he had spent only brief periods of time and then only when the court had chanced to be in proximity to the city of York, the functions of his office having been performed as needed by local bishops and monsignors.

With the blessings of King Arthur, who worshiped this gentle, erudite man who had seen him through so many illnesses, who had been his loved father's friend and confidant and was his as well, and with a retinue of clerical advisers and specialists loaned by Osbert Norton of Canterbury, Harold Kenmore had made his way back to the city that had for long been his home.

Throughout the widespread, protracted fighting that came to be called the War of the Three Marriages, Harold lived peacefully in York and its environs, leaving on only two occasions, both of these to rush to the bedside of Arthur and restore his threatened health with doses of the dwindling supply of longevity-booster capsules. Then, even as the war had ended, a fresh bout of the dreaded Priests' Plague had rampaged through Europe and into England, Wales, Scotland, and, this time, even the Hebrides, the Danish Islands, Iceland, and Ireland.

Immediately upon receiving word of the advent of the pest, Harold had prepared his archdiocese as well as he quickly could and removed to court, fearing for the well-being of the ever susceptible Arthur, the monarch's brother, Duke Henry, being even then already dead of the plague in Aquitaine.

This second visitation of the murderous disease upon England, Wales, and those parts of Scotland which had suffered in the first episode was not as costly of lives as had been the initial one, but still was it bad enough, following as it did the very same pattern of striking principally nobility and their immediate retainers and servants, large abbeys, well-to-do country gentry, ports, cities, and larger towns.

Even as before, a goodly proportion of the court were badly stricken, but this time not so many died, and of those who did die, Harold noted but few who were then old enough to have been alive at the time of the initial onset of the deadly pest.

King Arthur, however, very nearly died of this second outbreak, and by the time he was once more on his feet and reordering the realm, Harold had less than two dozen of the longevity-booster capsules remaining him.

But the king, recalling his sire in identical circumstances, had performed splendidly in the crises. After decreeing the burning of corpses and their flammable effects, the stringent cleaning of the interiors of buildings, the filling in of cesspits, the scourings of towns and cities, and the towing out to sea and burning of hulks filled with corpses, he and the court had set out on a procession around the realm, avoiding castles, manors, halls, or abbeys and biding in pavilions set up in fields and leas, moors and forests, under the sky.

With Osbert Norton dead (not of the Priests' Plague, but rather of an infected ratbite) and Canterbury once more depopulated of the clergy and their retainers, Arthur had designated Yorkminster to henceforth be the paramount archdiocese of his realm and had empowered Harold to fill all vacant sees. Once again, Harold Kenmore performed the bidding of his monarch, then made his way back to York and Yorkminster and the multitude of tasks that there awaited him. But he was nothing if not a consummate administrator, and within the year he had set matters once more aright and running smoothly.

So seldom indulging himself with a single longevity-booster capsule lest in so doing he possibly doom the sickly monarch, so beset constantly with the cares and worries of his high office, Harold Kenmore had aged—not so much or at all so fast as those about him, of course, those never treated with the longevity drugs at all—but he remained unaware of the fact until he again saw Emmett O'Malley.

As paramount churchman in all of England and Wales, his court and establishment at Yorkminster was grown as large and complex as the court of his king, with a never-ending stream of visitors of all stations, supplicants, messengers from the royal court and from Rome and from high-ranking churchmen in foreign lands, nobles bound on one errand or another, and, it sometimes seemed to him, fully half the population of the realm. Naturally, he could not himself spend all day every day doing nothing but meeting with suppliants and the like, so he had of course surrounded himself with concentric layers of men whose task was to winnow out the never-ending streams, and see the most of them met by and handled by lower-ranking subordinates, with only the business that could be performed properly by no other man eventually appearing before the Archbishop of York himself.

Of course, it did not always work out in just the ways Harold had envisioned upon setting it all up. Even men vowed to poverty right often fall to the insistent temptation of silver and gold, and what with the decimations of the clergy by the Priests' Plague, not all of the men making up his insulating layers were men of the cloth, anyway. When, one morning, he was presented with the usual list of those with whom he was to meet this day, he just glanced at it briefly, not even noticing the names, just the numbers of the suppliants and the times of their appointments. But even had he looked more closely, he later determined, he might well still have passed over the clerk's rendition of the name: "Sir Ymit Mc Badrag Ui Maile, said to be a high noble of the Irish Kingdom of Lagan."

Although not really aged in appearance, the Emmett O'Malley who at length had been ushered into Harold Kenmore's audience chamber had still shown unmistakable evidences of much suffering, sorrow, and worry. His once-sparkling green eyes now were more dull and filled with a soul-deep sadness, woe had carved deep lines in his face, and seldom anymore did the once ever-ready smile or merry laugh bring up the downcast corners of his mouth.

Immediately they two were completely alone in a smaller room off the larger, Emmett had tensely demanded, "Harold, hoo mony o' the capsules hae ye left?"

Harold had sighed and shrugged, replying, "About a score or so, Emmett."

A light, but a light of wildness, had come into the green eyes then, and the hard, bejeweled fingers had clamped down on Harold's arm with crushing force. "Nae, Harold, mon, not whatall ye hae *wi'* ye. Hoo mony in a', I mean?"

"That's it, Emmett," the archbishop had said, while peeling back the calloused fingers to free his punished arm. "I have exactly twenty-four longevity-booster capsules left. You look awful, Emmett. Are you well? Should I send for a restorative for you? A bit of wine, perhaps?"

Upon Harold's words, the blood drained from his flushed face and all the strength, seemingly, from his solid-looking, still-powerful body. Stumbling, tottering backward, he sank into a chair, all animation gone from his features, his appearance now become that of a hopeless man who has seen his certain doom.

At last, he had spoken in a soft, hushed voice filled with utter despair. "Och, the God an' His Holy Saints help us both, then, auld frind, for we be sairtain sure noo tae age an' die lang afore oor time. Where went a' the hunnerds ye owned, mon?"

Harold shrugged again. "They were used, Emmett, a dozen here and a dozen or two there, over the years, to keep Hal and Arthur and Henry alive. I could have done no less for my old friend and his little sons. But what about your own capsules, Emmett? You had just exactly as many as did I when we parted in Scotland."

Then the red-haired, onetime twenty-first-century scientist had related the terrible tale of his recent misfortunes. His wives, immediate family, and household almost all wiped out in mere days by the ferocious effects of the Priests' Plague were sorrows that still oppressed and haunted him.

"When first it come ain us," he had said, "it's I thocht me o' hoo' ye had cured the auld king wi' y'r capsules, so it's I took a party and rode hard f'r Fora, the gude fithers there havin' had the keepin' o' the casket wherein was hid me ain f'r mony's the lang year. But, och, hoo' turrible a sight we found there! The curst Plague had struck a' there doon the week afore, and wi' a' o' the gude men dead, the monastery had been looted an' burnt oot, ainly the black, sooty stanes left o' it. Still, I knew o' some dozen I had hid away back in Tara, sae we turnt aboot and rode back as fast nor we'd come . . . but ainly death were there tae greet us a'. They a' lay cauld and dead of the plague—my new, bonny wife, my other wives, my slavegirls, a' me children young an' older, near all me servants, e'en. And, worse, a' Tara were like that, too.

"The *Ard-Righ* an' a' his ain family and the most o' his great court had a' died. It were a' that we few survivors could do tae luck ontae a bastard half brother of Brian tae replace him. Mony as disliked the idea o' a bastrad, a rough mon as had been lang a' mercenary fightin' a' o'er Europe an' Ifriqa, bein' set 'pon the Stane, f'r fear it would move 'neath him and shriek oot his unworthiness, but it a' went well an' it's a fine *Ard-Righ* he's made us a'."

Gently, Harold had touched his old friend's red-furred hand, saying, "It must have been bitter-hard, Emmett. You lost all your family, then?"

"F'r lang an' lang I so thocht," replied the big man. "But then ain o' me grandsons, Tim, sailed back tae Ireland frae Great Ireland, which happy land had not been touched by the plague. Och, foin indeed it were that blessed day tae find that at the least ane o' the get o' me loins had not died. Sincet then, it's I've come tae learn o' a few ithers—grandchildren, great-grandchildren, some o' them legitimate, some bastards—scattered aboot in this kingdom or that.

"Och, but whin Tim appeared, it's nane o' t'other I was a-knowin', ye ken, an' t'were me mind tae do f'r the bouchal the best I could be doin'. So wi' the generous help o' the new *Ard-Righ*, t'were settin' him on the throne o' Lagan—it just thin bein' empty an' the bouchal w' as much or more rightful claim tae it as ont thin extant, too, both his mither an' his grandmither havin' been out'n the royal hoose o' Lagan an' hisself havin' happened tae be foaled in Lagan, more's t' luck. So noo he be t' legal king an' wed an' a' an' a-gettin' his dynasty a-started."

The brief flush of happiness which had colored his face and put life into his green eyes abruptly was replaced with the same old woeful spiritlessness as he sighed and said dolefully, "An' it's I can but hope that it's I'll be livin' lang enough f'r tae see Tim's son succeed him, is a', Harold. I noo own but twa o' t' capsules tae me name an' you hae twenty-two; sae mony betwixt us might maintain us anely three-score or less years. Aye, an' thin we'll surely start in tae age. Tae *age*, mon, tae become old an' feeble, infirm, stiff-jinted, unable e'en tae tumble a lassie an' tek joy frae her as a mon should. What can we do, Harold, f'r the love o' God an' a' His holy saints, mon, what can we do? Can ye fashion more o' the capsules? D' ye recollect how, arter a' these lang years?"

The Archbishop, too, had sighed and said, "Yes, I could make more longevity-booster capsules, Emmett . . . but not here, not anywhere in this primitive world. I could make them only if I had the run of the chemistry research building at the Gamebird Project Facility, back in our own time, on our own world. There exists here simply no way to manufacture the ingredients or the things and equipment necessary to compound or even refine them. Further, I have no trace of an idea how to go about making the machines that would be required to make the machines that would make the machines with which the lab equipment would be made. The levels of technology are just too low here to even dream of any of it, Emmett, I'm sorry.

"There's no choice, so just surrender gracefully. Both of us have now lived far longer in this world, alone, than is the norm for people of it, people born into it. Fifty or sixty years is not a short remaining lifetime by any manner of measurement. Accept it, accept your fate, and live your remaining years as fully and as enjoyably as you can, as will I. Remember, the longevity process, even under optimum conditions, was never designed or intended to provide immortality, only to prolong life, to slow the aging of bodies to acceptable—"

"No!" the red-haired man had roared so loudly that one of the poleaxemen outside the door of the larger room had felt impelled to come to see if His Grace was in need of help. When Harold had reassured and sent away the well-intentioned guardsman, Emmett had spoken on, in quieter tones, but no more temperately. In his clearly disturbed condition, he unconsciously reverted to speech that was much more like the basic English dialect of the twenty-first century with only a few words and nuances of the thick brogue peeking through here and there, now and again.

"Harold, ye were of middle age at least before e'er you took your first longevity treatment, so it's easy for you to think on growing old, *really* growing old, and from all I hear you took your vows of chastity and celibacy seriously, too, as damn-all clerics do in this time, so you have far less tae lose from aging than a lusty, vital mon like me does. Harold, I'd far liefer be cauld clay, wormfood, than end me days an old, doddering, toothless mon as could eat nothing save gruel and syllabubs, all me strength gone and unable to properly swive even the youngest, bonniest, liveliest girl. So, no, I'll not surrender. If ye must have the chemistry research building from Gamebird Project Facility . . . well, there just may be a way to get it intae this world, for a while, if not tae stay. Ye ken me? We twa must ride up tae Whyffler Hall. We must leave tomorrow.''

But they did not. There was absolutely no way, with the press of his duties and affairs, that Archbishop Harold of York could have departed his seat on such short notice. Therefore, fretting and complaining and protesting mightily and constantly, Emmett O'Malley had had no option but to bide in York until Harold was able to make a time and a way to prepare for the trip.

Even before they could think of heading northwest to Whyffler Hall, up in the wild border country, Harold knew that he must get to wherever the king happened to be and obtain his permission in writing to break his father's seals set in the walls that had been built so long ago to block off access to the ground floor of that ancient tower, for James Whyffler—if still he lived and his heirs if he did not—took his oaths and the royal trust seriously, and, despite the old friendship with the now-Archbishop, would be as likely as not to take Harold and all his party, confine them straitly, and send word to the king.

Twice, over the months that the matter dragged out, Harold had been on the very point of leaving York for long enough to intercept the king and court in their endless rounds of travel, but both times sudden affairs requiring his continued presence in York had frustrated him and Emmett. Then, one happy day, the king and court and entourage arrived in the environs of York and made the thing relatively short and simple. Arthur II, of couse, like his late father

before him, had long been privy to Harold's strange
provenance. The appearance and function of the singular device that still squatted on the earthern floor
of the old defensive-residential tower at Whyffler
Hall had been described to him in some detail by
Harold, but the always-busy monarch had never been
able to himself go up and view it. However, upon
hearing his old friend and savior out, the harried
king readily had properly prepared and recorded a
document which granted to "our faithful and most
trusted mentor, His Grace Harold Ceanmoor, Archbishop of York" lifetime permission to, at his dis-
cretion, break or have broken all royally sealed
repositories, and leave to examine or bear away any
or all contents of said repositories.

The court stayed in proximity to York for about a
month, then moved on in its accustomed progres-
sion, but Harold, still bogged down with a work load
that had not been helped at all by the fact that re-
placements for staff members and functionaries dead
in the Priests' Plague still were learning their jobs
and functions while blundering their ways through
them, still found himself unable to get away from
Yorkminster. When Emmett at last began to grate
upon his host, Harold had documents drawn up des-
ignating the Irishman a lay deputy of the Archdiocese of York, empowered to act in the name of the
Archbishop. Then he turned over the royal document
to Emmett, provided him with a sizable escort of his
episcopal horse guards, a packtrain, servants, and
all other necessities for the lengthy, overland trip,
and sent him off ahead to Whyffler Hall to break the
royal seals, open the walls, descend to the ground
level of the old tower, and begin the alterations of
which he had spoken over the months. Harold prom-
ised to join him as soon as he could get away from
York.

Emmett's first letter from Whyffler Hall had told

of ferocious fighting against attacking brigands twice on the ride up to the border country. He said that Sir James was long since dead of camp fever during the War of the Three Marriages in service with the army fielded by Duke Henry Tudor in Aquitaine and France. The fee now was held by James's eldest living son, Sir John Whyffler, who had gained his own accolade during the same war wherein his sire had died, his service, however, having been with King Arthur's amphibious force on the Mediterranean coast of France.

O'Malley had gone on to remark that the documents had, after careful scrutiny by Sir John's chaplain and clerk, been accepted as genuine and binding and that he and all his household and retainers had then bent their every effort to assist in any needful way the Archbishop's deputy and his party. The ground floor of the old tower now was opened. He had cleaned off the console and was going about alterations of those parts needing such. He had obtained large sheets of parchment, ink, and quills and was now at work pacing off distances and transferring his notes and all that he recalled of the other place and time to the parchment. He now awaited Harold's arrival and his assistance in the attempt to project the chemistry research facility entire into this time and place, that more longevity-booster capsules might quickly be compounded.

The second letter, delivered at last by the one wounded survivor of the party of three horse guards who had set out through the bandit-infested intervening country with it, made reference to an earlier letter that had never arrived at all and urged Harold to come up quickly, before worsening seasonal weather made a hard and dangerous trip more difficult if not impossible.

After the elapse of far more time than either he or, especially, the frothingly impatient Emmett would have preferred, Harold had accomplished the next thing to impossible—he had gotten out of York and had made the arduous journey up to Whyffler Hall in company with his sizable retinue, half a hundred horse guards of his own establishment, and two dozen more mounted men-at-arms hired on for the length of his sojourn from the households of various noblemen residing in the vicinity of York.

But in the end, it all had been in vain. Using Harold's twenty-first-century wrist chronometer—his own having been smashed into so much junk during the course of some long-ago battle or personal combat—Emmett had meticulously set the altered console (which through some arcane phenomenon still was connected to—across who knew what vastnesses of time and space—and could draw power from the massive banks of machines at the Gamebird Project Facility, a phenomenon which Emmett with great patience for him had tried earnestly and repeatedly to explain but which Harold still could not say he understood), then had raced up the flights of steep stairs to the battlemented roof of the old tower that he might himself observe the appearance of the building.

That building never materialized. True, in the light of the rising sun, he and Harold had seen a part of the intervening ground seem for a brief instant to look like muddy, swirling, rushing river water, with an even briefer flickering beyond it of tall, slablike walls that might have been a part of the Gamebird Project Facility, but that had been all which had occurred.

After screaming frightful, incredibly blasphemous oaths, stamping, beating his big hands bloody against the grey merlon-stones, while tears of frustration had bathed his red-stubbled cheeks, Emmett had at last calmed enough to go back down to the

console, reset it, and try it all again . . . and again
. . . and yet again, with even less result.

The frantic, desperate O'Malley had kept at it for
almost a full month, day and night, eating and drinking whenever he thought to so do at his labors, unwashed, unshaven, his hair and chinbeard and
moustache wild and unkempt, clothing dirty,
stained, and sweat-soaked. At last, he had collapsed
of exhaustion and malnourishment, and Harold had
seen him borne up from the ground floor of the old
tower, unclothed, washed, shaved, and put to bed in
the gracious manor that the late Sir James Whyffler
had had built incorporating the ancient tower and the
royal trust it contained to the honor of his house. By
the time Emmett O'Malley was sufficiently recovered of his self-imposed ordeal to quit his bed,
Archbishop Harold had long since had the ground
floor once more walled up and the seals of his dead
friend King Henry VII Tudor replaced, nor would
he hear aught of again letting Emmett near to the
console.

"Let be, Emmett, for the love of God, just let
be," he had said firmly. "Your idea was good, but
it just didn't work. Surely you can admit that much,
can't you? You came near to killing yourself, as it
was, and I'll not see you try it again, I cannot. I'll
freely give you half—all, if you must have them—of
my own capsules, for I have not the morbid fear of
aging and death that you do; I'll accept the years
God sees fit to give me, be they many or few. I also
have two injectable doses, back in York, hidden away
at Yorkminster, and I'll give you one or both of
those, too. But I'll not allow the seals on those walls
just rebuilt to be again broken for you."

And so they had ridden back down to York, Emmett O'Malley's mood as dark and foul as the
weather. He spoke few words to anyone and only
seemed to come alive when there were brigands to

fight or the prospect of such, and then he fought like a berserker, taking terrifying chances, killing without mercy.

He had remained in York only long enough to prepare for the trip back to Ireland. When he had left, he had taken with him only half of the two dozen capsules that remained and one of the injectable doses. He had spoken few words in parting from his old friend.

"I'll not take them all, Harold. These dozen and the injectable will give me at least fifty years, maybe half again that long. It was said that the monastery at Fora was looted between the time the most of the gude fithers died of the Plague and the time it was set afire, so mayhap, somewhere in Eireann unbeknownst tae any, rests my casket, its shrewdly concealed false bottom and sides still a-holdin' me ain capsules. And I mean tae search ivery kingdom, county, and eke barony until I find it. And the sooner I start me search, the better. So, bide you well, Harold. Goodbye."

Dr. Harold Kenmore had never seen Dr. Emmett O'Malley since that day, and had, as he sat in his alchemical laboratory in a tower of his episcopal seat at Yorkminster so many years later, good reason to believe his old friend years dead, killed in battle.

Out of his several wives, King Arthur II Tudor of England and Wales had sired six sons and four daughters. However, two of the sons and three of the daughters had died before reaching puberty, one son had died in his teens while tilting in a tourney, his sole remaining daughter had died in childbirth at fifteen, another son had drowned while fording a river on Crusade in Bavaria, and the second-eldest had gone in the way of his grandsire—dead of mischance while hunting boar in Aquitaine. The eldest of the ten children, Prince Henry of Wales, had been early betrothed to Princess Astrita of Hungary; when he had been fourteen and she sixteen, they had been wed, and by the time he had died at the age of twenty-nine, he had had by her two sons and five daughters. Although all five of his daughters had died before him, the sons—Richard and Arthur—outlived both their sire and their grandsire, who—mostly thanks to Harold's longevity-booster capsules dispensed so lavishly over the years—had enjoyed a reign much longer than normal for the times.

Bare months prior to his own demise, King Arthur II Tudor and his council had arranged a marriage of Prince Richard of Wales with the daughter of the Pope of the West, Angela Hasheem. Harold of York and not a few other churchmen and nobles, all well aware of just how devious and acquisitive was the Moorish Bishop of Rome, designated Pope Awad, had protested this choice in the harshest terms, but had found themselves ridden over roughshod by the councillors just then in ascendancy and well in control of a senile king in his dotage.

Angela had brought a full shipload of Moorish, Spanish, and Italians of various sorts in her entourage, and no sooner was her regal father-in-law decently interred than even more southerners flocked to her husband's new-formed court, displacing countless English men and women, making plain their disgust with England and English folk and customs.

Though loving, good, and pious, Richard IV Tudor did not prove a good king, for he was weak and all too soon his scheming, strong-willed Moorish-Italian wife had both him and his kingdom dancing willy-nilly to her Roman-Moorish tunes, while appalling amounts of the wealth of the Kingdom of England and Wales streamed out of the realm and directly, not a small amount of it, into Roman coffers.

Moreover, everyone at court and not a few outside it seemed to know that which her overly trusting husband did not know or would not, could not admit even to himself: In addition to a crown, she had been setting horns on his head ever since he had ascended the throne.

Since the very first of the Priests' Plagues and the sudden elevations of once-humble commoner priests to the English prelacy, anti-Roman sentiment had been rife in England and Wales, and under King Richard IV, it burgeoned, becoming both widespread and outspoken in all quarters and classes—noble, ecclesiastical and common. Then when the rumor began to circulate that the devious Angela—known by then, country wide, as the Roman Tart—

was hard at work persuading her loving, well-cuckolded royal spouse to go on pilgrimage to Rome, there to give over his kingdom to the Holy See, then receive it back as a feoff from the papacy, matters really began to boil.

The political, very nationalistic petard was already set and its fuse was sparked and spluttering, a delegation of high nobles had already surreptitiously journeyed to Aquitaine, closeted with Duke Arthur Tudor, Richard's younger brother, and he was upon the very point of sailing for England when word reached all of the death of Pope Awad, Angela's sire (although he himself had always in public referred to the young woman as "our niece, Angela") and the election of a replacement of the Italian Faction, one Boniface XI.

It had been decided by all and sundry in England, Wales, and Aquitaine, at that point, to hold fire and wait to see what might now develop in the changed circumstances. The faction of cardinals called Italian had always been less dogmatic, devious, and money-or land-grubbing than that opposing faction called Moorish. But then, all too soon, had come word that the new Pope had been assassinated, to be replaced with yet another Moor, Abdullah of Tunis, the godfather of Angela. It had been for this reason that Duke Arthur Tudor of Aquitaine had been already in England—though none within the court circles and very few others anywhere else had known of his presence—when the sudden death of King Richard was announced along with the fact that the royal council had met and declared that they had intent of summoning Duke Arthur back from his duchy.

As was later to be revealed, the widow had vociferously objected to and protested the council's decision, declaring herself to be even then pregnant with Richard's child and thus deserving to be named regent, but the council, after a fiery-hot debate which had raged on for many days and resulted in actual bloodshed on at least two occasions, had finally made their decision, announced it, and in a gesture of mollification directed at the storming widow, indicated their intent to suggest that Arthur at least consider himself marrying her.

But with the crown upon his head and all the realm rejoicing, King Arthur III Tudor had flatly declined the "honor" proffered by the royal council, saying, "Gentlemen, the stenches raised by the open dalliances of her who was married to my late brother are such that they were wafted clear to Aquitaine and beyond. I would as lief couple with a brood sow as with that Moorish-Roman harlot. No, we shall find us a chaste girl out of some other house, that I may be certain that the children she births are of mine own loins, not the get of some mincing, perfumed foreign courtier . . . or worse."

Of course, his words quickly reached the ears of the widow, and within his first week as king, two of Arthur's tasters died horribly of poisons. But as he quickly cleared the court of the coterie of Angela's importation, replacing them all with loyal English and Welsh, there were no more overt attempts on his life.

Sooner than might otherwise have been the case, King Arthur III had taken to wife a daughter of the Holy Roman Emperor, one Ilke. The wedding took place about two months after Angela had been delivered of a male infant; for all that the boy bore not one iota of resemblance to the line of her late husband—indeed, looking amazingly alike to her then lover, the Neapolitan ambassador—she almost immediately had begun to crow that he was the rightful King of England, that King Arthur was a usurper and should be deposed if not slain.

But her words reached precious few receptive ears in England or in Wales. Long disgusted with the weakness of his brother where his adulterous wife and her larcenous clique of foreigners had been concerned, all sorts and classes within the kingdom had mourned the dead king for a scandalously short time and then had rallied unrestrainedly to his successor. The very last thing that most in the kingdom desired to see was a return to the bad old times, and such would surely come to pass if Angela should be named regent for her probable bastard.

But others—powerful others—elsewhere heard the woman's pleas and these others took them to heart, one other in particular. Pope Abdul wrote from Rome during Arthur's first year of reign, suggesting that in all fairness, he should step aside in favor of his late and lamented brother's son. Arthur dictated three letters, each one far more heated than the one preceding it, before he finally turned the matter of answer over to his council.

But their diplomatic, courteous, infinitely reasoned letter did not mollify Abdul. His next letter, though still courteously phrased and couched in friendly terms, bore the bare trace of an edge of threat; so bare indeed was the trace that some of the councillors failed to even notice it on first reading and others had to point it out to them. These men, taking their initial letter as a framework, reiterated in greater detail all that they had said before—all that could be said, really, to such a demand—and duly dispatched it to Rome.

The third letter from the south was, though addressed to the king, delivered by papal messenger to the Archbishop of York, at Yorkminster, along with another letter from His Holiness Abdul to "Our esteemed Brother in Christ, Harold of York." Taking both letters, Harold had immediately set out for London, wherein the king and court were just then residing.

In cold fury, Arthur had waved the two letters before the full council before handing them over to be read by the hastily summoned men, declaring, "That despicable Moorish camel's turd! Know you, gentlemen, old Abdul is even as we speak here suborning, inciting treachery and treason against your king, in divers parts of our realm. Of course, you all know His Grace Harold, Archbishop of York, here. Well, the first of these two letters was sent to him. You will note that His unholy Holiness endeavored to bribe His Grace of York, to bribe him most blatantly, and a quite handsome bribe, too; indeed, we do not know if we could have so quickly refused it, had we been in the place of His Grace of York.

"But thanks be to God that His Grace recalled— and we repeat *his* very words, mind you all—that he was an Englishman before he was a priest. We can but pray our Savior that all men of power in our realm recall that sentiment when they are offered bribes by this most dishonorable Bishop of Rome."

Musing, now, in his alchemical laboratory, the aged man called Harold of York thought, "All that the late Abdul had offered me then—for the performance of what he called my 'holy duty' of moving to see King Arthur III deposed and/or slain and Angela named regent for her son—was a mere cardinal's hat. Now he's dead—some say of poison— Angela and her bastard are dead, Arthur is firmly on his throne, and, with a multinational movement afoot to make of York another papal city, like Rome, Constantinople, and Addis Ababa, two of the most powerful cardinals of the Italian Faction have sent a secret letter offering me, once more, a cardinalcy with a strong hint of even more wonderful things to come do I but give over plans now afoot, deliver up England, Wales, and Scotland back into the Roman papal camp, and travel myself to Palermo in Sicily for consultation with my two benefactors.

"Just how am I to answer these powerful churchmen? That is the question. Am I ambitious enough a frog to trade my small puddle for a bigger one? Here I am a very big frog indeed; in all modesty, I think that I can state that I'm the second most powerful man in this kingdom. Would I own so much power in Rome? I strongly doubt it.

"Oh, I know well what Sicola and D'Este are about. Northern Europeans, especially, have been disenchanted by the bickerings of Rome for years now; the power there has rocked unsteadily from Moorish-Spanish Faction to Italian-French-Hungarian Faction and precious little in the way of power or gain has gone to those of any of the smaller factions. If our schemes and conferences here succeed, if York is established as a new papacy, Sicola and D'Este and certainly not a few others are terrified that York will soon come to completely replace Rome, just as Addis Ababa replaced Alexandria long ago under similar circumstances. So can they really prevail upon me to bring this kingdom, the hotbed of the scheming, back under the sway of Rome, it will be well worth anything they need to give me to achieve that end. They haven't written such, of course—they'd be fools, and fools is one thing they certainly are not!—but I doubt not for one minute but that were I to mention a desire to sit on the Throne of Saint Peter, they'd offer me that, too . . . maybe even deliver on that promise, though just how long I'd live after that is anybody's guess; assassination is a fine art and a hoary, honored profession in Rome.

"Ah, but how can I go to Italy, no matter what the inducement? No one questions my incredibly long, unnaturally long life here, in England, but there surely would be questions in plenty there, and no good answers, no answers that could or would be believed by Renaissance churchmen, and I'd more than likely end up burnt at the stake if the preceding tortures didn't kill me first.

"If young Emperor Egon and his army have purged Rome and Italy as thoroughly as it's said they have, have broken the back of the Moorish-Spanish Papal Faction, truly, then I believe that this new papacy business should be ended, here and now, and that all participating kingdoms should return to Rome, go back under Roman power and go about strengthening there the smaller factions, trying to combine them into a Northern European Faction strong enough to fairly compete with the Italian-French-Hungarian and the certain-to-become-resurgent Moorish-Spanish Faction. But how to say these thoughts of mine, how to word them without seeming to be betraying those who have come here from their own lands to attempt to form something new and, hopefully, better than the sorry kakistocracy Rome has projected of the most of the last century?

"However, I must come up with some kind of an acceptable reply soon, for there is a definite limit to just how long I can expect to keep D'Este's messenger, that papal knight, Ser Ugo D'Orsini, cooling his heels here in Yorkminster. For, for all my vaunted security measures, I can be damned certain that a whole host of folk here know just who and what he is, maybe even why he came here to me, though I doubt strongly that anyone else knows just what was the gist of the correspondence he brought and it would take more technology than anyone in this age owns to get to that correspondence where it now is reposing."

Glancing down at his notes, he smiled. "And it would take a person from my own world and time to read any of this, too, while not a few of this age and world can't even read their own language or write any more than their names. A spy would find little but discontent in my private chambers, God be thanked."

Then, thinking better of the matter, he corrected himself. "Well, Bass Foster or Rupen Ademian both have enough education and a provenance close enough to my own time to probably absorb the gist of these notes, anyway, though some of the words and usages no doubt would be obscure even to them." Then the old man showed worn teeth in a grin, adding, "But Rome and her minions would play merry hell trying to get either of them to spy against the interests of me or the kingdom. And they're neither of them any more of this particular time and world than am I. And it's clearly my fault that they're here in this time and world, too, dammit, for all that the both of them—fine, caring men that they are—try to reassure me and tell me that the two malfunctions of the projector console that precipitated them and the folk who arrived with them were merely happenstance. No, I know the truth of the matter full well; I should have either made Emmett cut it off after his last failure of so long ago or, myself, at least axed through the power cable that still connected the wretched thing to our old world, Emmett's and mine."

He sighed deeply. "But, of course, had I then done so, there is an excellent chance that Rome and her crusader minions might long since have conquered this kingdom. Lacking the very valuable knowledges and abilities of Bass Foster, Peter Fairley, Buddy Webster, Carey Carr, and, yes, even that egocentric, treasonous lunatic Professor William Collier, that accursed adulteress might reign even now, and King Arthur and all the rest of us loyal subjects might be dead or forever exiled and the wealth of the kingdom be flowing remorselessly into the bottomless coffers of Rome.

"And Rupen Ademian is every bit as invaluable,

in his own way, too, as any of those who were projected here before him. Peter Fairley attests that the man is a constantly flowing fountain of detailed information regarding the manufacture of nineteenth-century firearms and accessories. Furthermore, thanks almost entirely to the experiments of Rupen and Peter to improve upon the cannon primers Peter had been making, we now have matches in this world and time—not very many, just yet, true, but due to the meticulous records of their experiments kept by Rupen, we now know just how to make them. And Rupen says that that knowledge wasn't gained in our old world until at least two and a half centuries beyond the current date in this world, and that is a big something; I can but speculate just how far and how fast this world may go on to develop on the basis of that one tiny invention alone.

"And, better, they did finally come up with the cannon primers. They're just simple, waterproofed tubes of metal filled with a dried mixture of sesquisulfide of phosphorus, with a twist of wire at one end to which to attach a lanyard and to serve when given a sharp jerk as the friction device for striking into fire the compound, the fire thus produced then proceeding down the tube, melting out the waterproof seal and igniting the propellant charge in the chamber of the cannon.

"The king was almighty pleased when these were demonstrated to him, for he's nothing if not a great captain, all too conversant with all aspects of war and warfare, and he knows just how many lives the implementation of such a device will save, especially on the crowded gundecks of ships at sea, where open casks of powder and linstocks holding smoldering slow-matches have presented a very real and ongoing hazard to the lives and well-being of all aboard since the very first cannon was mounted onboard a ship.

"And when Rupen and Peter remarked to His Highness that, even as they spoke, Carey Carr was back at the Royal Cannon Foundry here in York hard at work on the development of waterproof primer caps for use on shoulder arms and pistols, explaining to him just what such a development would mean to an army in the field, Arthur saw Peter and Rupen initiated into his new Order of Royal Champions, Carey Carr to be so initiated and sworn immediately he can find time from his labors to get to court, declaring him an esquire of the order, meantime, and that's a signal honor in itself, in that it makes our Carey officially a gentleman in this society.

"Alas, these are things that I possibly should have thought of and at least experimented upon over the years, but so very much specialized was education become in my old world that I simply lacked any in-depth knowledge of anything save my particular field of endeavor, it just required men from a less specialized age to find ways to adapt their knowledge to this age, this world.

"But it's not only in weapons of war, new and more efficient ways of killing, that these unspecialized men have helped and are helping this new world into which they were projected, either. Thanks mostly to Bass Foster, the royal camps now are much cleaner, healthier places, with latrines and royal orders that they be used, refuse pits, and water sources upstream or uphill of both, and regular details of soldiers to tour the camp and keep it clean of litter, fill in standing water, chase off swine and stray dogs or chickens and scoop up the dung of horses, mules, and draught-oxen. After he became Lord Commander of the Royal Horse, Bass implemented such measures in the cavalry camps, and so impressed did Arthur become at the exceedingly low incidences of the usual camp fevers and diseases in those camps that he sent for Bass, questioned him at length and in some depth, then rode roughshod over the many objections of his other commanders and promulgated the present strict rules to apply in future to all royal encampments as well as to encampments of the court when traveling.

"Not only that, but thanks to Peter Fairley, the king, the court, and not a few others—my episcopal self included, God be praised—are bodily cleaner and sweeter-smelling these days, while the coffers of the archdiocese are now blessed with a new source of most welcome revenue, and all these blessings of the same cause.

"Bass Foster, sick and tired of either going dirty or burning his skin with the caustic semisolids that passed under the name of soap in this world when first he arrived here, appealed to Peter to apply his inventive genius—a very real genius, too; the man had precious little formal education in his own world and time and still speaks what I am told is a very crude dialect of twentieth-century English—and with no real knowledge of chemistry, Peter proceeded to go by trial and error until he had produced a fine, hard-milled soap that was not only far less caustic than current products but was scented with oil of lavender. When gifts of it were sent to the king, it created such a sensation at court that an immediate and impressive demand for it was created, and far more was needed to fulfill orders than Peter could produce in the small corner of the Royal Cannon Foundry and Powder manufactory that he had allotted to it.

"When he came to me with the problem, I offered him a charter and my full backing, for it looked to be portending a virtual gold mine of income, but that honest, selfless man insisted—finally, profanely, and blasphemously insisted over my objections—that I and the archdiocese stand to receive the bulk of any profits if I backed the venture. So that is how

Yorkminster now is operating and tremendously profiting from a manufactory of scented soaps and now a fine deodorant Peter has developed of common parsley and certain other plants in a paste form.

"Nor is that the end of the man's inventiveness, either. When he was advised by one of his blacksmiths—thank God he didn't go to one of the Guild of Physicians; he'd most likely have been bled half to death if not poisoned—to chew willow twigs soaked in ale for relief of headaches, and found that the folk remedy actually was efficacious, he and Rupen went to work on several bushels of willow twigs right here in this very chamber, using my equipment, and have developed powder which, when stirred into a gill of ale or light wine and swallowed, rather quickly acts as a fine analgesic. And that is a something of which *I* should have thought, long ago. I also should have thought of something that Rupen recently broached: primitive—well, primitive in my time on my old world, at least—antibiotics were compounded of the same chemicals as are found in wheatbread mold, and God knows there is more than enough of that always around in this world; therefore, I've been myself conducting some experiments along those lines.

"And how could I do all of this, take a part in all these so very important projects in Rome, whether as cardinal or pope? I suppose I could take Peter and Rupen with me on loan from Arthur, but I find little enough time for experiments as a mere paramount archbishop, and I doubt me not but that the schedules of more senior churchmen are even more crowded and hectic. No doubt, Ser Ugo D'Orsini could tell me much of the schedules of cardinals, were I to inquire of him . . . hmm." The old man scribbled yet another cryptic note on the sheet of vellum.

* * *

Far away from Yorkminster and from York, across
most of the whole width of England, then across the
restless Irish Sea, then across more land, near to a
place called Lagore in the personal lands of the *Ard-
Righ* of Ireland, sprawled an impressive palace complex. Although only the nucleus of it was built for
defense or really defensible, it still was called by the
old name of that nucleus: Castle Lagore, and the
presently reigning *Ard-Righ* or High King preferred
it to all his other residences, even the more formal
palace near Tara Hill.

As Harold Kenmore sat in his private alchemical
laboratory that grey day, musing and thinking hard,
so too did High King Brian VIII (known as Brian
the Burly to his subjects) sit within a private chamber of his own, brooding, musing, and thinking very
hard indeed. But his chamber of thoughts was much
different from that of Harold Kenmore. Many men
knew that such a chamber must exist somewhere in
either the Lagore Palace complex or in the Tara Palace, but only a mere handful of his closest advisers
knew exactly where it was, and only three men in
all of Ireland—himself, his eldest son and presumed
heir, and Baron Slane, his chief minister—knew how
to gain entry to it or safely exit it once they had
entered, for the ancient builders had sown the way
with deadly traps to ensnare the unwanted and un-
wary.

Though fairly lofty, the chamber was far from
large and was so crowded with chests and caskets as
to leave barely enough room for a refectory table and
a backed armchair. Windowless, it needs must always be lit by lamps or tapers. It was built into the
very fabric of the oldest part of the palace, the ancient Castle Lagore, so walls, floor, and vaulted
ceiling were all of bare grey stone, nor was any door
visible to the uninitiated even from within the chamber, and more than one interloper in past centuries

who had chanced to find his way into the treasure room of the High Kings had died of thirst and starvation within long before his moldered remains had been found and removed. Others had succumbed to the deadly traps along the way, and although the castle had fallen to assault, sieges, and treachery a few times in its long history, no one ever had found, breached, and looted this chamber.

Knowing full well that no one could possibly disturb him in this so secret retreat, Brian often came to it to talk out problems with himself under circumstances where no living soul could hear aught which he spoke aloud. On previous visits, he right often had unlocked one of the treasure coffers and laid before him atop the table a tray of jewels—those of the Magical Jewels of Ireland, the ancient symbols of sovereignty of the various kingdoms which went to make up the island, which he owned or at least held, while he had schemed and planned how to best and most quickly acquire possession of the others— but in the hideous light of all which had so recently occurred in Ireland, the sight of the Jewels and the subsequent thoughts of how terribly his careful plans and schemes had gone astray so upset him as to almost deprive him of the power of reason, so he instead had placed atop the table on this day a bronzen coffer of ancient coins—some of them dating back to the old Roman Empire—that he might absently finger them as he thought.

Looking down on the worn visage purporting to be that of the Emperor Severus, he demanded, ''Were ever you so vexed as I've been this last year, old-timer? I doubt it. Things were so much simpler and easier for rulers in those olden days. These accursed modern times age a king well before his natural time, I trow.

''This time last year, I not only held my patrimonial lands, but I'd made clients of the kings of

Lagan and Airgialla, my armies were sitting siege before Corcaigh, the capital of Muma, and also had marched into Connachta, defeated everything that stood before them, and driven that plaguey king of theirs and his scarbrous sons into their burrow and were set to smoke them out.

"I should rightly have let matters rest there, taken what I could as soon as I could with the force I then owned. But, oh, no, I had to outwit myself, cozen Cousin Arthur of England and Wales into making me the loan of his famous great captain, the Duke of Norfolk and his condotta, that owning the use of an additional striking force I might win more quickly the whole of Ireland, that I might then become a real High King, ruling the entire island, not merely a couple of counties, as Cousin Arthur rules England and Wales.

"Well, I'm hoist by my own petard, now. I got the Duke and his condotta, right enough, and along with them more trouble than I could have imagined would come my way. It's not that he's not all he's reputed to be, this Sir Bass—he and his can do and have here done stupendous things, militarily speaking; his private war-fleet is almost as large as mine and better armed, too, and those fine, light little field pieces, which can be taken apart and packed on mules or horses and so go anywhere horsemen can go, have given a rude and deadly surprise to not a few on this island. But the other things he's done and the things that have happened simply because of the fact that he's here . . .

"And having talked with the man, come to know him very well, in fact, I don't think he has done any of it deliberately, has not ever entertained any thoughts of harming me or discommoding any of my plans for Ireland. By his lights, he's always done the things he considered right, what was needful of the doing in order to carry out my orders to him. Yes,

I'm convinced that the obedient man truly meant well . . . but, oh and alas, what he wrought for me!

"I first sent him up to Ulaid to somehow get the then Jewel of that kingdom from off the foul finger of the Ui Neill bastard cousin who then was the usurper-king there. He did it, too, and I still can't say I understand completely just how he did it all, based on eyewitness reports. Well, the bastard king is dead and I own his Jewel, but it's no longer of any save intrinsic value to anyone—just another big, yellowish diamond set in a heavy gold ring with a trick band that expands and contracts—for while the Duke was up there, one of his men, an Italian knight, fell into muddy peat at the edge of Lough Neagh and was dragged out with the centuries-lost original Jewel of Ulaid stuck into the flesh of one of his plaguey feet, and now *he's* the King of Ulaid.

"Nor is that the end of this sorry mess of slops up there. My client of Airgialla, both he and his queen, along with some of the court, were murdered and their only child, an infant, was taken away, all in a night.

"*Righ* Roberto di Bolgia of Ulaid, meanwhile, knowing the real weaknesses of his new little kingdom and of my designs upon it, betook himself to Islay by galley, gave over Ulaid to the Lord of the Isles, the Regulus, and received it back as a feoff. Oh, that piece of filth, that shrewd, scheming, conniving Italian turd! He knew that I would not dare to attack—well, not openly attack anyway—a vassal of that grim old man. Hellfire, alone, the damned Regulus is near as powerful as I am, and if he brought in his other vassals—as he would—he could crush us like so many beetles. So, he succeeding in his end of protecting his little kingdom from me, it's as safely out of my reach now as if a steel wall surrounded it all. If only the bastard had let matters go

at that. But oh, no, trust a damned Italian assassin
to twist the dagger in the wound.

"Lo and behold, when I sent part of the Duke's
condotta up into Airgialla to oust some crackpate
nobleman who had declared himself 'Priest-king'
subsequent to the royal murders, what should con-
front the column but *Righ* Roberto of Ulaid and a
not-inconsiderable and well-armed force of fighting
men holding a fortification of timber built squarely
across the road at a shrewdly chosen point. This
miscreant that they call *Righ* in Ulaid now informed
Sir Bass's troops that as he now is fostering the missing infant heir to the throne of Airgialla, he has also
assumed the title and duties of regent to rule and
sustain that kingdom until the child's maturity. I was
in receipt of those foul words at about the same time
that I was in receipt of the damned letter from that
forever-damned Regulus Aonghas and God alone
knows what kept my wits in my head and the hot
blood from bursting forth from my poor body that
ill-omened day.

"Nor is this mother's mistake, *Righ* Roberto, the
only di Bolgia who seems set on plaguing me as old
Saint Job of Scripture was said to have been plagued.
Cardinal D'Este had sent to Muma a condotta of
Italian and Ifriqan mercenaries under command of a
famous captain, His Grace Ser Timoteo, *il Duce* di
Bolgia, to aid the then *Righ,* a congenital lunatic,
Tàmhas Fitz Gerald, in keeping his throne. I arranged to meet with this Ser Timoteo and—as he was
becoming very much aware within a very short time
of the necessity of . . . ahem, 'replacing' the drool-
ing idiot Tàmhas with a man whose ideas of modern
military tactics did not all concern an all-or-nothing
charge of heavy cavalry—I set up other meetings and
at last arranged for him to replace *Righ* Tàmhas with
another of that mad ilk of dangerously inbred Nor-

mans, one Sean Fitz Robert, a man who seemed at least willing to and capable of learning.

"Well, *Righ* Tàmhas died of a cracked skull, said by right many to have been taken in a drunken, accidental, and well-witnessed fall down a flight of granite stairs. The first time ever I set eyes upon that treacherous lout of a Ser Roberto di Bolgia, indeed, was when he and Ser Ugo D'Orsini rode up here with the Star of Muma, the Jewel of that kingdom, that I might replace it with a cleverly wrought forgery. They'd lifted it in the very hour of the funeral of *Righ* Tàmhas." The big, muscular man chuckled at the memory of so humorous an act of posthumous lèse majesté wrought against an old enemy.

"So, Sir Sean Fitz Robert was crowned *Righ* of Muma and things briefly appeared to be progressing in the direction I had nudged them. But then that howling pack of addlepates, the Fitz Geralds, trooped into Corcaigh and, cozening Ser Timoteo with a need to invest *Righ* Sean as *ri* or chief of Fitz Gerald, managed to get the poor bastard to themselves long enough to murder him, then roused the townsfolk, somehow won to them the Ifriqan mercenary cavalry, and first attacked the royal palace, which was defended by the condotta of di Bolgia, then poured out of the city and threw themselves at what was by then left of my besiegers. Well tenderized by my entrenched troops outside the walls, the survivors fled back into the supposed safety of Corcaigh only to be shot and cut and stabbed and speared and clubbed down to almost the last man by di Bolgia and his condotta, looking for blood and finding it.

"Ser Ugo D'Orsini had fought his way out of Corcaigh during the darkest-seeming hour, when it had looked as if di Bolgia and his force would be hard pressed even to hold the palace against the Fitz Geralds, the foresworn Ifriqans, and the howling mob, and despite his terrible wounds, had ridden to me, here. But by the time I, with my bodyguards and part of the Duke's condotta, came before the walls of Corcaigh, bodies were being tossed down from the walls or dragged in wainloads out from within the city that they might be thrown into the trenches that my troops had vacated when the siege was lifted, and di Bolgia rode out to tell me that he again had the reins firmly in hand.

"I should have sent Sir Bass home then, but I didn't! I can damn myself for a fool for the rest of my life. But how was I to know then that which I know now?"

CHAPTER
THE FOURTH

As the Archbishop of York mused in England and the *Ard-Righ* Brian VIII mourned his undeserved reverses in Ireland, that day, far and far to the westward, across the width of Ireland, the vast reaches of the Atlantic Ocean, and many leagues of land on its western shores, in yet another fortified dwelling place of dressed stone and timber and packed earth, a group of men and women sat in conference. The Archbishop might have recognized a few of them; the High King would have recognized none.

Those gathered together in the spacious chamber were clearly, to any objective observer not knowing more of them, of several races or subraces, this easily evident from faces, body shapes and sizes, skin tones, and differences in hair, beards, eyes, and suchlike. Although all were sun- and weather-browned, some were so much darker that it was obvious their skins had been darker to begin, and the males of this segment, for all that they owned long thick braids of coarse black hair, sported beards that were either skimpy or nonexistent and very little visible body hair. Most of the lighter-skinned males, on the other hand, wore full beards and thick, flaring moustaches, and some of them had arms, legs, and bodies almost as thickly furred as those of many apes.

Within the high-ceilinged, stone-walled and paved chamber, it was far cooler than the sun-baked, scorching, windless outside world; nonetheless, all the men and women were sheened in sweat and wore only as much clothing as each felt he or she had to wear. They sat or squatted around an empty firepit of smoothly dressed stone, passing two large, long-stemmed pipes of smoldering tobacco and a porous, clay *olla* of tepid water. However, despite the heat, a number of them wore on their heads plain, unadorned hats that looked to be—and were—of gleaming silver; and though periodically the wearers would doff the helmet long enough to wipe the forehead beneath it and the front rim of the metal with a bit of rag, they always replaced it on their heads.

Through the doorway another of the lighter-skinned variety of man strode rapidly, streaming perspiration from seemingly every pore. "Sorry," he panted to no one in particular. "Me and some the Creek fellers were down in the basement of the magazine loading cartridges for the rifles all morning and Bear Claw just come to find me and tell me about this shindig. I miss anything?"

A slender, striking blond woman answered him, saying, "No, not a thing, Haighie. Arsen and the Micco are still in the back room talking to those four young Creeks that Soaring Eagle's patrol brought back up here with them from their reconnaissance of the Spanish settlements and fort down near the mouth of the river. Sit down and have a drink of water. You look like you could use a salt tablet, too." Reaching into her shoulder bag, she proffered a bottle.

Nodding his thanks, the hirsute man tossed the tablet into his mouth with gunpowder-blackened fingers, then accepted a gourd dipper of water. But when he had swallowed both tablet and water, he made a face. "Muthafuck! That stuff's hot as horse-piss! What I really need's a ice-cold beer or six. When in hell's Arsen gonna take the carrier back to where we come from and bring us some beer and all like he use to, Ilsa?''

Ilsa frowned. ''You know the answer to that question without me telling you again, Haighie. Arsen just doesn't like to steal without some very good or pressing reason, and he has none of the little gold bars left; he had to use most of them to keep that wretched, greedy, good-for-nothing Squash Woman and her clique overfed and happy before the Micco came.''

''But, good God, Ilsa,'' expostulated the newcomer, ''he goes back and talks and works out things with his papa all the time, and Uncle Kogh is rich as I don't know what, and no way he wouldn't lay some bread on Arsen was he to ask him for it. You know that good's I do.''

''Bills have serial numbers, Haighie,'' she replied. ''That means they and their travels can be traced, especially bills of higher denominations. It's just not the same thing as taking goods and leaving behind plain, unmarked, flat ingots of pure gold.''

''Arsen doesn't like to steal, huh?'' said Haigh Panoshian, with a tinge of bitterness. ''Try telling that to the Spanish downriver, there, what he's stole at least a half of ton of gunpowder from, not to mention all the swivel guns and sacks of grain and whatnot. If that ain't stealing, then what is?''

Another of the lighter-skinned men, this one with a full, dark-brown beard but no moustache, replied, grinning, ''It's what your dear cousin chooses to call a 'military expediency,' Haighie. It's the old and quite honorable practice of letting your enemy supply you such as you need in order to better fight him. Both my people—the Greeks—and yours—the Armenians—used it against the goddam Turks for hundreds of years; too bad those old fellows didn't have some of these carriers and projectors. I tell you, it must be driving the Spanish down there up the fucking wall how their barrels of powder and guns off their boats and off the very walls of their fort just keep disappearing without a damn sound in the middle of nights no matter how many guards they mount and keep around.

"If only Arsen and the Micco and Swift Otter would do what I've been thinking about, we could drive those Spanish so fucking crazy, so damn bananas, that they'd shag ass out of that fort and town and go bother somebody else. But . . . oh, hell, there's no point in trying to argue with him and the Micco anymore. They don't want to hear psychological warfare, all they seem to want is blood."

The blond woman spoke again. "Oh, John, you know better than that. If all Arsen had in mind was killing Spaniards, he could've . . . we could've wiped out every one of them that he purposely let escape from that island base of theirs, the night we freed the pen of slaves they were holding. For that matter, you know how awesome the power available to a person in a carrier. Don't you think he could've wiped out the whole settlement and fort by now if he wanted to? Or sink that big ship instead of just damaging it and setting it adrift that night? You have a very fine brain, John; think with it, not with your emotions. There's more than enough brainless thinking going on around here, anyway."

"What the fuck's that s'posed to mean, huh, Ilsa?" demanded two of the other bearded men, almost in chorus.

"Methinks my lady's roving shaft hath fleshed," said another. This speaker was a man of a skin tone lighter than that of any of the others except the blond woman. Though not so big and large-framed as the other lighter-skinned men, he was extremely muscular, his limbs and body bearing not a few scars.

His brown hair hung in two long, thick braids bound with strips of dyed doeskin, and his flaring moustaches soared up into points resembling the horns of buffalo. His beard, however, had been neatly clipped into a spade shape, while small reddish-gold rings—taken from off the body of a dead Spaniard—depended from the smallish lobes of his flat ears. His few articles of clothing were exactly alike to those of most of the darker-skinned men, and like them he squatted on the calloused heels of his bare feet rather than sitting on the floor.

One of the two men who had yelped now turned to him of the golden earrings, demanding, "Who the fuck asked you to put your big mouth into it, Simon, huh?"

He got no immediate answer, for Simon Delahaye was just then sucking a great lungful of smoke from out one of the circulating pipes of strong tobacco. Of them all, only he, Arsen Ademian, and Mike Sikeena seemed to really relish the stuff, the others taking as few shallow puffs as Creek or Shawnee courtesy required.

"Aw, you leave Simon alone, Greg," said another of the bearded men, Al Ademian, " 'cause I warn you, you get into another fucking donnybrook with him, you're on your own this time; I'll just let him clean your fucking clock for good and all."

"Any time, buddy," said Greg Sinclair in brittle tones. "And I don't need no kinda help, neither, Al, yours or nobody else's . . . long's it's just Simon and me, long's some his fucking redskins, his fucking blood brothers, his bunghole buddies, don't pitch in to help him."

Before Simon could exhale his smoke, voices were heard from outside the room, then seven more men entered it, still conversing. When all within the chamber once more were seated or squatting, and a very old, white-haired darker man—the Micco of the

Creeks—and a younger, lighter-skinned, black-bearded man—Arsen Ademian—positioned on a slightly elevated dais made up of a thick slab of waxed hardwood covered with colorful cloth, Arsen began to speak.

"Everybody got his helmet on? Look, everybody here that speaks English except Simon, take off your helmet and loan it to one of the ones who doesn't, huh? When we get into discussion, you can have them back. That way, we won't have to waste a whole lot of time while Simon translates into Shawnee and Creek, see."

The transfers of silver headpieces effected, he began by saying, "Crooked Knife, here, and three other members of the Turtle Clan of the Creeks took French leave of the Spanish fort down by the mouth of the river and Soaring Eagle run on to them on his way back up here from there. The Spanish have brought in a bunch of new Indians, see, what Crooked Knife and the Micco call Worm Hunters and some other things that are flat insulting any way you translate them; some of this lot are half-breeds and most of them speak Spanish, too. Crooked Knife and the other three Creeks didn't think they could get along with them, didn't like them one damn bit, and, besides, had some way heard that the Micco was somewhere up here, so they just deserted one night."

"Arsen," snapped Greg Sinclair, "how you know them redskins ain't pulling the fucking wool over your eyes, huh? They could just as easy been *sent* up here by the spics to spy on us, too."

"Don't worry, Greg," replied Arsen, "I already thought of that angle. I checked with the carrier control and found out how to go deep enough into their heads to find out whether whatall they were saying, were telling me and the Micco and Swift Otter, was the truth. It was, buddy, every fucking word of it.

"But back to what I was going to say, now. Any the rest of you got questions, wait till I'm done, hear? Like I've told you and the rest of the guys and gals who've been downriver in the carriers have told you, the Spanish are gearing up down there. They've towed that big ship from off the mudbank back up to the basin near the fort and rerigged it and took some of the biggest guns off it so it doesn't draw as much water and that can't mean anything else but the fuckers mean to come upriver in it.

"But it was another thing I noticed but didn't bother talking about because I didn't understand about it, but after talking to Crooked Knife, I do. The Spanish have cut down enough big old trees to make them a couple of humongous rafts that right now are both pulled up on the riverbank just upstream of the town or village or whatever you call it. I seen them, but I thought when I did that the fuckers just were leaving them there until they had got around to cutting them up for timber or firewood or something, but Crooked Knife says different. He says that the Spanish mean to partially deck them, mount big guns on them, tow them up here, and use those guns against this place, that they call a *fortaleza*. All they're waiting for right now is a supply ship with more gunpowder—seems their powder keeps disappearing, ever so often, out from their magazine, barrels of it at a time." He grinned, and not a few around the circle chuckled, snorted mirth, or laughed merrily.

"Also, they're expecting shipsful of more soldiers from some other forts down south of here, maybe Cuba or Florida, I don't know, and some more of these Hunter Indians, too. The ships are supposed to be to the fort anytime now, and we can fucking bet our ass the Spanish will be up here after our blood very soon after that. And that's why I called ever'body together, now: We need to talk this whole thing out and figure what's going to be the best thing for us to do—cut and run up to that valley up north or stand and fight the fuckers off here, then go up to the valley.

"Before I say what I feel about it, I'll tell you what the Micco told me. He knows I want to draw other tribes into a real sizable confederation that can cut the Spanish and any other fucking Europeans over here down to size and make the fuckers give up slaving and killing the Indians just to be killing something, the way they've been doing. He says the only way I can attract the kind of Indians I want in the numbers that'll be needed is to beat the piss out of the Spanish a couple of times and then just pass the word around. And he thinks this here is a damn good time and place to start out. The old man's prob'ly right, he usually is, you all know that."

"But what do *you* think we should do, Arsen?" demanded Ilsa.

He shrugged his hirsute shoulders. "Hell, honey, I don't know. I never did get a kick out of shooting fish in a barrel, and you can't call us going after guys armed with single-shot muzzle-loaders and cannons and swords and crossbows when we're in flying carriers and APCs that their weapons can't even scratch anything else besides shooting fish in a fucking barrel. Think of the cleared space between here and the river. Got it in your mind's eye, honey? Now, think of it with dead and dying Spanish soldiers and Indians ever place you look. That's just what it's going to be like after we've sunk enough of their ships and boats that they decide to launch a frontal attack and get to see the business end of a couple of medium machine guns face to face, not to mention all our cannons and swivel guns and the flintlock rifles and pistols that are better, more accurate, and faster to load and fire than anything they've got. We sure Lord don't have enough medical supplies to go in after any battle like that, so do you think you've got what it takes just to wait and listen to the poor, wounded fuckers scream, and whine and moan and whimper and gasp until they finally die? Or could you go out there and shoot them in the head, put them down, out of their misery, honey? You think you could—''

"Stop it, Arsen!" she ordered from between clenched teeth, her slender body shuddering strongly as if in some spasm.

"I'm sorry, honey . . . Ilsa," he said softly, gently. "I . . . I guess I just got carried away, said it all stronger than I needed to is what. What I mean is, I don't want to have to fight them here, not because I'm afraid of fighting them, just the contrary, because I know they can bring more men up that river in ships than they could march through the woods or crowd into rowboats and canoes to get farther up the river where it's too shallow for ships to sail. The more they bring up, the more we'll have to kill or wound and let die, see. So what I want to do is start the people toward the valley, either cross-country or up the river in the boats we captured or the dozen or so Shawnee canoes.

"I'll keep just enough warriors here to hold the fort if we have to and to get everything ready for transporting when the time is right for it and the rods are in place up north there to guide the loads in right and all. Us who stay here can take turns flying a carrier up there to choose places for everything to go and setting the rods, even before the people get there. I mean to take the whole damn fort, hill and all; we've put too damn much sweat and time and effort into this place to just go off and leave it for the fucking Spanish is how I feel, Ilsa."

John the Greek chuckled evilly. "I like your plan, Arsen. I'd just like to be a fucking bird in a tree when the fucking Spanish come sailing up the river, loaded for bear, and find nobody to fight, no fucking fort, no nothing.''

Arsen shook his head. ''Give the fuckers credit for more know-how than that, John. They are pros, no two ways about it. They're not going to just come sailing up here blind—no, they'll send a patrol or two through the woods and prob'ly another one in small boats up the river, too, to feel out the defenses, see just what we do have to throw at them. If I was them, I'd set up an advance base and CP on that island where what we left of their little fort is, keep the ships and most the men down there till the patrols come back in and are debriefed. Then—''

''So what we oughta do,'' interrupted Greg Sinclair, ''is to fucking rig that whole damn island, Arsen. That is, if you don't wanta just take all three of the carriers down there one night soon and stop the fuckers afore they can get started. Go back to your papa in our old world and get him to give you some land mines and grenades and booby-trap kits, and maybe some plastique, too. And we could show the fucking Shawnees and Creeks how to make up and set a whole bunch of punjee sticks, soak the fuckers in the latrine for a few weeks first, and you know.''

''God, but you're bloodthirsty!'' burst out Ilsa, in horror and disgust. ''Bullets and metal shards are bad enough. But have you ever seen, ever had to try to correct, the damages of barbaric devices like you're thinking about? Well, have you?''

He nodded, grimly. ''Two and half tours in the Nam, Ilsa? You fucking-A right I seen whatall Charlie's shit and ours, too, can do, a whole fucking lot of it to friends of mine, too. But goddamm it, honey, it fucking works; it does the job without exposing none of us to return fire, without us even having to fucking be around, see. And come to that, you done worked on enough Shawnees to know mosta the damn fucking common things them fucking spics done to them they took for slaves and the worser things they done to the ones as was too old or too young or sick or crippled up, too. You think they got anything better'n whatall I'm thinking about comin' to 'em?''

Coldly, she snapped, "Greg, two wrongs do not make a right; never have, never will, and . . .''

The silver headpieces Arsen had made up according to directions of what he had come to think of as his carrier's "brain"* were admirably efficient at their intended function—that of allowing the wearer to understand the speech of others no matter what language they spoke, while projecting the wearer's own intended thoughts directly into the minds of those to whom he spoke in such a way as to convince them that he was speaking their tongue—but these crude copies contained only a small fraction of the functions of the "operator headpiece" which was a part of the full equipment of one of the enigmatic carriers and which were currently being worn by Arsen, John the Greek, and Mike Sikeena, the last ones to have used one of the three carriers the group owned.

Arsen waved a hand impatiently. "Look Ilsa, you want to hold a philosophy class with Greg or somethin', do it when we're not so pressed for time, huh? Besides of which, the Indians can't any of them figger out just what the hell's got your bowels in a fucking uproar anyway, and are wondering if you've fucking flipped your lid or somethin', honey. Honest, you don't b'lieve it, swap hats with John there, and see if I'm not telling you the gospel truth, honey.''

To Sinclair, he said, "Thanks for suggestions, buddy. I'll keep them in mind. But I figger we got

* See *Of Chiefs and Champions*, Signet Books, 1987, and *Of Myths and Monsters*, Signet Books, 1988

more than enough going for us here as it is. All I want to do now is to get the noncombatants away from here before the Spanish get up here, see, and that means starting them north by the end of next week, anyway—all of the Shawnees, excepting Swift Otter and three or four of his bucks, and at least two-thirds of the Creeks—all I want around here when the fireworks start up are some of us and the warriors, no kids, no squaws, no old people except the Micco here, 'cause I don't think we could get him out of here until after the fight, 'less he was tied tight to a fucking ICBM.''

None of the whites could be certain just how the allusion was translated by the far-future technology into the Creek and the Shawnee languages, but there were clear indications of general mirth among the Indians.

Another of the women spoke then. ''Arsen, there's a problem with your time schedule. It's the crops. The Shawnee garden patches mostly aren't ready for harvest yet, won't be for weeks, and those foods will be needed to see them through the winter, since they'll be getting up into that valley far too late to sow another crop. Game and wild foods can only go so far, you know, and since you can't get much more from home . . .''

Arsen Ademian sighed. ''Look, Rose, push comes to shove, I'll go back with a fucking Class Seven projector and flat fucking clean out a supermarket or grocery warehouse or meat packer before I'll let these folks starve. You oughta know me well enough by now to know that, honey. I do have a little bit of the gold left, anyway, but I'm saving it for really important things, like medicines and like that, 'stead of wasting it on canned beer like some y'all'd like me to. But I'm not going to need it for this. See, I'd thought about that angle when I first started thinking about moving all the folks north this summer 'stead of next spring like we'd thought we'd do, at first.

"We've been stealing gunpowder and cannonballs and cannons and piglead and whatall from the Spanish fort right along, no pain, no strain—and you can bet your ass that's slowed the fuckers down, not to mention driving them half crazy wondering just who the fuck was taking ever'thing and how they was getting it out of locked rooms under the fucking noses of the damn sentries and all. I don't read spic and not even one the carrier hats can help you do that, so I ended up with a barrel of their wine, on one run, remember, thinking it was gunpowder. But the fucking stuff smells like vinegar and tastes like cat puke and the onliest one really liked it was Simon, so I never lifted any more of it."

"On the contrary, Friend Arsen Silverhat," remarked the aged, white-haired, wrinkled Micco. "I, too, relish the Spanish liquid. Of old, in the south whence I led my people here, I found it most tasty and found too that it owned the effect of easing the pains that cold or damp weather brings to old bones and joints almost as much as do the little pieces of white, powdery rock that Friend Ilsa has me swallow with water now. So take all of it that you can find and bring it to me. I promise to share equally with my friend the mighty warrior and leader of warriors Captain Simon."

Arsen chuckled. "One barrel of wine coming up, *Der* Micco . . . among other things. See, Rose, you know damn well if the Spanish are going to be bringing in more troops, they're damn well going to have to have laid up rations to feed them while they're on hand. So I mean to just flit into there from time to time and project back enough of their grub to feed our folks through the winter and the early spring, up north, in the valley; I'll project it up here and then once we get the crypt in place up there, so there'll be a varmint-proof place to keep it, I'll project it all up there. It, some of it, might be things the Indians aren't too familiar with, but if the Spanish live on it, so can we. You know, rice, rye, oats, dried onions and garlic and chili peppers, loaf sugar, cured meat, pickled vegetables, lard, stuff like that—least, those are things I've seen stored down there. Plus more barrels of hard crackers—and when I say hard, I mean fucking *hard,* too, hard as pieces of fucking slate hard—than you could shake a fucking stick at.

"But I won't take enough of anything to do more than just slow the fuckers down, see. Just like we won't try to wipe them out when they get up here, just hurt them bad enough to send them back down-river to lick their wounds and get ready to hit us here again. Only by the time they get back up to pay us another social call, not only will we all be gone but the fort will be, too, and that ought to be a real kick in the balls to them. But they're tough fuckers, professionals, and sooner or later, they'll get over it and still be madder than hops at us, so they'll cast around till they find the trail and they'll send the best force they can after us, or maybe just a sizable patrol, first off, to locate us and then a bigger unit.

"But if they come up the river, find out they can get up there that way and do it, they're going to have to leave all their big, deep-draught ships behind, and that means no big guns, nothing any bigger than swivel guns. And with nothing but fucking deer trails through the woods, they're gonna play hell getting any of their guns that're bigger than men can break down and carry on their backs to use against us up north. But that'll prob'ly be some time next summer or fall."

"But Arsen," pleaded Ilsa, "if you truly feel the way you say you do, why fight them at all? Why not just get completely beyond their reach? Why not project everybody and everything up to the valley, not leave a trail of any kind they can follow?''

The black-bearded man sighed and shook his head, setting his thick braids of hair to swishing. "Because it won't work, honey, not in the long run. The Indians in our world, that's just what a whole lot of them did as soon as they found out they couldn't drive the Europeans back, out of their lands—they moved away from the parts of the country that had been theirs and that the whites were then occupying, only to see their children and grandchildren go through the same things they had as more and more whites came from Europe. Despite all the wars and diseases and starvation in Europe in this world, just like it was in our world, it's flat running over with people; from what I heard and understood while we were in this world's England and what the Micco has told me, I'd say it's prob'ly more people living on that one island than there are Indians in this whole damn continent, and Spain is bound to have more people than England, too. And there's Irish up north of here, along the Atlantic coast, and French north of them and Norwegians or Swedes or Danes up north of the French, so none of these Indians are going to stand a fucking chance unless they all get together, stop fighting each other, and stand up against the whites, see.

"But according to Micco, I could talk myself blue in the face to the various tribes within traveling distance—Tuscaroras, Shawnees, Cherokees, Powhatans, the other Creeks, Choctaws, and so on—and the best they'd do would to be to listen politely, accept anything I'd give them free, give me a good feed or two, see me on my way, and then go back to doing things no different at all. But if they can be gotten word that a bunch of redskins has beat the shit out of the Spanish once or twice or three times, then they'll want to come to us, learn how we did it, and see if they can do it too to whatever kinds of Europeans have been plaguing them and their folks over the years.

"So, no, Ilsa, I don't want to fight and kill and wound a bunch of Spanish—hell, I admire them, sometimes, in a way—but I'm still going to have to do it if I want to see a real, meaningful Indian Confederation that can hurt the Europeans here so bad that they'll maybe not do in this world what they did in our world to the Indians. Goddamm it, this fucking country is big enough to share—there never was any need to try to kill all the Indians off."

John the Greek shook his own head of brown curls. "But Arsen," he said sadly, "didn't you know it wasn't warfare that killed off most of the Indians in our world? It was VD, smallpox, measles, mumps, chicken pox, even, things the poor bastards had never gotten any racial immunity to. How the hell're you going to stop that kind of decimation, huh? And it's already started, too. You're not the only one has been talking to the Micco and some of his council, you know, and considering what passes for long-distance communication in this part of the world, it's amazing just how much they all seem to know about things.

"The Irish seem to be able to get along with the Indians, in wherever they settle. They were in Florida a long time before the Spanish got there, you know. They were living and farming and all tooth by jowl with the Indians for years before the Spanish came and ran them out and they sailed up to where they are now. What they call Great Ireland seems the best I can figure to be coastal parts of Virginia and North Carolina and a little bit of Delaware.

"But when the Irish first went to Florida in any numbers, and the Micco leads me to believe that was as much as two hundred years ago, there were a fair number of Indians living there, living well, at least one tribe of them with what the other Indians considered to be a high degree of culture or civilization or whatever you want to call it. But over the years they lived completely at peace with the Irish, something like eighty percent of them died of various diseases, while the Irish lived on happy as clams among them.

"Now the Irish have been up in their new areas for something over a hundred years . . . and lo and behold, the Powhatans and the Tuscaroras are dying off from diseases, too; they're dying of diseases they'd never had before the Irish came.

"So, Arsen, if your planned confederation does come off, get off the ground at all, how the hell are you and it going to fight a bunch of bacteria, viruses, and what-have-you? How will all the godawful weapons in all the Ademian warehouses combined keep tens of thousands of super-vulnerable people from dying of what you and I consider kid's diseases? Tell me that before you start planning a bloodbath for those Spaniards and Moors downriver there."

The Irish, who had been the first white men in the place, had called their settlement Corr Torpur—the Well of Cranes—and had dwelt thereabouts for at least a century, farming the rich riverside land, and cutting timber for many and varied uses, which included the burning of charcoal for use in the conversion of bog ore out of the swamps to iron. Their little colony had been virtually self-sufficient, and as they had lived in peace with the nearest Indians, they had neither built nor seen a need for any sort of defensive excavations or structures. In the time of their long tenure, the low, rocky hill at the riverside just above the deep anchorage inlet had been the site of their church—the largest building of any kind in the settlement and the only one partially constructed of rough stone.

Then, a Spanish-Moorish pope having declared all of the lands in the west to belong properly to the kingdoms of the Hispanic peninsula, a great and well-armed force of Spaniards and Moors had come sailing up the river on a dark, ill-omened day and attacked the settlement without even the trace of an attempt to resolve the matter in less bloody fashion. Those poor Irish folk not butchered by the red-handed invaders had fled to their Indian friends for safety, and eventually some of them had found their way northward to the lands their fellow Irish held in the north, arriving there with nothing save their lives, having been bereft of the hard labors of many of the generations of their ancestors and the lives of full many of their nearest and dearest.

The conquerors had burned the church and most of the other structures of the former Corr Torpur, when once anything of any value had been looted from out them. They had killed, or first raped or tortured and then killed, every white of any age they caught. They had killed many Indians, taken almost as many to be chained aboard their ships, then left the charred ruins to return to wilderness.

More than two score years later, French ships had picked a way through the dangerous maze of sand and silt bars at the mouth of the river, and negotiated the meandering channel up from that mouth to the one-time site of Corr Torpur. They were attracted to it not by ruins, for none of these were easily visible, but by the fine, deep anchorage so very close to shore along the south side of the wide river, then by the spring-fed pool of clear, cold water on the hill above that anchorage.

They were consciously trespassing on Spanish-Moorish territory and were so doing because that was what they had been sent south to do—nibble bits here and pieces there away from the Spanish and Moors to the glory of France.

Their leader decided that this hillock would be an excellent location for a fort, and he and his military expedition immediately set about the building of one. They had not even thought to question the provenance of the roughly worked stones they found in the clearance of the hilltop; they had simply set them aside and later used them in their own fortifications.

Having been periodically subjected to raids of Spanish and Moorish slavers for forty years, the Indians resident along the riversides to the north and west and those to the south of the river had happily traded labor for these newcome white iron-shirts' promise of protection from the rapacious other iron-shirts' long predations. As time had gone on, the aborigines had conducted an ongoing and peaceable trade of furs, hides, freshwater pearls, the stray semiprecious stone, and oddities with the new, relatively friendly iron-shirts in exchange for iron tools and weapons, beads, copper pots, brass scissors and needles, thread and cloth, and cheap spirits of various sorts. Their braves had more than willingly joined the French in the occasional foray against Spanish-Moorish settlements to the south, while the squaws had regularly bartered food to the garrison of the fortification that was going up as fast as worked stone and brick for the walls, guns to go on those walls, and slate and tiles for the roofs could be obtained and emplaced.

By the time the Spanish authorities in Cuba had had enough of the impudent French settlement and its clandestine raiders and dispatched an overwhelming force against it and them, the Fort de St. Denis had been almost completed, though at the time of the attack, the garrison had been far from numerous, due principally to an unfortunate outbreak of pox which had virtually exterminated the nearby friendly Indians and caused not a few deaths among the French themselves.

Unlike the force which had so brutally dispossessed the Irish so many long years before, this Spanish-Moorish military expedition had not been intent on performing a massacre, only wanting possession of the fort and settlement and to get the French interlopers out of easy raiding range of their own more northerly settlements; therefore, when the beleaguered French commander had asked for terms of surrender, he had received them, generous terms, which had been honored even after he himself had committed a messy form of suicide—blowing up the fort's magazine and himself along with it.

With the French sailing north, the Spanish had rechristened the partially demolished place El Castillo de San Diego de Boca Osa and rapidly set about repairing it with shiploads of soft coquina limestone for the walls, lumber and brick for the interiors, and red tiles for the roofs. There being so few indios left at all close to the refurbished fort, settlers had been brought in from Florida, Cuba, and other places to engage in farming and stock-raising, while the soldiers to make up the new garrison had been encouraged to bring families, as too had the necessary craftsmen for the envisaged community. Within very few years after the takeover, the newly rebuilt fort was strong and comfortable for what it was—a primitive fortification set in the midst of a primitive wilderness—the old, Irish croplands had been recleared and once more were producing fine yields, herds of swine and goats and flocks of chickens battened in the woods, and a saw pit was reducing cured timber to planks for the church under construction in the riverside settlement.

He who had led the victorious expedition against the French had been one *Capitán* Don Guillermo ibn Mahmood de Vargas y Sanchez del Río, and, his mission accomplished, he had in due time returned to render his official report to the Governor for King and Caliph, in Cuba. A part of his reward for his valuable services had been his appointment as lieutenant governor of the newly reconquered northern territories, which meant that he—a European of noble antecedents but bastard birth—thereby had achieved to dominance over an extent of territory larger than that ruled over by most reigning European kings.

Considering, as too would have any of his peers, the office to be a business opportunity, Don Guillermo had carefully, meticulously picked and chosen the proper men to fill out his staff. As partner in the business aspect and second-in-command of the garrison, he had selected his old friend and battle-comrade of many years *Capitán* Abdullah de Baza, for not only was the man a proven and doughty warrior, a born leader of men, and a pious Christian of well-proven loyalties, but he had had the invaluable experience of large-scale slaving on the Río Kongo, was level-headed, and rational, and possessed a turn of mind that had allowed him to turn disadvantages into very distinct advantages in both military and business senses, over the years of his life in the New World.

For a few years, the various business enterprises of the two knights had gone quite well. With a strong and constant demand for slaves from the colonies to the south, their seasonal predations on Shawnee, Tuscarora, Southern Cherokee, and Eastern Chickasaw clans and tribes had not only fattened their Cuban accounts, but had allowed them to clear more lands, bring in more colonists, and begin thus to produce more grain and suchlike than was needed by the settlements, this giving them other exports than slaves, furs, hides, timber and other natural products.

Settlements had been made near the mouths of navigable rivers elsewhere in the vast tract which Don Guillermo held in trust for the Governor in Cuba, each with a triangular *fortaleza* of timber and rammed earth and rocks, four to five *halcones* and *saqres*—light cannon for the gates and corners—a few swivel guns, and a small, part-time garrison of soldier-farmers under command of a creole sergeant.

One larger and several smaller slaving stations, usually occupied only during the best slaving seasons, had been established on islands in the rivers and their larger tributaries. These stations allowed the relatively small parties of whites, creoles, and their indio mercenaries not only to operate more easily in the more populous, inland territories, but to do so for longer periods of time, in conditions of enhanced safety from indio raids aimed at rescues or revenge.

Then, suddenly, unexpectedly, inexplicably, disaster had struck. Despite their constant warrings amongst themselves, all of them often abetted by Indian allies or mercenaries, the various groups and nationalities of whites—Spanish-Moorish, Portuguese-Moorish, French, Irish, and Norse—had always honored an agreement—for long unwritten, but finally formalized by all parties—that under no set of circumstances would the Indians be allowed to acquire, possess, or learn how to use firearms of any description. This stricture had applied, of course, only to full-blood, wild Indians, not to the many varieties of mixed-blood creoles, who were generally considered by pure-blood Europeans to be not Indians at all but rather a much inferior sort of white.

The first inkling of the disaster then looming so near had come to Don Guillermo in the form of a boat-borne message from Don Abdullah; that worthy then had been occupying the largest of the slaving stations set upon a well-fortified island high up the reaches of the Río Oso, among some clans of the Shawnee. Don Abdullah had tersely reported the destructive rout of a slaving party at the hands of an awesomely armed white man who had spoken, it had been averred, pure, erudite Spanish or Moorish or both. Several boats had been captured, along with small swivel guns, casks of powder, and a quantity of other weapons, three creole soldiers had been killed, and some dozen or so Creek mercenaries had deserted to the enemy.

Hard in the wake of that boat-borne message had come another: An expedition by boat upriver had

been met by one or more of these same strange
whites and turned back with some losses of boats,
weapons, and life. Don Abdullah had noted some
wounded, as well, and had reported his dispatch of
one of his young Spanish knights with a patrol to
ascend the opposite bank of the river and spy on the
site of the first incident with a Venetian long-glass
lent him for the purpose.

The report which had followed the return and de-
briefing of the young leader of that patrol had been
the first, though not the worst, bombshell. The young
knight had said that he had observed not merely one
or two but as many as a dozen whites—both men
and women—in and about the indio village. Its pal-
isade—badly damaged by the slavers—had been rebuilt, incorporating the wood that the indios always
had used and finely dressed stone which they never
before had been known to employ; earthen-and-
timber mounds had been raised at the corners and
flanking the main gate, and some of the captured
swivel guns had been there emplaced, along with at
least two carriage guns—full-size *saqres,* by the look
of them. But worst of all, the knight had watched in
horror while a white man had imparted European
drill to a group of at least a score of indios, *all of
said indios being armed with a short, light-looking
firearm of unfamiliar pattern and design!*

This hellish revelation had been sufficient to impel
the horrified Don Guillermo to dispatch a message
directly to the Governor of the Indies himself.

And this alarming message had barely been well
on its way when Don Abdullah's largest watercraft,
a pinnace, had come limping down the Río Oso,
laden with dead, dying and seriously wounded—Don
Abdullah himself among these latter—they being all
that now remained of the slaving station and party.

The story pieced together from the reports of survivors had been grim at best. There had been some

elements of the fantastical in those reports, but Don Guillermo had initially regarded the chaotic circumstances and the well-known superstition-ridden imaginations of ignorant creoles and had discounted the wildest of the yarns in their entireties . . . but that had been before Don Abdullah had sufficiently recovered to render his own cool, unemotional report.

For reasons unknown save to God, the magazine had exploded in the night, setting fire to many areas of the *fortaleza,* including the garrison carriages of all of the guns. Then a pair of armored and wheeled *tortugas*—which siege devices had apparently been rafted down the river unseen by any sentries on the dark, drizzly night—had broken down a stretch of the already-fire-weakened palisades and entered the *fortaleza,* and the armed whites and indios contained in them had opened fire with light arquebuses, *pistoles,* probably some swivel guns, and quite possibly one or two old-fashioned multibarreled volley guns. As a result, all of the Spaniards, Moors, and Creoles who had not managed to get aboard the pinnace now were certainly dead, along with those of the Creek mercenaries who had not joined their fellow savages in deserting to these strange, white-skinned enemies. The gathered slaves all were lost, as too were the boats and everything else that had been in the *fortaleza* or upon that island.

Digesting these unsavory facts, Don Guillermo had dispatched a second, far more urgent message south, then set about preparing El Castillo de San Diego de Boca Osa for repelling a now near-certain attack from the north. He was dead sure that the accursed, hell-spawn French must be responsible, for why else commit the heinous sin of firearming and drilling and training the redskinned barbarian hordes, then leading them in a deadly and destructive raid-in-force against that upriver *fortaleza* but to season them in combat against and defeat of Spaniards and Moors in preparation for a quick attempt at seizing back the lands from their rightful and God-sanctified owners?

The assault was yet to materialize, but that was not to say that some happenings of an exceeding strangeness had not been occurring in the castillo during the time since the pinnace had straggled in. First, two large barrels of corned cannon powder had somehow been stolen from out the magazine, along with three casks of finer powder for use in arquebuses and a barrel of a passable wine (stored in such place for reasons of both security and coolness). Somehow, in some way, the thieves had managed to get these unwieldy, world-heavy items out of the locked and bolted magazine, up stairs, down stairs, and along corridors without a noticeable sound and under the very noses of generally alert guards, then through barred gates and—supposedly—aboard a ship or boat, since a more than merely thorough search of the environs of the settlement had not found so much as a trace of any of them; moreover, not one scrap of the wood or the valuable hardware had ever showed up anywhere.

Nor had this been the sole theft, only the initial one. Despite all manner of enhanced security precautions and procedures, doubled and redoubled layers of guards and the like, the maddeningly impossible thefts had continued unabated—more powder of both sorts, of course, but also garrison guns, sling guns, and long calivers off the very sentry-patrolled walls, and food stores, along with an assortment of hardware for the servicing and laying of cannon and round shot for cannon, pigs of lead, and a brass gang-mold for the casting of caliver balls. And just as Don Guillermo was beginning to wonder why no coins or jewelry had been stolen by whomever, a good three troy pounds of gold *onzas* and *medias* disappeared from out his office strongbox, *without damaging the fine locks at all*—indeed, said locks did not even look as if they had been opened, yet the three purses were gone along with their precious contents.

Long and thorough experience at properly handling the ignorant, superstition-prone creole common soldiers had allowed Don Guillermo to nip in the very bud rumors that the thefts were performed by no mere earthly person or persons, but rather by the revenant of the one-time French garrison commander, a suicide, forever damned to remain in the place of his death. He had tracked the rumors back to their source, and had the miscreants put upon the triangles and lashed mercilessly, the pain and blood loss achieving true wonders in curing their overvivid imaginations, much as a chiururgeon's cupping and purging cured fevers of the body. Unlike not a few of his peers, Don Guillermo did not really like witnessing whippings or maimings or torture, but recognized and accepted that such were the only proven ways to maintain discipline among the commoner sorts and the slaves, so he steeled himself and observed those punishments he had ordered as sternly and blankfacedly as a hidalgo knight should.

In due time—and not overmuch time, considering the snaillike creep of progress among the Cuban bureaucracy, not to mention the vagaries of seaborne communication and the exceeding delicacy of treating with such sworn enemies as the European interloping, excommunicant trespassers on lands that Rome had long ago given solely to Spanish-Moorish keeping—a *guarda costa* from Cuba, an armed sloop, had arrived in the basin below El Castillo de San Diego de Boca Osa with a message from the Governor of the Indies noting that neither the Norse, the French, the Irish, nor the Portuguese would any of them admit to knowledge of this dreadful firearming and training of the savage indios . . . not that it had been expected that any of them would admit to such knowledge. All had offered aid—types, amounts, and exactly when it would come, all unspecified, of course—in eradicating this dangerous situation. Sanguinely, Don Guillermo and the still-recuperating Don Abdullah had decided not to try holding their breaths until such ephemeral aid actually materialized, and therefore they sent back a letter on the sloop's sailing requesting the temporary loan of additional men, guns, ships, and supplies that they themselves might scotch the upriver menace independently of their European enemies, none of whom could be trusted, anyway.

The guns and supplies, for which Don Guillermo would be expected to pay out of his Cuban accounts, of course, had arrived quickly enough, in varying quantities and qualities, but troops had been another matter, as had usable ships. Slowly, only a few at the time, some Appalachees and a very few of the generally better Creek indio mercenaries had been landed by sloops out of more southerly mainland ports, but not many creole soldiers and no white men at all.

Then, on a day, a shallow-draft pinnace had tacked upriver from the sea to bring advance word of the imminent arrival of a *guarda costa* which was escorting two French ships-of-war, both of them fully armed and packed with troops, French troops, all under the command of a French knight and sent down from the north to aid Don Guillermo in combating the common menace of indios illegally armed with firearms. A second, tightly sealed message directly from the hand of the Governor had warned Don Guillermo that, knowing as both hidalgos did the well-authenticated tendencies of all Frenchmen to duplicity, treachery, and truthlessness, he and his officers and garrison should receive these "allies" politely, treat them with exceeding diplomacy and tact, but not trust them any farther than a knight could throw an old-fashioned bombard.

The commander, his officers, and the garrison had taken the note to heart, and it had been as well that they had stayed alert, for in the night following the arrival of the French, the large, two-decked *frigata*— too deep of draft to tie up at the wharf in the basin and therefore moored in the channel just opposite the castillo—had loosed off a treacherous broadside which had fired portions of the waterfront, damaged the stern of the *guarda costa,* and done a certain amount of harm to the smaller French vessel moored on the other side of the wharf, then slipped her cable and tried to ride the current downriver.

But Don Guillermo's men had been ready and all his guns had been fully charged in preparation for the chance of just such an instance of French perfidy. The well-laid wall batteries had fired as the current brought their target to bear, wreaking horrific damages to both hull and upper works of the *frigata,* cutting almost all the rigging and even severing the rudder cables (as examination had later determined), so that the unmanageable ship had been driven, willy-nilly, from out the main channel at the first turn below the castillo to plow deeply into the silt and sand.

What with the massacring of the landed French troops in and about the town, the fires to be fought there and aboard the two wharfed ships, and other necessary considerations, it had been a full day before Don Guillermo had been able to take a well-armed force by boat down to where the *frigata* had ended up. They had boarded her without incident, the only Frenchmen aboard her being either dead or dying of wounds by that time. They had discovered the vessel to have sustained severe damage, both by

cannon shot and by subsequent fires; her hull had
been holed in several places and only the shallow-
ness of the bank on which she had finally foundered
had prevented her sinking. Her keel was cracked
through and her mainmast sprung, and officers of the
guarda costa had advised Don Guillermo of their
doubts that she could ever be completely salvaged,
though as she was no more than about ten years
old, European-built and well—almost lavishly—
appointed and armed, she still constituted a lucrative
prize even in her deplorable condition. The estimated figure that the captain of the *guarda costa*
rendered regarding the salvage of the unquestionable
prize-of-battle brought a broad smile to Don Guillermo's face.

Never less than generous wherein circumstances
so permitted him to be, the commander handsomely
gifted the captains of the *guarda costa* and the pinnace from the salvage of the French *frigata,* saying
that it was in appreciation of their seamen's aid in
stripping the wrecked ship, most of his garrison, then
under command of one of his lieutenants, Don Felipe, being out in the riverside swamps hunting
Frenchmen. But then, before the two small vessels
beat downriver for San Agostino, Don Guillermo
hired away one of the officers to captain his captured
French sloop-of-war and some half-dozen seamen to
man her and train selected creole soldiers in her
proper handling.

Due principally to an unfortunate spate of over-
enthusiasm on the parts of their Appalachee and
Creek mercenaries—who seldom got the chance to
hunt down and kill white men legally—the only prisoners taken by Don Felipe's force had been two black
slaves who, even under torture, could impart to the
commander of the castillo no reason why their de-
ceased French masters had so suddenly and treacherously fired on the town, harbor basin, and

fortification. Therefore, all that Don Guillermo had been able to send in his letter to the Governor had been the bald facts of what had occurred and his reactions to said occurrences. He also had sent his superior the two black slaves—by then a little the worse for wear—that that high man himself might have them more thoroughly questioned in his more modern, more sophisticated torture chambers in El Castillo del Morro.

In the aftermath of the incident, however, Don Guillermo found himself and his garrison in possession of a true abundance of the sinews of warfare—small arms of all kinds, sling-pieces and cannon up to a size of full culverins and demicannon, piles of equipment, so much powder of various grades that he was obliged to set his men to digging a new, temporary overflow magazine to hold it all in safety, plus a small mountain of assorted supplies which had been intended to feed and maintain a force of Frenchmen while on campaign . . . or more likely, all things considered, thought Don Guillermo and Don Abdullah, to maintain the new, French garrison of the treacherously retaken Castillo de San Diego de Boca Osa. Now all the two knights needed was a force of troops to bear and use the small arms, service the larger arms, and crew the available sloop, pinnace, and whaleboats.

Also, in the wake of the short, brisk, bloody, and lucrative action against the French, Don Guillermo thought that it might be a good idea to beef up the garrisons of the small satellite strongpoints to the north, so he set the pinnace and his fine sloop to bearing additional cannon, sling-pieces, powder, and other supplies to them, along with the promise of more soldiers whenever they should become available. The heavier armaments and a sternly couched warning to be wary were the best he could do under his circumstances; he could then only pray God that they would be enough until he could provide better without dangerously stripping the larger, more important castillo.

"Of course, my friend," he remarked of a night over some of his rare, sweet wine of Málaga which he was sharing with the now convalescent Don Abdullah and Don Felipe, the young knight who showed such promise, "to call this pitiful little pile of stones in which we sit tonight a castillo or presidio, or even to so name the larger one down on the Ría Matanzas at San Agostino is to laugh with much heartiness."

"Agreed." Don Abdullah nodded. "But even so, ours has now proved itself more than a match for that well-armed and fully manned French *frigata*. Do we not now own the loot to prove it?"

"We do, of course," answered Guillermo, still looking worried. "But what if a larger, a stronger and better-armed ship should sail in and set her guns at our walls and anchorage and town, eh?"

With a grunt of discomfort, Don Abdullah set down his silver cup long enough to use both hands in carefully shifting his still-healing leg on the cushion-covered support. "However, I would not like to have to be the sailing master or the captain of any larger ship-of-war essaying to negotiate that ever-shifting, ever-deadly, ever-treacherous maze of bars and false channels between here and the sea."

Brightening a little, Guillermo remarked, "Yes, you are of a rightness, my friend, there is that natural outer defense. In fact, I now recall, we grounded at least two vessels on our way up here to drive out the French, years back, and those were in no way ships with a requirement of truly deep water under them."

Politely, the youngest knight cleared his throat and looked the question at his two superiors, whereupon Don Guillermo smiled expansively, saying, *"Hijo mío,* in such discussions as is this, we three all are equals in all ways. When you thirst, you take up the decanter and fill your cup; when you have words to be spoken, speak them. Please to understand, your weighted thoughts are of as much value to me as is your strong swordarm and your well-proven courage.''

The slender, olive-skinned young man glowed visibly under the unsolicited praise from the lips of this man for whom he bore so much respect. So he then told them his thoughts on making the approaches to the settlement from the sea even more incipiently deadly, and these thoughts pleased the two older knights mightily.

Pinky Boyette, Gabe Lauderback, and John Peeples, having earlier boosted a box of thirty-six candy bars, a jug of pink chablis, and some chips from a corner convenience store, were lazing around the old, rotting bandstand in the park, washing down mouthfuls of gooey chocolate with swallows of wine and awaiting the onset of darkness, the time when they could begin to prowl the surrounding streets in search of prey, for the morning would come soon enough and with it would come the need for money to buy the wherewithal to feed their habits.

The top edge of the westering sun was not yet down behind the bulk of the sewage-treatment plant when a seeming miracle occurred. A shiny four-door sedan turned off the paved drive and moved slowly along the narrow, grass-grown way that once had been a graveled drive almost up to the bush-and-weed-shrouded bandstand itself. Its finely tuned engine making almost no noise at all, the car came to a stop not ten yards from the three hidden predators, and they watched as a man got out of the expensive-looking automobile, half unbelieving that a victim should come to them this way.

''Man,'' murmured Pinky Boyette, his candy-smeared lips barely moving in his thin face, "that damn car don' even soun' like it's running. It sure is shiny—mus' be bran' new. How much you reckon we c'n get fer them wheel covers, Gabe?"

"Should oughta look good, asshole," was the hissed reply of him addressed. "That's a fuckin' German car, one the ones costs thirty-five, forty *thousan'* dollars, new . . . an' it sure looks new to me."

"Forty thousan' dollars?" breathed the third of their unwashed, stubbly, sore-infested number, in a tone closely resembling that of a fervent prayer. "Man oh man! Sheeit! That kinda bread, we could go inta big-time dealin', you know . . . at leas', stay stoned out for a fuckin' long time, you know."

"How much you thank ol' Perlman, the fence, he'll give us for the whole car, then, Gabe?" this from Pinky Boyette.

"Aw, how the shit we gon' get it to him, asshole?" that worthy demanded. "Les you done learned to drive recent, 'cause I sure Lawd don't and neither does John Peckerhead here, you know."

"Well," suggested Peeples, taking no offense at what Gabe had called him, most of his concentration going toward the removal of a particularly itchy scab from one cheek, "then why don' we go over and git one them gang fellers to drive it over to Perlman's for us, huh? All these damn country yokels lives down here drives, you know—ain't like it is up home where it's subways and all and don't hardly nobody need to drive, you know."

"Asswipe," said Gabe disgustedly, "you better be goddam glad you and this other shithead got somebody got some brains to do your damn thinkin' for you, hear? You go tellin' that bunch of asshole punks 'bout thishere car and all, they'll take it 'way from us faster'n you can cut a fart and prob'ly beat us half to death or off us in the bargain, too, you know. Naw, you and Pinky and me, we'll settle for whatall we can carry our own se'fs—the wheel covers, anything we can get from outa the inside, mebbe some the fucking tires and wheels, too. But first off, we gone see how much we can get off that honky drivin' it, see, you know. I got me *my* screwdriver— you and Pinky got yours, brother? Good. Minnit he gits out they car, we goes for the ofay, hear?''

But when the three actually saw the automobile glide to a halt, heard the engine cut off, and watched the big, stocky, well-dressed man get out and carefully lock the door, then pocket the key, Pinky shook his head and whisperingly whined, ''Gabe, man, I . . . he looks *mean,* man, mebbe we should oughta . . .''

''Lissen, chickenshit,'' Gabe growled in quiet reply, ''I don't give a rat's ass how mean he look—it's three of us and only one of him, and we got our fucking screwdrivers, too, you jerk, good as any fucking wop stiletto, too, but legal to carry. Now, c'mon!''

But when the three footpads burst through the thick growth of bushes that masked the entrance to the bandstand, the man was not anywhere in sight!

Led by the snarling Gabe, the three searched every clump of unpruned bushes within the distance he estimated the turkey could have moved in the few seconds of elapsed time. They looked under the car and in it, all in vain. Raving at this sudden unexpected, patently unfair deprivation, the three kicked at the locked car and deeply scored its finish with the honed points of their Phillips screwdrivers, and, at length, Gabe picked up a sizable rock and used it to smash out the driver-side window, then reached inside and pulled up the lock knob before opening the door.

He was lying prone across the two bucket seats trying to pry open the locked glove box when a scream of terror in two voices erupted from outside, followed by the thud of running footsteps. Next, a pair of powerful hands took firm hold upon his ankles and easily jerked him out of the car to a face-first and very painful landing on the imbedded gravel. But he retained a grip on his screwdriver, and immediately his skinny legs were under him, he went for the torso of the stocky white man with his needle-tracked arm fully extended and pure murder in his mind.

But fast as was the raging Gabe, his intended victim was far faster. His body swayed just far enough to the right that the needle-tipped screwdriver and the needle-scarred arm propelling it missed, and the thin body itself would have slammed into the thicker, meatier one had not two big hands stopped it; one of these hands clamped onto the weapon arm and the other took hold of the shoulder of the free arm. Then both thumbs unerringly found certain spots in those body parts and the pressures they commenced to exert suddenly created an explosion of unbearable pain that seemed to suffuse every fiber of Gabe's entire being. The sharpened screwdriver slipped from nerveless fingers even as consciousness departed his agonized body.

The erstwhile victim of Gabe's rage looked emotionlessly down at the unconscious junkie-mugger, started to step over him to get into the automobile, then noticed the spiteful damages inflicted to the body finish by Gabe and the other two earlier. His face indicated no slightest change of expression, but rather than getting into the automobile, he took off his suit coat, folded it carefully, and laid it across the back of the driver's seat. He softly closed the door, thus extinguishing the courtesy lights, then took a grip of Gabe's shirt collar and dragged him toward the dark bulk of the old bandstand, taking care to pick up the screwdriver from where it lay among the weeds.

Gabe Lauderback lived for about five minutes after he was brought back to full consciousness, but to him that few minutes seemed at least a century long and could not have ended soon enough.

Neither the police, who found the roach-crawling, fly-buzzing, rat-chewed mess that had once been a heroin addict named Gabriel Lauderback some days later, nor the city pathologist to whom the fast-decomposing, maggoty organic rubbish was finally delivered for examination had ever before seen the like. The body had, to all intents and purposes, been virtually disassembled, and seemingly by main strength by the perpetrator; no traces of any cutting had been found anywhere on the parts.

At the outset, it had appeared that there should be comparatively little difficulty in apprehending the clearly deranged killer, for the flaking woodwork and the warped floorboards inside the trash-filled bandstand bore numerous bloody handprints, fingerprints, and even prints of shoe soles. But in point of unpleasant fact, the case never was solved and eventually was filed under the catchall of "a drug-related killing" by the baffled police. None of the hand or finger imprints showed the slightest trace of any identifying lines or whorls or palm markings, the shoe soles told them to be of a commonly sold if moderately expensive oxford, size nine, and the extraneous material those soles had left in the dried blood had all seemed to be from plants and soils found in the immediate vicinity of the bandstand.

If he had been asked, which he was not, the city pathologist could have told them that it was utterly impossible for one lone man or woman—no matter how strong—to have done barehanded all the things that had been wrought upon the flesh and bone of the late Gabriel Lauderback. But as said pathologist worked in a department that was chronically under-staffed and continuously overworked, both he and his superiors were more than content to let well enough alone, agree to the police conclusion, and close the files on the grisly case of the dismantled junk.

On the morning following the dismemberment of Gabe Lauderback, the stocky, powerful man who had terminally rent the addict sat at a desk in a Victorian-mansion-become-expensive-office-building near the center of the city. The polished brass plate affixed beside the paneled walnut doors read: "Samuel Vanga, Investigations by Appointment Only, Secu-rity Advisor." Beyond those doors, in the comfort-ably appointed outer office, an attractive receptionist sat, filing her nails by the silent telephone; neither she nor the older but no less attractive secretary (just now typing personal letters in her own office) would or could have believed their soft-spoken, kind, con-siderate employer capable of coldly, methodically taking a man's body completely apart with his bare hands. And if you had told either woman that the creature they knew and revered as Mr. Vanga was, though an excellent copy, not a man at all, they would most likely have looked frantically for the men in white coats who must surely have been diligently searching for so patently certifiable a loose lunatic as you. And they would have been completely wrong in almost everything they knew or thought they knew about Sam Vanga.

By order of their Great Khan, a sizable horde of yellow-brown, slant-eyed Kalmyks and their kindred allies were, in fits and starts, withdrawing from the ravaged provinces of northeastern France; behind them, they left a howling wilderness within which squatted a few of the stronger, better-defended castles and walled towns which never had fallen to them, but otherwise, the only accurate word for the lands was desolation. In those so recently populous and productive lands, the now most frequently seen living creatures were sleek wolves, vultures, and carrion crows, though from out the wilder reaches, boars, bears, and even a few lynxes had come out to feed upon the carnage lying unburied upon the land in the wake of battles, fights, and massacres. Those croplands not burnt provided ready sustenance to hordes of smaller vermin, and these beasts, in their natural turn, fed vast numbers of raptors, reptiles, and the smaller felines. Unmolested by hunters, deer browsed in grain fields, while the bodies of the men who might have pursued them went to sate the hunger of the beasts who might have hunted them.

The unfortunate provinces all had been thoroughly looted, raped, ravished, and ravaged by the eastern horsemen, and those few survivors as remained alive on the lands were become as chary as game, crouching and trembling in the deeper reaches of forests, in hill caves, or among the blackened ruins of homes, farms, towns, villages, and the weaker castles.

The Kalmyks had proved pitiless. After the last armed resistance to them had been overcome, they had moved across the face of the land like a cloud of locusts, killing man, woman, child, babe, and beast impartially, as the mood struck them. The killings would have been bad enough, but they had not been all or even the worst of the savage barbarities inflicted upon the inhabitants. Wave after wave of the swarthy, fur-clad, stinking riders on their shaggy, big-headed ponies had crisscrossed the lands, each horde trailed by a heterogeneous collection of carts, waggons, wains, pack beasts, and coffles of chained, brutalized, and terrified slaves, folk of all stations and both sexes, for the primitive Kalmyks did not recognize the practice of ransoming war captives.

Those merely subjected to multiple rape, otherwise abused or beaten, and then taken for slaves were actually the luckier ones, for the hordes of raiders were capable of and gleefully practiced much more and far worse against their helpless prey. Multiple rape followed by disembowelment or impalement was far more common than was enslavement for women and little girls, while in the cases of men and boys, an amusing session of savage tortures and deliberate maimings which invariably included castration was most often followed by slowly roasting them alive, although if the horde happened to be in a hurry, they might cut leg and arm tendons, pull out tongues, gouge or burn out eyes, and just leave the bloody, blind, croaking, flopping sufferer to bleed to death.

Anything the Kalmyks could not bear away with them was if living killed, if inanimate burned or pulled down or broken or befouled. It was not a new practice; such had always been the way of the nomadic Kalmyks and their ilk. They did not either sow or reap; their sole use for lands was a place whereon to erect their yurts and graze their flocks and herds before packing up and moving on to fresh pasturage; it was the only way of life they and their forefathers ever had known. They loved their untrammeled existence and they had no understanding of or even bare tolerance for any settled peoples or their works.

On the way back to their own steppes and plains, the hordes rode through lands no less rich and populous than had been those lands they just had left, but there could be no mere thought of rampaging through these as they had through the others, for all that there were precious few fighting men in evidence, for these were the lands of the mighty Khan of the West, the Holy Roman Emperor, by whose leave they had been afforded the most recent fun, loot, and slaves, and by order of their own Great Khan, these lands were sancrosanct and any rider who misbehaved against them or their peoples would long for death weeks before it finally was vouchsafed him and all his family.

The Great Khan himself was seen at least once by each group of Kalmyks as they rode back east through Empire lands. With him rode a big, towering white warrior, his blood brother, the uncle of the present Khan of the West, *Reichsherzog* Wolfgang. Now and again, as the Great Khan's party rode up the slow-moving columns, this white Kalmyk would spy a slave, talk with him briefly, then seek out his owner and buy him of the Kalmyk. The nomads thought it odd that the Great Khan's blood brother never bought females but only males, and potentially dangerous warrior males at that, but then who could ever know or understand the souls of white Christians? The brown Christians of the south and the white animists of the north were far easier to fathom.

As he forked a decent rounsey beside his benefactor's well-bred ambler, *Sieur* Charles de Brienne, despite his verminous rags and the ceaseless pain of suppurating whip weals on his back and shoulders, could but silently offer up prayers of thanks that he was miraculously delivered up from out his odious bondage to the savage heathen. No matter that with the current devastation of his family's lands he would no doubt be very, very long in accumulating even a modest ransom and so would probably end for a good while as a virtual military slave to one of the hated and hateful noblemen of the Empire, still he would at least be swinging steel as he had been bred and reared to do, and moreover would be doing so in the service of an honest Christian.

Also, there was this: So far as he knew, he now was the last extant scion of his family, so that would mean that younger son or no, all familial estates and privileges would be his when once he won back to claim them. He had witnessed the deaths of his father and his eldest brother, Jules, and he had it upon the reasonable testimony of surviving servants that his other two brothers also had been slain during the hellishness of the intaking of their ancient fortified home and the city which had grown up out of its onetime bailey.

Even after the town itself had fallen to the howling horde, the old Marquis, Charles's sire, and his family and retainers had made to hold the venerable castle on the hill. They had held it, fought it, fought it well and hard for weeks, not only bloodily repelling the barbarians' every assault, but with their bombards, cannon, engines, calivers, and crossbows making it deadly dangerous for the savage victors to mass anywhere within range of the walls of that castle.

But it had been a defense doomed before it had started for lack of adequate supplies and foodstuffs. The old Marquis had known that messengers had alerted the king of this sudden invasion and had but hoped that he could hold out until a relieving royal army could be marshaled and marched the distance. But the long weeks had rolled on, the stocks of gunpowder had dwindled alarmingly, and still no royal banners were visible from even the highest tower of the castle. When there had been no more rabbits in the hutches, not one dove or pigeon left in the cotes, no milch cows, not a single cat or hound and precious few rats left to be caught and cooked, the old Marquis had sternly ordered the inhabitants of the mews—even his treasured gyrfalcon—to the stewpots, that the garrison might remain strong enough to fight on a little longer. Then it had become the turn of the horses, one or two at the time, taking the rounseys, amblers, and palfreys first, rather than

the high horses and trained destriers. The fewer
numbers of horses to be fed released quantities of
grain, pease, and bran, of course, and these helped to
lessen the need for more immediate horse-butchering.
But even so, it could not last forever, all knew that,
and still no royal army came to break the siege and
save them from the Kalmyks.

Then, of a day, as if they did not have enemies
and to spare, the stubborn, valiant little garrison was
struck with an outbreak of the bloody flux, and
within a week, several of the oldest and youngest—
these including both of Charles's twin daughters—
were dead of its ravages, while more than a few of
the survivors were seriously ill or weakened.

Of course, that was the time when the pagans in
the town below, reinforced by the arrival of another
group from the east, had set about assaulting the
castle in earnest, raking the wall tops with arrows,
quarrels, and musketry fire, dragging bombards from
off the city walls to batter at the castle stonework
and main gate. Behind, in the streets of the town,
the defenders could see a timber tower under rapid
construction and knew all too well what that por-
tended.

Rapt in his own thoughts, his bitter memories,
Charles did not at first realize that the big man beside him was bespeaking him, but when he did, he
replied, "Uh, yes, my lord Archduke, please to for-
give your servant, his mind was far away."

The broad, loaded shoulders under the rich fabric
of the *Reichsherzog*'s brigandine rose and fell, and
he nodded shortly, his deep voice speaking in his
fluent—if Burgundian—Franch, kind and sympa-
thetic. "Think nothing of it, my good *Sieur* de
Brienne. I was but merely saying that when we reach
the lodge wherein I am making my headquarters in
this principality, you will be provided all your immediate needs—servants to bathe you, the services

of my barber, who also happens to be a fair to middling leech, cupper, and drawer of teeth, clothing and accouterments commensurate with your true rank and station, and, do you give me your parole, weapons.

"You will meet at meat today certain other gentlemen of France whom I have bought, as I did you, from their Kalmyk captors. Like them, you will be decently mounted, and when I move on in company with the Great Khan, you and they will accompany my retinue. When the last of the Kalmyk raiders are back out of France and these more populous lands of the Empire, then I shall repair to my own principal residence and all of you with me. Until that time, you all are my noble guests, and if you want for aught, you need but to ask of the servants or of me, your own servant, Herr Wolfgang."

"My lord Archduke," said Charles slowly, haltingly, "as regards my ransom . . . my lands . . . well, my family's lands are now completely despoiled—crops burned, orchards felled, vineyards chopped down, kine and peasants all butchered or driven away or enslaved, towns razed, fortified places slighted, everything looted away. So it may well be years, even a decade, before I could raise and deliver to you a decent ransom . . . But you have my sacred oath that—"

The large, powerful warrior on the ambler made a clucking sound with tongue and palate. "The time will come to discuss such things, my good *Sieur* de Brienne, but that time is not now. As I just said, for now and for some time to come, you brave gentlemen of France are my guests, a part of my retinue. I now ask only that you enjoy my hospitality and repay it with your company and conversation."

At journey's end, Charles found the so-called lodge to be nothing less than a sprawling, comfortable country mansion, its main building four stories

high and its three wings, three and two, plus a full
quantity of outbuildings, gardens, and a pleasant
park, all within the compass of its walls. Atop a
small but steep hill within the park crouched an aged
round tower of dark-grey stone; this ancient motte
now was almost entirely overgrown with ivy and its
outer stockade was become only a barely visible ring
of rotted wood, but a well-used track leading up to
it showed that the motte still was being put to some
kind of use.

Observing his newest guest's scrutiny of the elderly fortification, the *Reichsherzog* beckoned him
to his side and remarked, ''For many years, despite
the general lack of internal war, it has been the order
of the emperors that places such as that remain in
repair and defensible in emergencies, and that one
is, despite all its outward appearance. Within it, for
the length of my stay hereabouts, I am billeting many
of my Kalmyk mercenaries, survivors of the squad-
ron I took with me to England, years ago, to help
my dear cousin, King Arthur III, retain his rightful
throne and lands against all the might that the late
and unlamented Pope Abdul could hurl against him
and his loyal subjects.''

Charles nodded. ''Two of my cousins took the
Cross in that Crusade, my lord Archduke; one
drowned while fording a river in northern England
somewhere, the other died of camp fever, it is said.
May the good God ever keep their souls.'' He signed
himself, piously.

The *Reichsherzog* emulated his guest, saying solemnly, ''May it be so.''

At first, Charles automatically recoiled, almost
cringing, when the four Kalmyks entered the chamber used for immersion bathing in the *Reichsherzog*'s
almost palatial lodge, but the short, yellow-brown
men were deferential, though all conversation between him and them had needs be in German, since

none of them spoke even so much as a single word of French. But although they all bore the unmistakable and honorable scars of proven and veteran warriors, they were equally adept at the role of gentleman's servitor, and their ministrations were as gentle and considerate as the Frenchman could have wished.

His bathing completed, a fifth Kalmyk entered the chamber, this one bearing with him the basin, razors, shears, and other paraphernalia of the barber, plus a chest of *cour bouilli* slung over his shoulder.

In better German than that spoken by the other four, he said, *"Mein Herr von* Brienne, this speaking is Rukh, barber to His Grace, the *Reichsherzog*. To trim your hair and beard this one will, and also to rid them and your body of parasites, but first, please to allow that this one see to and treat your injuries. The black rot more warriors kills than sharp steel, my lord."

Gaping his leathern casket widely, the little man squatted on his heels beside it, had Charles stretched facedown upon a swath of coarse cloth before him, and used another, softer cloth to dab away the pus, serum, and diluted blood which the necessary handling in the bath pool had caused to exude from the knight's whip-wealed back and shoulders.

Charles gritted his teeth and breathed a prayer, expecting more and worse to come . . . but he was wrong. The Kalmyk took from out the casket a broad, round container filled to the very brim with what looked to be a viscous, greasy brown mud. He dipped out a goodly handful of the stuff and dumped it between Charles' shoulder blades, then began to spread it over all sites of injury, and in the wake of the gentle fingers, all pain ceased, to be replaced with a coolness. Such pain as the Kalmyk's work caused after that was easily borne.

When he and one of the others had assisted the knight to sit up on the cloth, Rukh rose to his feet and filled his basin from a steaming kettle set on one of the chamber's glowing braziers, but when he examined the scalp beneath the damp hair, he hissed between his teeth, turned, and spat a rapid-fire stream of instructions in the Kalmyk tongue to one of the others, who then left at a run.

Sinking once more onto his heels to face his patient, he asked diffidently, "Please, my lord *von* Brienne, how and when were the wounds upon your pate done you? With what were they done, does my lord know?"

Charles nodded and shrugged. "The older were done when a wall or a part of one fell on me, killed several of my retainers, and sundered my helm. That is how I was captured. A party of pagans, desirous of the arms and armor they could spy beneath the stones, uncovered me, and when they found that I lived, enslaved me. The more recent injuries were wrought when one of my captors belabored me with the butt of his riding whip."

By then, the Kalmyk sent out had fetched back a small flagon and a brass cup. These he handed to Rukh, who sniffed at the neck of the flagon, then poured a goodly measure of the liquor into the cup and set it on the floor. From out the casket, he took a small, horn container. He unstoppered it, added its brown-black contents to the liquor in the cup, then stirred the resultant mixture vigorously with one long forefinger.

Raising the cup and proffering it to Charles, he said gravely, "Please to drink this draught, my lord *von* Brienne. Men of the west find its savor abominable, so swallow it quickly, but be certain that you swallow it all, even the very dregs of it."

"What is it, this stuff you want me to drink?" demanded the knight warily.

"The flagon contains a fine brandy, this one, from the Sandlandt, I believe, from out the *Reichsherzog*'s own cellars. The potion which I have added was discovered by a former student of mine, one Nugai; it is composed of certain rare herbs, and when combined with liquor, it will render you into a deep sleep for some hours."

"Why must I be put to sleep merely to get a haircut and to trim my beard?" probed Charles suspiciously, still fearing and deeply distrusting any Kalmyk and his motives.

Patiently, the squatting man answered, "In order to treat the wounds now dangerously festered in your pate, it will be necessary to shave your head, entire. Then, after those wounds have been all opened afresh and cleaned, it may be found best to cauterize them, and for all that this one is aware of just how brave you are, he still knows that the body, unbidden, can flinch at inopportune times, is it not soundly asleep and unfeeling. My master, the *Reichsherzog*, values you most highly, my lord *von* Brienne, and would so be much wroth were you not to be treated and so die. Therefore, please to drain the cup . . . but here, please to allow this one to once again stir it."

When Charles at last awakened, he lay in a large bedchamber and in the finest and largest feather bed he ever had occupied, as large was it even as his late father's had been. For the first time in a long, long while, he awakened to no pain at all, only the feeling of coolness under the bandages he could detect on his back and shoulders and atop his head. But he awakened to a raging thirst.

Wordless, the Kalmyk, Rukh, arose from where he squatted nearby, helping the knight to sit up, then poured and placed in his hands a pint beaker-cup of a cool, pale wine. Immediately he had quaffed the contents of the cup, Charles felt sleep once more claiming him, dashing against his halfhearted de-

fenses of consciousness in wave after irresistible
wave. He thought to feel the wiry arms of the Kalmyk lowering his body again to the bed, then he felt
nothing.

On the next time he awoke, he not only again
thirsted ragingly, but hungered as well. And Rukh,
apparently anticipating just such hungers, was once
more waiting, squatting on the dais beside the great
bed, this time accompanied there by two ewers—one
of the same pale wine, the other of a rich meat broth,
fragrant of the odors of onions, garlic, herbs, and
Malabar pepper with a hint of cinnamon.

With all of the hearty broth in his belly, Charles
felt much better—alert, vital, strength having seemingly returned to all his being—yet when he made to
swing his legs out of the high bed and make use of
the convenience, he found that said legs would not
support him, and that though use the convenience he
eventually did, it could be done only with the help
of Rukh and another of the surprisingly strong little
Kalmyks, Mankas.

Rukh would not allow the knight to return immediately to the bed, but rather placed him in a chair
with both arms and back to take his wine in sips,
while Mankas went out of the chamber on an errand.
The younger Kalmyk soon returned with Rukh's *cour
bouilli* casket slung from his shoulder and a folded
length of thick linen under his other arm.

Once again, he was asked politely to swill a
smaller measure of the awful-tasting concoction he
recalled from his first night in the *Reichsherzog*'s
country palace. He did so and shortly knew no more
for time unreckonable. But Rukh was squatting on
the dais by his bedside when he again awakened,
again with broth and wine and his wiry strength to
aid him in reaching the necessarium. That matter
accomplished, a brace of Kalmyks entered the chamber with a simple arrangement of a light armed chair

and poles for carrying it. It was thus Charles was borne belowstairs to the chamber of the sunken bath and all his body save the still bandage-swathed area above his eyes laved again. Then he was carried back up the stairs and put back into the bed. Shortly, his noble host joined him.

With the customary, polite amenities between two noblemen out of the way, Rukh and the Kalmyk who had accompanied the German both squatting soundless near the door, and a decanter and cups on the table between their chairs, Wolfgang remarked, *"Sieur* de Brienne, you are an exceedingly lucky young man. God must truly love you or have important plans for you if not both together. Did you know that?"

Charles had no slightest idea just what his host was talking about or getting at, but he simply answered, "No, Your Grace."

"Then I must tell you of the unquestionable miracles which have resulted in your sitting here and drinking with me this night," said the *Reichsherzog* with a brisk nod. "Know you, sir, that more than nine and ninety men out of any hundred would never have for one minute survived the first of your head injuries, much less the long mistreatment, the additional head injuries, and the protracted forced marching from out of France and halfway through my own lands to where I found and bought you of your captor. Rukh says that you aver a wall fell on you. Tell me about it, pray. You must have been full-armed—no other way you could have lived through such."

Charles began, saying, "Then know you, Your Grace, that the town of Brienne grew up from the extended outer bailey of the Castle of Brienne, starting centuries ago when still it was a part of the old kingdom of Burgundy, before my ancestors conquered it and its lands for France. With the recent years of peace, the town had expanded, despite the misgivings of my late sire, *Sieur* Rupert, Marquis de Brienne, not a few more recent structures had been raised beyond and even hard against the outer faces of the town wall. Upon the incursions of the first waves of the pagans, right many folk—of all classes and stations—fled to the supposed protection of the town, but the external construction—confirming my poor sire's very worst fears—not only prevented proper use of bows, crossbows, cannon, and smaller arms from the towers and bastions but provided the attackers quick and simple means to scale the walls themselves in numerous places. The town was packed with refugees from the countryside, and their milling mobs prevented the quick redispositioning of such few trained troops as we had, so before long the pagans had gapped a gate and the wolves were within the fold.

"We fought them in the streets and spaces of the town until we found ourselves driven back to the walls of the old inner bailey, wherein were the town homes of our extended family and some few minor nobility of the Mark. Vastly outnumbered by the heathen horsemen, my sire had us gather as many fighters and such quantities of arms and supplies as we quickly could, then retreated into the inner bailey; however, as he knew the walls to be too weak and low to hold attackers for long, no matter how well defended, he set most of those at his command to stripping the houses of anything that could be of use to a garrison under siege and borne up the hill into the walled castle itself, while the rest of us strove to hold the bailey walls, keep the barbarians back long enough that the Marquis might complete his purpose.

"Upon being apprised that the most of our force was within the castle, we spiked our few old bombards, bore away with us the port-pieces, sling-pieces, wall calivers, and suchlike with the shot and powder for them. Just before enough of the pagans had come over the walls to really fight us, we fired every building we could reach on our line of retreat, then entered the castle ourselves, and barred the gates behind us.

"The pagans immediately flung themselves against the castle, of course, charging right through the blazing high-town and along the tops of the flanking walls. They are long on courage, though often short on any sort of caution; they kept charging the walls on their big-headed little ponies even after we had shot down so many of their predecessors that they needs must jump or clamber over the twitching bodies to get at those walls which they could not have hoped to scale anyway, without at least a few ladders, at gates they could not have breached lacking any tools save bows, swords, axes, and bare hands."

The German nodded. "Yes, the initial waves of Kalmyks lost a very large number of warriors, not only at Brienne but elsewhere as well. I blame that on the fact that the most of that wave was composed of the young, the hotheaded, the loot-hungry, not a few of them riding their very first large-scale raid, with the more mature and level-headed men among them being almost entirely from clans only recently arrived from far to the east and so owning precious little experience at the conditions and dangers of this kind of warfare. Out on the far steppes, you see, young sir, most walls are of wood and can be burnt down by enough fire-arrows, nor are large, modern, longer-ranging cannon at all that common out on the steppes, and there are there far more bows, axes, and swords or spears and lances than there are dags and arquebuses. But I ramble on. Continue with your tale, please."

"The castle itself was as strong and secure as ever, of course—it had fallen but once since completed in its present form; that was when my great-grandsire took it, and he had been quick to see the single weak point that had helped him and his force to conquer quickly and thoroughly corrected—but the force that had followed my sire into it was actually too small to serve as any adequate form of long-term garrison, and not even all of those were trained to arms. There was no lack of water up there, at least; all of that area is rife with icy-cold springs that flow freely in even the worst of droughts, and one such was within the castle walls. But of weapons and supplies we were in want almost at the very inception of our resistance.

"Had we had more powder, we might well have just sat up there and driven the pagans from out the town as we soon were able to do from the inner bailey, but we did not, and therefore my sire soon forbade the loosing off of cannon at any save very large groupings of the heathen, small arms to be employed only against assaults on the walls. Meanwhile, he set men to making cartridges of various sizes from paper and waxed cloth, then filling them with exact measures of such powder as we did have that none of the precious stuff be spilled and wasted to our use during loadings.

"My sire, all of us who understood warfare knew that unaided we could not long hold the castle, even against such primitives as those we faced, not lacking gunpowder, supplies, and more men, but we were certain that the king must even then be marching an army to the relief of us and the other invaded desmesnes; we knew that many gallopers had been sent to His Highness and could not imagine him just leaving us to fight and die alone. And so we held our place, cutting rations until they could be cut no more and still keep us alive with the strength to fight, watching our supplies of powder shrink and watching continually from the towertops for the lily banners of salvation.''

"Some few, small, uncoordinated forces did try to come to the aid of you and the other holdouts, you know,'' said the *Reichsherzog,* "but they were not either led or ordered by your dear king. No, they were raised and led, if you can call it that, by certain nobleborn nincompoops—the *Comte* de This or the Baron de That—all of whom apparently rode under the impression that they were leading forces to something on the order of a mere Italian tourney. And by the time that any of them actually got into combat situations, the main waves of the Kalmyks were arrived, better armed and led by sagacious, blooded veteran chiefs and sub-khans. Under them, the warriors virtually exterminated the pitiful little scratch forces of the French noblemen. But as regards your esteemed king, he gathered the most of his available troops in and around Paris, and for all I know he is still squatting there, no doubt having halberdiers peek under his bed before he takes to it of nights, lest there be a file of Kalmyks lurking there. Such is not a monarch I could either respect or serve, no!

"But, then, it had been the considered opinion of my nephew, the Emperor, and his councillors that His Highness of France would behave in just so shameful and cowardly a manner were his eastern frontier marks attacked suddenly and forcefully by the likes of a large number of Kalmyks. It is to me regrettable that you and your peers and people had to so suffer and die, but whilst you are blaming the Kalmyks, my nephew, and me, reflect that an even larger part of the blame should lie upon the narrow, quaking shoulders of your greedy, feckless, unprincipled, and cowardly king.''

"Way it looks," said Greg Sinclair to Arsen and the other whites assembled that night in one of the commodious chambers of Arsen and Ilsa in the fort, "this here brave, this Snake-and-a-half, was sent up here for to see if it was really true we'd kicked some shit out the damn spics before they got around to sending any more their braves to join up with us."

"Well, thank God," breathed Arsen feelingly. "This is the fucking beginning we've been waiting and hoping and praying for. Did the Micco ever figure out where he came from?"

"No." Greg shook his head. "He allowed as how he'd heard of the tribe, long time back, but he didn't know exac'ly where their stomping grounds was. We was all stumped till old Swift Otter come by and he knew right off. These Sis-ip-aw-haws are from east and north of us, somewhere between the next two rivers north of this one, but closer to the coast, see. Seems like it never was too many of them, just one of these small tribes, and the damn fucking spics have been hunting them for years, like everbody else, too, around here, so it's fewer now than there might've been.

"Not even Snake-and-a-half is a Sis-ip-aw-haw, his own self; he's one of the last of a costal tribe from down near the mouth of thishere river was wiped out by the spics, years back. It's just the Sis-ip-aw-haws took him in, adopted him into the tribe, and he married one their squaws.''

"What does the Micco think of him?" asked Ilsa Peters.

Greg replied, "Well, he told me that for a warrior so young—I'd say Snake-and-a-half is maybe thirty, thirty-five—he is very wise, resourceful, moves gracefully, looks strong, is clearly an accomplished killer of men. He later said that he wished he'd gotten the chance to take him into his tribe first."

Arsen nodded and smacked a fist into his palm. "Well, I'll take that sharp old man's word on it, then. Simon, issue him a full kit—rifle, pistol, powder, everything—then you and Swift Otter teach him the ropes on them. When he leaves here for home, we'll give him another set for his chief or sachem or whatever, too. But I say we should keep him around here for a while, get to know him."

"Ahhh, there's a problem about him, Arsen," said Greg. "He can't really talk to nobody don't have a helmet."

"Now wait a fucking minute," yelped Arsen. "I thought you just now got through telling us Swift Otter knew his tribe and all?"

"Oh, yeah," said Greg, "he knows his tribe, knows where they live and all, but he still can't talk to him, and neither can the Micco or any the others, 'cept in sign language is all. The way the Micco explained it to me, the Sis-ip-aw-haws speak a language as diff'runt from Shawnee as Shawnee is from Creek or either one is from spic. The Micco, he says all the Injuns speaks diff'runt languages, too, even the ones live almost on top of each other; some of the ones some of them talk is close enough related to Creek that they can sometimes talk to each other pretty good, but most of them ain't, and that's how come they had to come up with sign language and why all of them has to know it and have all the signs down pat. I'm just glad as hell now I took a merit badge in Injun sign language back when I was in the Boy Scout Troop at St. James's Church and ain't never forgot the most of it—lots of them signs is the same ones or close to the same ones these Injuns here uses, see. But Arsen, teaching him how to shoot and load and prime and cast bullets and all and not blow off his own head or at least a hand in doing it by just sign language is gonna be a bitch and a fucking half, buddy.''

Arsen shrugged. "Okay, then, *you* teach him, you and one of the other braves, and all three of you wear helmets all the time you're doing it, that's all I can figure. But I want him won over for us, Greg. I want this Sis-ip-aw-haw Tribe for my Indian Confederation. By the way, did he mention how many braves they have?"

"Yeah, Arsen, he told the Micco wasn't many left, way the damn spics downriver from them has been riding them so long and all, you know. He's one, and it's sixteen more where he come from. It ain't many, Arsen," Greg concluded glumly.

"Maybe not," Arsen agreed. "But it's still a beginning, buddy. We get together enough little bunches of sixteen, seventeen braves, arm them all with Uncle Bagrat's finest flintlocks, we'll be able to flat put the Spanish and all the other fucking slaving whites in this place on the run."

"Arsen," spoke up John the Greek quietly, "I hate to throw water on your righteous wrath, but not just the white settlers here hold Indian slaves, you know. Holding slaves is an old and quite accepted Indian custom, too. The Micco and his people, they brought up a fair number of slaves with them when they came north to us; and Swift Otter tells me that in the old days, when they were more numerous and strong enough to make war against other tribes, these

Shawnees did, too. Now and then, here and there, in fact, I'm told various tribes have held white slaves, captured from settlements or coastal shipwrecks or out of fights with cross-country expeditions that the Spanish send out from time to time. So if you and Ilsa mean to play Lincoln, maybe you'd better stop bum-rapping the Spanish long enough to emancipate the Micco's slaves.''

In the wake of that meeting, Arsen Ademian went looking for the leader of the Creeks, the Micco. He finally found the aged leader of the Indians squatting in a shaded area, interestedly observing two of the braves—Soaring Eagle and Lizard-Upsidedown—melting pigs of lead Arsen had lifted from the Spanish fort in a large iron ladle from the same source in order to fill a gang-mold and produce cylindrical bullets for the .50-caliber rifles with which almost all the Indians now were armed. Nearby, in another spot of shade, a brace of other braves squatted, industriously knapping gun flints from a core of the rock, smoothing and perfecting their creations by use of antler picks and small, heavy mallets.

The old Indian's thin, wrinkled lips twitched slightly—the closest anyone had ever seen him come to a smile—when he spied Arsen bound in his direction, and, belying the expected infirmities of his more than ninety years of hard life under primitive conditions, he arose from his deep squat onto his feet in one smooth, easy-looking movement.

Arsen had often reflected that his own father's father, Grandpapa Vasil Ademian, would probably have gotten on fabulously with the old Micco, for like the aged Indian, the old man had been both smart as a whip and tough as rusty nails until the very day he had died after helping to reshoe a fractious horse; Arsen's memories of his grandfather were not of some doddering near-invalid, but of a powerful, still-vital, and very masculine man who even in his last years of life smoked like a chimney-pot, ate and drank anything he damned well wished, worked like a man a quarter his age, engaged in strenuous Armenian and Greek folk-dancing for hours at a time, and still had more than simply an eye for attractive females. Although of an entirely different time, culture, and world, even, the Micco of the Creeks was, Arsen thought, from out the same, identical mold as old Grandpapa Vasil Ademian. Needless to say, he deeply respected the Micco as he had respected his grandfather and still respected his father and his uncle, Rupen Ademian.

"Micco," he said, "we two need to talk over some things. Let's us do it inside, huh? It's cooler in there."

Inside the big council room of the fort, where the comparative coolness began to dry the sweat bathing his hirsute body, Arsen was relieved to remove his silver helmet—there was no need for more than one of them to be wearing one in order to communicate, and the Micco seemed to wear his constantly. That done, he got up while the Micco went about the preparation of a pipe of the incredibly strong, sharp, biting Indian-cure tobacco and set into motion the Rube Goldbergish, clockworklike arrangement of springs and weights that Greg and Al had recently rigged up in several of the rooms in order to move ceiling-mounted two-by-three-foot screens of woven reeds and thus increase air circulation.

When he had taken a pull at the fancifully carven pipe trimmed lavishly with bits of fur, colorful feathers, and strings of tiny wampum beads, he asked, "Micco, are there many of these smaller tribes like this Sis-ip-aw-haw Tribe, hereabouts? I'd only heard of the larger ones—Creek, Shawnee, Tuscarora, Cherokee, Catawba, and so on—before today."

The old Indian nodded. "There are more than two

hands' worth of fingers, Arsen Silverhat, though most were larger and more powerful before the Spanish came to hunt them and take much of the land. I remember that the Eastern Creeks used to often war against the Santee, the Pedee, the Wateree, the Congaree, the Cheraw, the Lumbee, the Sugaree, and the Waccamaw, all of which were allies of the mighty Catawba, but not even they were able to stand for long against the steel-breasts and their firesticks, fire-logs, and such deadly wonders. The other steel-breasts who came and first built a walled place where these Spanish now are brought with them a great and fearsome sickness which as good as wiped out all of the Pedees and not a few of the Santees, as well. Snake-and-a-half states that his tribe-of-birth, who lived along the other side of the next big river north of this one, died in that same way, of a terrible sickness brought by the Spanish, who have a small fort in what were their lands beside the river. I am told, indeed, that even the gentle White-Robed Ones bear deathly sicknesses with them.''

Distracted from his purpose for the moment, Arsen asked, ''Micco, I heard of these White-Robed Ones from Squash Woman soon after we first came here to help the Indians, but she didn't seem to really know all that much about them. Do you? Are they white-skinned? Where did they come from—inland somewhere, or what?''

The aged man nodded. ''Yes, Arsen Silverhat, it happens that I do know much of these, for years ago a small party of them came wandering into the lands we then owned and I talked long and frequently with their tall leader, whose hair and beard were much like the color of that of Ilsa Sunbrighthair, though also hued so as to look more like pale fireflames. Yes, his skin was whiter even than yours, though not so white as is that of Ilsa Sunbrighthair. His strong body was not so hairy as is yours, though. He called himself Bhán-Damh, which words he said mean White Stag, and he and his were all-powerful in the ways of magic, obviously servers of and much loved by the Great Spirit.

"White Stag told me that his many times ancestors had come to this land from another land beyond the Bitter Water, long, long ago, and had lived in small groups along the coasts before other white men came, to either slaughter them or drive them inland. He said that many of these small groups had finally joined together and dwelt in the Land of the Thunderbird until their omens had told them to move on to other places."

Arsen said, "But Micco, I thought you told me that folks weren't allowed to live in the Land of the Thunderbird? Didn't you say that?"

The wrinkled man nodded again. "Yes, I said that, Arsen Silverhat, and it is true for folk who hunt beasts and eat meat, but the people of White Stag do not, and so Thunderbird allowed them to dwell in peace in His land. No, the White-Robed Ones eat only plants, fish, eggs, and honey. Their robes, even, are woven of some plant they grow for the purpose, and they protect their feet with moccasins made cunningly of wood, bark, cloth, and the firmly compressed hair of certain beasts, but they do not ever kill the beasts in order to obtain the hair, rather persuading them to allow it to be plucked in seasons of shedding hair."

"Persuade animals? How, Micco?" queried Arsen puzzledly. "By trapping them?"

"Oh, no, Arsen Silverhat," answered the old man. "These White Robed Ones, through the mystic arts granted to them by the Great Spirit, can converse with all beasts, as all true men once could do, you see. They are the true friends of all beasts, and the beasts sense this; even the most savage or the hungriest of beasts will not ever do harm to them, and if a maddened beast should charge or threaten any one of them, they have but to stand still before them and sing a lovely, soft song of strange words and the very sound takes the rage or the fear from the hearts of the beasts. I know, Arsen Silverhat—I saw the one called White Stag do just that on a long-ago day, stopping a huge buffalo bull in full charge, so that the shaggy creature stood pawing at the ground and making low whuffling noises such as a little calf might make, then the one called White Stag walked slowly up to the massive bull and spoke with him for a long while, all the time caressing his muzzle and nose, which the beast held low enough for his hands to reach easily.''

Odd as it might have seemed to another, Arsen believed the tale of the Micco, for with the aid of the silver cap and the carrier, he had himself communicated after a fashion with the long-haired, tusked things that he thought of as elephants and that prick Bedros Yacubian insisted were mastodons, over the mountains in the strange Land of the Thunderbird. Once they were finally convinced that the man meant them and their precious calves no harm, they had become rather chummy, actually. He also had established communication of a sort with some of the super-lions, twice so far having been able to guide prides of the massive, lightly spotted felines close enough to pairs of the hairy, predatory, apelike things that the cats had been able to catch, kill, and eat them; ferocious as the pithecoid creatures were, they still were no real match for even a single full-grown super-lion and seemed to do their best to avoid close proximity to the scattered prides and individuals.

The super-lions would eat any creature they could get their claws or teeth into, large or small, but seemed to harbor a clear preference for the herd animals—bison, horses, a weird-looking antelopish creature that Yacubian had called a hayoceros, and some towering and longish-necked things the exact nature of which Arsen still had not decided, whether they were almost-humpless camels or slightly humped and oversized llamas. They and all the other predators would avidly consume any carrion they chanced across, no matter how ripe was the carcass or part thereof, but the lions studiously avoided confrontations with either the mastodons or the thick-furred, slow-moving, strictly vegetarian ground sloths.

These oversize beasts seemed to be preyed upon almost exclusively by the rare predators Arsen had taken to thinking of as bear-cats. These were composed of a strange combination of parts and traits, he had discovered. Viewed from a distance, they seemed to be mostly catlike—a Canadian lynx squared, Greg Sinclair had said the first time he had seen a pair of them—with large ears, thick bodies, short tails, and curved upper fangs that jutted their sharp points well below the lower jaws. John the Greek, an armchair paleontologist rather than a big-game hunter like Greg, had named them some kind of sabertooth tiger, but when at last Arsen had brought the professional into the Land of the Thunderbird, Bedros Yacubian had said that they were actually nothing of the sort but rather some hitherto unknown variety of something he called a homotherium.

These bear-cats apparently lived and denned and hunted in only mated pairs or small groups consisting of the pair of adults and the most recent litter of cubs. They were most often found near to the haunts of the small herds of mastodons or the thick woods which made up the feeding grounds of the sloth, which two beasts seemed to be their principal prey animals. Arsen's attempts to establish rapport with these particular predators had frustrated him some-what; the bear-cats seemed to be at least as intelligent as were most of the super-lions, perhaps even more so, but they also seemed to move in perpetual distrust of any creature not of their immediate kith and kin, showed no interest in anything other than their accustomed prey species, and more often than not just ignored attempts at communication by the man.

Though they were put together oddly, seemingly of spare parts from more than one kind of animal, and when immobile looked close up to be ungainly, Arsen had been witness to the facts that the bear-cats, while perhaps not as fast as the super-lions and far slower than any of the smaller cats, were easily able to provide for themselves and their mates and cubs or to protect themselves if attacked.

The first noticeable thing about them at close range was that, unlike the lions or any other cat, their backs sloped sharply to the rear like a hyena's, their hind legs seemed oddly misshapen, and they appeared to have no neck. Also completely dissimilar from felines was the thick, broad, very muscular body. Even closer examination—performed, prudently, by Arsen from a good distance with the optics of the carrier—revealed the truth of the matter: The backs did indeed slope, and this was because the forelimbs were much longer than the hind ones. Like those of any good cat, these forelegs were equipped with big, retractable claws, and only the toes normally came in contact with the ground surface, but it was the hind legs that caused Arsen to hang the bear-cat moniker on them. They were not deformed, but the creatures rather walked on the full flat of the foot, and although they could do quite respectable damage to skin and flesh with the bearlike claws of the hind feet, these claws were not retractable like those of the forefeet.

For all that even the biggest bear-cat Arsen had so far seen was, disregarding tail, shorter in body length than an adult super-lion, Arsen estimated that what with thicker bodies and more robust builds, they weighed just about as much, maybe even more. Their heads were about of a size with the super-lions', but their necks were as thick as the heads and were set to shoulders loaded and rolling with muscles. They varied widely in color, from agouti to an almost-bluish grey, some of them with more or fewer pale spots or streaks or, around the legs and stumpy tails, circlets of darker hues, these markings being fairly prominent on the cubs but fading as they matured; though not really long-haired, their coats were noticeably thicker and denser than those of either the super-lions or the jaguars.

Therefore, Arsen could believe that it was possible for men—natural telepaths, perhaps?—to "speak" to animals. "Where do these White-Robed Ones live at now, Micco?" he asked.

The aged Indian shrugged. "Everywhere, Arsen Silverhat, and anywhere and, really, nowhere. One must suppose that they gather somewhere, have villages whereat they can grow their cloth-plants, make their garments, beget and birth and rear and train those who will come after them, but the one called White Stag never spoke of such things, only saying that he and those like him journeyed over the lands wherever the Great Spirit bade them, He speaking to them as He always speaks to mankind in dreams. For all his youth, he was strong in his wisdom, and I learned very much from him."

"Then you've never seen any of them again, Micco?" probed Arsen, intrigued. "Or even heard so much as rumors of them, of where they might be found?"

"Only in dreams and visions have I seen White Stag since he and his party left my village and lands so many years ago, Arsen Silverhat, but one of those seeings was on the very march up to this place. Of a night when I was troubled, wondering if indeed I had made the best choice for my people by leading them so far from their lands to meet with white strangers, White Stag spoke with me from, I suppose, the Happy Hunting Ground—for he appeared no older than I remembered from so very long ago. He assured me that my way was right, was the best choice for the people, that although white-skinned, you and your tribe were also of the Great Spirit and were none of you evil, as are even the best of the steel-breasts. He went on to say that you would teach us new and better ways to do very many things. He said that you would show us many wonders, forever changing many of our customs and our lives while we lived and fought the steel-breasts with you. He said that in the end, it would be through you that the True People would be delivered to a world wherein there were no steel-breasts.

"As to where the White-Robed Ones may live, Arsen Silverhat, I cannot say at all. However, twenty-two winters ago, a warrior came to dwell among us for a while. He was one of those with a skin bluish-black in color and hair growing all in tight knots upon his head. Once a slave of the Spanish steel-breasts, he had been taken by his white master on one of the long marches that these and the other sorts of steel-breasts often mount around the lands in every direction for whatever purpose.

"This particular pointless march had taken them far, far to the north and west, then back across the Father of Waters to the east, then back a little way to the west and south, then again due south, until at last the few who were left of that party fetched up at the coastal place near to what were our lands, that place they name San Mohammed de Zaragosa. His white master having died of hunger on that march, he learned that it was the intention of the steel-breasts to sell him to a place where he would be worked to death quickly digging certain things out of the ground, dirt from which metal is made or something of the sort. He therefore made good his escape from the coastal place and was living alone when Creek hunters found him and brought him to me.

"In times past, others of that color of escaped steel-breast slaves have lived among the True People and other tribes of the various kinds of half-men, so when I was certain that he spoke words of truth with a straight tongue, I took him first as a guest in my lodge. His name in our tongue meant Deadly Spear, and a well-balanced spear in his hands was nothing less than deadly, we soon discovered. He soon learned our tongue, showed his skill in the hunt, and took over the lodge of a widow, and in the next war against the treacherous half-men who call themselves Choctaws, he became a noted warrior, as well."

"What became of him, Micco?" asked Arsen. "Is he still among you? I've seen no black warriors."

The Micco shook his head. "No, Deadly Spear lived among us for nine winters only. He fought with us against Choctaws and other half-men, but his greatest hatred was for the steel-breasts, and on several occasions he persuaded young warriors to follow him on raids against the smaller steel-breast settlements. On the last of these, his great, long-legged, black body was torn into pieces by a shot from a fire-log.

"But while still he lived, we two talked often, for he was of a turn of mind to learn all that he might of the True People and our history and customs. I was more than glad to tell him these things, while he told me of the strange lands beyond the Bitter Waters, the stranger peoples there. He told of his capture in war, of his being sold as a slave to the steel-breasts, who packed him and hundreds others into a great winged boat and kept them all chained in hot, stifling darkness, wherein rats scampered over and fed upon them in their weakened helplessness and many went mad or died for want of water and food.

"And that, Arsen Silverhat, confirmed in my mind much of the stupidity of these steel-breasts, for slaves are valuable. It is nothing less than stupid to so confine and starve and kill them; it is wasteful and, therefore, an affront to the Plan of the Great Spirit.

"But Deadly Spear, while we talked, also spoke of the great, pointless, and rather silly march of the steel-breasts around the vast lands to the north and west and east of where our village then sat. He said that far up the Father of Waters, that great river to the west, another river almost as mighty flows from farther west to join the Father of Waters. Up that river, two weeks' march along its northern bank, the part of the marchers with which Deadly Spear was proceeding came first to broad fields of plants bearing upon them what looked to be tufts of a fine white fur, all partly enclosed in shells of brownish-green. While the steel-breasts were still studying and discussing amongst themselves the possibilities and significances of this wonder—for it was clear to any who had looked that the even rows of that field were the work of none but mankind—a man robed all in white garments and shod came walking down a path towards the fields and the men of the marchers. He had, said Deadly Spear, long hair that was white as new snow and a long beard no less white; he used a long staff of peeled wood to aid his steps along the way, and when he saw the marchers, he raised it high above his head, smiled, and hurried on.

"The leader of the steel-breasts, Deadly Spear's master, bespoke the old white-skinned man as he

neared the group, demanding to know how and
when and why he was trespassing upon lands owned
by, given by the god of Rome to, the chiefs of Spain,
León, and certain others. He was answered politely,
Deadly Spear swore, in his own tongue and in such
manner and terms that Deadly Spear's master
abruptly changed his hostile behavior, telling all his
followers as they followed the old man to his village
that he thought this to be a very holy man; if not a
true priest of God, then possibly one of a community of monks or anchorites, probably come out of
Spain itself, since the old man's Castilian had been
pure and idiomatic of Deadly Spear's master's own
natal village.

"But then the other type of accomplished warrior
the steel-breasts call a knight, one who had come
from the tribe ruled over by the great chief the steel-
breasts call the Caliph, disagreed most forcefully
with the Spanish knight, swearing that it had not
been such a language the old man had spoken, but
rather a purer Berber than he had heard since the
first day he had set foot in Cuba. The two, recalled
Deadly Spear, both were hot-tempered and had almost come to blows in debate on the subject before
the party arrived at the village.

"According to Deadly Spear, they were all freely
given all the fruits and vegetables and meal prepared
in various ways that they could eat, along with the
lightly fermented juices of certain plants. Enough of
the strange stone huts built mostly below the level
of the ground were evacuated by their inhabitants to
house them, and all of the folk of that village—
young and old, male and female—behaved toward
these newcome strangers with courtesy and friend-
liness. The one who first had met them, who was
called something that sounded to Deadly Spear like
either Zagard or Zakairdot, was the chief of these
people.

OF BEGINNINGS AND ENDINGS

"This aged chief, his son, called something like Calf of the Plain, and that younger man's woman, called only Servant of the Mare, often spent long hours conversing with one or the other of the warriors called knights.

"Now Deadly Spear said that this group of marchers had all been near to exhaustion and starvation when they had chanced upon the old chief, having lost all their horses and mules in various ways, along with many of their supplies and some of their weapons. Only by dint of the efforts of Deadly Spear and a few of the kind of men the steel-breasts call *criollos* had they all had enough small game and wild plants to keep them alive that far. Therefore, weak as they had mostly been, it took them some weeks of plentiful food and rest to recover their strength. When they were all once more fit and healthy, Deadly Spear's master had assembled them all in the open space of the stone-lodge village and drawn his sword and declared that he was claiming the place and its rich croplands, fields, forests, waters, and any minerals in the names of his chiefs over the Bitter Water. He then called the old man to him, drew from his garments a thing that many of the steel-breasts wear about the neck, this one made of two bands of the yellow metal fastened one to the other as they do, and demanded that the old chief kneel before him and kiss that metal thing.

"In his ever mild voice, the old chief said only, 'Serve and reverence your own gods as you wish; that is the natural right of any and every living creature. But I must follow the old way, my way.' Then he departed the gathering and all of his people, too.

"When once the inhabitants all had drawn away some distance from their village and guests, the leaders of those well-served guests drew their followers close together and, in low words, told them that their hosts were none other than godless pagans,

not true Christians at all, and therefore no evil
wickednesses wrought upon or against them was or
could be considered to be a sin, but rather a certain
act of faith.

"Then did they all commence to rifle all the stone-
lodges, taking sacks of meal and shelled maize, nuts,
dried fruits and squashes and beans, salt, honey, and
gourds of the fermented juices. They found none of
the metals they so strangely prize anywhere in that
village, said Deadly Spear, only a few tools and or-
naments of red copper and another metal whose
name I misremember, now. When they had taken all
that they wanted, they fired the roofs of the lodges
and set out east and south, the way they had come.

"Deadly Spear said that not all those of that village had been in it there, that morning; he said that
some of those white-skinned men and women often
were absent for days and nights, only to come back
bearing plants of various sorts, rolls of bark, hon-
eycombs, baskets of eggs, and the like.

"The steel-breasts had been on their way only a
few hours when they came upon a young man of the
village walking toward it bearing a string of fish and
a fish-spear. Ignoring his smiles and words of
friendly greeting, these steel-breasts took his fish and
his spear, struck him to the ground, and wreaked
terrible and shameful things upon his body before
hacking him to death with their blades. Then they
marched on.

"A few hours farther along that riverbank way,
the marchers sighted her who was called Servant of
the Mare bathing in a back water pool. The two
called knights dragged the woman from the water
and, while others pinioned her upon the grassy bank,
used her body most brutally, one succeeding the
other, until they were sated, then they laughingly
encouraged all the other men to emulate them. The
marchers willingly complied and the young woman

died under them, yet they continued to abuse her dead flesh until it grew cold, they then cut off her head and hung it from the branch of a tree by its long, light-brown hair leaving her mangled, greying corpse where it lay splayed on the riverbank.

"They made camp for that night only a few yards from where they had abused and killed the woman. After cooking and eating of the stolen fish and other foods, they set up a strong night guard and slept. Although Deadly Spear—who was one of the guards that night—says that there was no disturbance, no noises other than those that beasts make naturally, both the woman's body and the severed head were gone from the places they had been left when it once more was light enough to see these facts."

"Lousy fucking motherfuckers!" hissed Arsen, "They're as bad as the fucking Cong or the goddamn NVA. I knew it must be a good reason to fight these fucking Spanish cocksuckers."

"Yes," agreed the Micco, "it is but another example of steel-breasts' innate stupidity and wastefulness. A captive woman is a very precious thing, not to be so used, but to be brought back to work and bear children to the good of the tribe of her captor.

"But there is more to the tale of Deadly Spear, Arsen Silverhat. He said that most of the marchers became terrified when it was discovered that the body and head both were gone, speaking often of walking, undead corpses, witches and demons called something that sounds like 'afreets,' but that the two called knights struck down some with their fists, beat others, and finally convinced them all that bears had borne away the corpse and head, for all that there were nowhere about that place the tracks of any beast large enough to have so done. Then they all broke camp and marched.

"Deadly Spear averred that it was full, broad daylight when they rounded a turn in the trail and saw standing before them the old, white-haired and bearded man who first had met them, the chief of the despoiled and burned village, Zagard, with no anger, but rather a look of intense sadness upon his face, bearing no weapons of any description, only his peeled walking stick. Expecting an ambush, of course, the leaders of the march halted in place and those behind crowded close to their rear, and so all heard the old chief's words spoken.

" 'Men of honor, you call yourselves, prating loudly and often of it, yet you own no honor, truly, you know not even the meaning of that word in any tongue. You all came to this land of peace tired and hungry. Here, the People of Peace took you in and fed you, cherished you, gave you rest and friendship, which was but another way of serving the earth, Mother of All Creatures. And how did you depart your benefactors?' "

"In a low but penetrating voice, in tones of infinite sadness, the old, bearded, white-skinned chief stood there alone on that riverside trail and bespoke the heavily armed steel-breasts," said the Micco. "Nor, or so averred Deadly Spear, could any just then find voice to counter his or even to respond.

" 'You claim everything you see in the names of unknown chiefs and what you call God, yet you— who, in the sad fact that you do not even feel or understand gratitude for good acts done you, the simple gratitude felt by the humblest of beasts—truly only worship, reverence, a reflection of your own unnatural evil and senseless greed. When first I met you, I sensed this ancient strain of evil in you, yet I had hoped that living in peace among the People of Peace might loosen its insidious hold upon your spirits, that you might begin to become the good men you might have been, but I was proved wrong; too long have you been steeped in the deadly venom of that age-old evil. Such as that evil has made you, you steal things which would have been freely given you had you but only asked, you destroy for the unnatural love you take in destruction, you delight in the infliction of suffering and death upon other living creatures who had thought themselves your friends. You . . .'

"But then the master of Deadly Spear found again both his voice and his arrogance and lust for killing. To one of his soldiers, he ordered, 'Hernán, put a bolt into the belly of that *viejo babaso.*'

"The man dropped a quarrel into the slot of his crossbow and loosed, all in one smooth, practiced movement, but the bolt flew rattling off among the brush and little tree trunks beyond the figure of the white-robed old man, and his expression and stance never altered.

" '*Carcamal!*' snarled the master of Deadly Spear, adding a whole plethora of obscene and blasphemous insults, while withdrawing from its water-repellent case at his waist a wheellock dag, but before he could prime it and span it, the figure of the old man vanished all in an instant as if it never had stood before them.

"A hurried search could find no slightest trace of the old man or any other human thereabouts, nor was there so much as a single footprint in the soft, sandy soil of the path where he had stood. However, no sooner had the march recommenced, than he stood once more, berating them softly and sadly, in the selfsame spot, but now behind them.

"Deadly Spear, who had been at the tail of the column of marchers, was brusquely ordered by his master to drop his load of sacks and spear the bearded old man. Dutifully, he obeyed, hurling the largest of his spears with his famous accuracy, and all of the watching men gasped to see the heavy spear pass cleanly through the white-robed figure and bury its sharp steel point in the soil behind that figure, which simply spoke on slowly, sadly, softly, with never a pause as a half-foot of steel and four feet of hardwood shaft passed completely through it.

"This was when, said Deadly Spear to me, he came to the understanding that the old man was not really there where they all thought to see and hear him, but was most likely in trance state far away from that spot and projecting a semblance of his body, such as a few of the more adept men-of-powers of his own natal land had been able to do. His master, however, insensitive steel-breast that he was, did not understand that he faced no man of flesh and blood. Roughly pushing his way through the bemused marchers, he drew his long steel sword, raised it above his head, shouted a warcry, and ran back along the path. Then he stopped all at once with a cry of surprise and alarm, teetering upon the verge of a round pit that had opened before him when the old man had but raised his peeled stick of wood.

"Now, Deadly Spear had dashed back to steady his master, and he stated that the pit looked every bit as real and solid as the old man, being about five feet deep and walled to about a foot above the ground with fire-blackened stones. Most of the bottom of the pit was covered in ashes and smoldering, smoking bundles of half-burned thatching. Visible near to one wall, however, was what was left of a pine-wood cradle, and within it was what was left of its infant occupant, one black-charred, tiny, clawlike hand still raised to seek, to implore the succor that never came. He knew then, did Deadly Spear, that this too was a projection, a projection of one of the subterranean lodges that the steel-breasts had first looted, then fired back in the village of the White Robed Ones.

"Because he knew that that which he and all the others of the marchers were seeing—or, rather, perceived themselves to be seeing—was not real, was only pictures cast before them all by the magic of a powerful, trained, and intensely disciplined mind, he alone did not scream and quake and befoul himself with his own wastes wrenched from out his body by abject terror when, to the right hand of the old, bearded white-skinned man, there appeared suddenly the grey-hued corpse of the fisherman the

marchers had tortured and maimed and slain soon
after taking leave of the blazing village. The empty
sockets from which they had gouged the eyes stared
at them, broken teeth grinning gappedly where the
lips had been sliced away, the lower jaw hanging on
broken hinges to show the stump of the torn-out
tongue. Coils of gas-filled intestines hung from the
great, gaping gash in the belly and onto the dusty
ground between the toeless feet, decently hiding the
evidences of the hideous outrages which sharp steel
and cruel savagery had wrought between the legs of
the dead man.

"Deadly Spear stated to me that his master, save
for one cry, had held to his courage in the face of
the appearance of the murdered fisherman, simply
gripping his sword hilt hard and staring at the ap-
parition; but when the raped and brutalized corpse
of the woman was all at once in an eyeblink there
on the left side of the old wizard, her dead hands
holding her severed head between and just below her
tooth-torn breasts, the sightless eyes wide-staring and
seemingly fixed upon none other save the knight
himself, then did the steel-breast let go all his dung
and water, begin to cry and whimper like a child in
his terror and back stumblingly away from the grisly
trio, his trembling hands held before him as if to
ward them off, while his fine steel sword hung by its
knot from his wrist, clean forgotten, its point trail-
ing in the dust.

" 'Not all of you are so deep in evil as are others
of you,' said the sad-voiced old man, 'but those who
are the most evil have ordered and infected the rest,
have dragged to the surface proclivities which without their baleful influences your spirits—those parts
of you that are of the Universal Good—would have
kept safely locked away in the furtherest recesses of
your beings. Therefore, for all that you all have per-
petrated evilnesses, I do not find it truly meet that

all should be punished, though it is most likely that the Mother of us all will gainsay me in this regard and see the lives of others forfeit.'

"Then, said Deadly Spear, did the other one called knight say loudly, 'What recompense of us would you, foul, heathen witchman? We have little gold or silver among us all, precious little, but we will leave it for the death-prices of those two and leave also the food and other things we took from your village.'

"Then did the voice of the old, white-skinned man become of even greater sadness, as shaking his bearded head, he said, 'Only life can recompense the snatching away of life. Besides, you only treasure the bits of soft, shiny metals; we People of Peace do not. The food would have been gladly given to you, so keep it—it will nourish some of you and impart to you strength for the long and arduous journey that lies ahead of you.

" 'But know you, honorless, ungrateful man, that stolen food will only nourish from this day the least evil among you. From this very moment onward, the bodies of those most steeped in evil will reject this food and any other taken from the Mother, retaining only unnourishing water, so that day by day will the evilest ones of you weaken and sicken as their evil-steeped husks waste away and at last die, that their spirits may return to the Mother and be once more cleansed in the Sacred, Healing Fires. Three evil men of you will die—life for life, as is the Plan— and with each death you still alive will receive a Sign so that you will know that the death is not happenstance or simply the chance Will of Her, but rather a part of the price to be exacted for the wrought evil.'

"Then, stated Deadly Spear, did his cast spear pull itself from out the ground where his cast had sent it, reverse itself, and fly fast and truly as if

thrown by a mighty-thewed warrior to come at last
to be imbedded at his feet, and the old white-bearded
one said, *in the very language of the tribe into which
Deadly Spear had been born,* 'Take your weapon,
black-skinned man, for it was cast by order of another. There is but little evil in you, so go in peace
from this place. You will live more years, find freedom and happiness for yourself, and finally will die
in honor, while combating that which you perceive
to be evil.'

"The marchers had stood or knelt on the path during all of this, bunched together for safety, wailing,
whimpering, crying and gasping prayers in their unholy terror and horror, but when it all at once seemed
that the old man and his two ghastly companions
were without moving somehow drawing closer to
them, they turned, scrambled to their feet, and ran,
screaming mindlessly along the riverside, all of
them, the ones called knights and the ones called
criollos alike, nor did they cease to run and scream
until they had exhausted their abilities to do either
and then they made to crawl and moan for some
distance farther toward the east."

The Micco tried to draw smoke from his long-
stemmed pipe, failed, and after exploring the bowl
with a horny forefinger, dumped the ash into the
firepit, then began to restuff the bowl with more of
the home-grown, home-cured leaf. When it was
stuffed to his critical satisfaction, he took the stem
between his lips and made use of the disposable bu-
tane lighter gifted him by Arsen and now one of his
proudest possessions. With it lit and drawing, he
gravely handed it to Arsen and waited until the white
man had had a puff before taking it back and filling
his own lungs with the acrid but soul-satisfying
smoke.

"So, you see, Arsen Silverhat, there is at least
one village of the White-Robed Ones, and probably

more. But the one of which my adopted warrior, Deadly Spear, told me lies far and very far from this place here in the lands of the Eastern Shawnee half-men.''

"Now, dammit, Micco," complained Arsen in frustration, "there you go again. You have the very annoying habit of starting a good tale, then just breaking it off at the most exciting part of it and trying to change the subject to something else entirely, so that your listeners have to beg you to tell the rest of it. So, all right, I'm begging. What the hell happened to those damned Spanish butchers after the old man scared the shit out of them?''

With a jerk of his thin lips that indicated vast amusement, the old Indian nodded slowly. "Deadly Spear, not knowing what else to do in the strange country, trotted after the rest of the marchers, picking up sacks and pieces of equipment and weapons they dropped in their mindless flight until he needs must walk, so burdened down was he become with impediments. It was well after nightfall before he found them, all huddled around a blazing fire they had built, exhausted but wide-awake and so nervous that they came close to shooting him before realizing his identity.

"Thanks principally to the efforts and levelheadedness of the black-skinned slave, with the sunrise of the next day, there was food available for the famished men and pots to cook it in. But when the master of Deadly Spear had spooned down his plateful of meal and dried squashes, he looked suddenly green as grass, then spewed out all of the food he had but just gobbled so avidly. Nor, from that day, could he hold anything of more substance than water within his belly, but though he gradually weakened until he had to be all but carried along by the other one called knight and Deadly Spear, still he insisted that the party march every day from the rising until near the setting of the sun.

"At last, the camp awoke of a morning to find him burning with a fever and raving in delirium, so they did not march that day. He was given by the other knight water with a little of the last gourd of fermented juice in it, but his body rejected it, though it did hold unmixed water well enough. Deadly Spear sighted a rabbit and brained it with a shrewdly flung stone, skinned and dressed it, butchered it, and made of its flesh a nourishing meat broth, but not so much as a spoonful of it could his fever-racked master retain within himself.

"Deep in the following night, the sleeping camp was jolted into wakefulness by a succession of terrible screams from Deadly Spear's master, who was seen when once the fire had been stirred up and replenished to be sitting straight up and, still screaming, just pointing wordlessly at something outside the range of the firelight. When the other steel-breast knight and Deadly Spear and the most senior of the *soldados,* one Federico, armed with dag, spear, and sword, took a torch from out the fire and went to see what was upsetting the wordlessly shrieking chief, they found on the rotted stump of a tree a partially decomposed head, apparently the head of a woman, with long, light-brown hair. It was resting on the jaggedly hewn-off remainder of its neck, its dead and decaying eyes seemingly staring directly into the camp.

"With a snarl, the one called knight struck the head hard with the flat of his long sword, sending it bouncing and rolling off into the darkness, then furiously wiped his blade with moss to cleanse it of any rotten bits of flesh. By the time he was done and the three turned back toward the camp, the other had ceased to scream. When they drew nigh him, they found out why: He lay dead, a look of unmitigated, bottomless horror upon his wasted, shrunken face.

"After certain religious rites, they dug a hole and placed the husk of Deadly Spear's first master in it, along with the bit of shiny metal that was his medicine and his sword. Most of his weapons, clothing, and other possessions were given to those living and most in need of them, and the other steel-breast knight claimed Deadly Spear for his own property.

"They piled the grave with stones from the riverbanks that wolves and bears not dig up the corpse, then thcy marched on at the first light of the sun. However, that night in the new day's camp, Deadly Spear's new master vomited up his entirc meal of fish and beans and meal. He continued to march as had his dead chief, with at last the aid of Deadly Spear and the *soldado* named Federico that he might stay erect on his weak and wobbling legs and essay to put one foot before the other, breathing like a holed bellows, with great difficulty, and before many days coughing up gouts of thick, jellylike stuff that looked rusty in color. He did not last as long as had his chief. He was found stiff and cold in death one morning, with blood caked all over his lips and beard. Lying beside his own head was a rotten, maggoty, wormy severed head with some long strands of light-brown hair still clinging to the sloughing skin and flesh of the scalp. The others recoiled in horror and would not so much as draw near to the body of their dead leader until the *soldado* Federico, raging and cursing at them while scathingly questioning their manhood and mental balance, had taken the worm-crawling head by the hair and thrown it as far out into the river as he could.

"This Federico was something that the steel-breast leaders had called a *sargento* and alsò a *criollo*, though they had seemed to despise him less than the others. With both the steel-breast knights now dead, this man took over as chief of the party. He took all of the most recently dead man's possessions for his own, even his sword, tumbling his naked corpse into a shallow, hastily dug grave before marching on.

"But within bare days, the same identical fate that had struck down those steel-breasts called knights had afflicted this Federico, and when the others saw that he could not retain food of any sort, then they ceased to waste any more of their now-shrinking supplies on him, nor would even one of them help Deadly Spear to aid him on the march, more than one of them, indeed, suggesting aloud that the slave simply strip the weakened man of anything usable and leave him by the river to fend for himself or die, as God saw fit.

"But Deadly Spear said that while he himself squatted of a bright morning eating his share of the food, this Federico, burning with fever, crawled somehow to the edge of the river to apparently bathe his suffering body in the cool waters. His screams drew Deadly Spear and many another to where they could see that a huge alligator had clamped its toothy jaws upon the wasted leg of the *sargento* and was dragging him by it toward the river. No less than two spears merely skittered off the beast's armored back, and the crossbow bolt loosed by the *soldado* called Hernán missed entirely despite the short range and large target.

"Then did Deadly Spear snatch away from another of the *soldados* a poleaxe, run and leap down onto the little narrow beach, and deal the monster so powerful a blow across the head that it let go the thin leg of the *sargento,* gave vent to a mighty, hissing roar of pain, and backed swiftly into the waters of the river, bleeding. But when Deadly Spear saw the monster sink under the muddy, red-brown water and turned to his most recent master, it was to find him lying dead, not breathing and with no heartbeat.

"As the *sargento* had stripped the corpse of the second steel-breast knight, so did the *soldados* strip his, but they made no moves to bury it and were almost ready to move on when, once again, the old, white-haired and bearded white-skinned man in the white robe appeared before them all, the same sad look upon his face.

" 'I am the last Sign you will see. The debt of life has been now fully paid with life.' He spoke in the same, soft, sad, gentle tone that all remembered. 'You have been heretofore led by, ordered by the most evil among you, but their lives now have been taken to pay your debt of life to Her. Your health and lives now rest entirely at Her Will, but then all creatures always live or die finally at Her Will.

" 'Now I am an old, a very exceedingly old man. You would not believe me if I should tell you how many winters and summers I have lived since She breathed life into my present husk. I have learned much in my long, long life, and some of my learning I will now impart to you men.

" 'All living creatures in Her keeping possess within themselves elements both good and evil; those we call good are those whose spirits have learned best to suppress the evil and allow the good to flourish, while those we know as evil are those so spiritually weak or flawed that they have allowed the evil of their natures to drown and kill the good.

" 'You must in the parts of your lives still remaining seek to be good in all ways. Relish not the fleeting and unnatural pleasures of your own evil natures and reverence not the deeds of evil done by others, lest like the severed head of a murdered woman, the wraiths of your evil deeds and theirs pursue you to your extinctions.

" 'One last time, I bid you go in peace. Fare you as She wills.' "

The Micco puffed the pipe back into life, filled his

lungs, then said, "Deadly Spear and the others—or some few of the others, rather—at last recrossed the Father of Waters, made their way to the appointed place of rendezvous with the other parties of the steel-breast marchers—all of those which arrived there of far fewer numbers than those which had departed and some never returning there at all—then they all slowly retraced a way back to one of the forts of the Spanish steel-breasts at a place where even the largest of the white-winged boats can come close to the shore.

"Deadly Spear it had been who had been chosen as leader of what remained of his party of marchers, and yet, when the parties rejoined and had won safely back to a fort, the words of the men he had led so well were ignored by the steel-breasts called knights and they sold him to a man whose intention was to put him onto one of the white-winged ships, take him back to Cuba, and sell him to a man who would work him to death. That is why Deadly Spear feigned meek submission for long enough to lull his new owner into freeing him of his chains just long enough to go with the Spaniard to bid farewell to those with whom he had marched for so long and so far.

"In a dark and deserted place, he strangled his newest owner, then stole weapons and food and fled as deeply into the forest as he could quickly get. That is where a hunter of my tribe found him.

"Now you have the entirety of the tale, as I recall it after so long, Arsen Silverhat."

The second night after the day he had heard the tale of Deadly Spear and then had spent most of that day questioning and arguing with the Creek leader about tribal customs and practices, Arsen sat in his own quarters with most of his fellow whites. He looked glum.

"A'right, here's the way it's stacked. John was

OF BEGINNINGS AND ENDINGS

right the other day, the fucking Creeks do keep slaves—women, men, kids, too. Not only that, they're not about to let any of them go free or even promise to stop taking more where they can catch them, either. I've argued with the Micco until I'm blue in the fucking face and it all comes back to the same fucking place every fucking time, like a fucking cracked record.

"See, the way the Micco thinks, the Creeks are the only real, one hundred percent pure people here. All the other Indians are, at the best, about three parts human and one part animal, and so killing them or making slaves out of them doesn't really mean any more than hunting animals does and really is part of the plan of the Great Spirit and all, you know."

"Bullshit!" snorted Mike Sikeena. "That's the same kinda crap that slimy, lying, greedy old cooze Squash Woman used to lay down, Arsen."

Arsen just sighed and slowly shook his head. "I know, dammit, I know. It seems like every fucking different tribe of these fucking Indians are of the same damn fucking stupid mind—their own fucking tribe are the real people and every other fucking tribe are just imitation people, see. I talked to Swift Otter, too, after I talked to the Micco, and he swears the same fucking line of shit: The Shawnees are the only real people and the Creeks are all at least half animal and so should by rights be the slaves of the only real people."

"Well," snapped Greg Sinclair, "if they're the only real people, than what the fuck are we s'pose to be, huh? Some kinda fucking monkey, maybe? Or are we lower than that even? I've hunted and done a whole lot of work with these Injun fuckers, I tell you, and I was thinking the most of them was pretty good joes, 'for I come to hear all this shit today. But I tell ever' one of you right now, any fucking redskin

comes to try to make a fucking slave out'n Miz Sinclair's boy, Greg, better've made up his death song
and sung it all through, too, 'fore he sets out, 'cause
he ain't gonna live long enough when he gets near
me to sing airy a note or a single fucking word of
it. And buddy, that's fucking gospel and you can bet
I mean ever' word of it, too!''

"Don't worry about that much, Greg," Arsen assured the now-heated man. "All of these Indians
seem to be under the impression that we were sent
from or by the Great Spirit. Understand, they're not
exactly afraid of us, but they deeply respect us.

"But that's not the thing I tried to get everybody
together in here tonight for, see. When I first dived
into this thing, this situation, here, and dragged the
rest of you into it along with me, I thought we were
saving the poor, abused, primitive Indians from a
bunch of Spanish and Moors who had the technolog-
ical edge on them and were taking unfair advantage
of it—raiding, killing, slaving and all.

"But, hell, from what I learned from the Micco
and Swift Otter, yesterday and today, these fuckers
do the same, identical fucking rotten things to each
other and were doing it long before any of them ever
seen or even heard of a man with white skin and
armor. And even if someway we do manage to beat
the whites over here bad enough, often enough, to
make them start leaving the Indians alone, then I
guarantee you the Indians are going to start going
after each other and doing things just as bad or worse
to each other, too. And it's going to take a hellacious
long time and guys with a lot more fucking patience
than I've got to talk them around to trying to even
make a stab at leaving each other alone and figuring
everybody is really real people and not part animal.

"So, hell, I figure now maybe the fucking Spanish
and all ain't so bad, after all . . . . not any worse than
the fucking people they're going after would be if

somebody turned the tables on them. And that makes me wonder if maybe we—all of us, here—don't really have a place in this thing, if maybe what we really should ought to do is use the carriers and projectors to go back over to England and get Uncle Rupen and Jenny Bostwick—if that's where they still are—and then project everybody back to our own world and time and let these fucking bloodthirsty, slaving savages—both red-skinned and white-skinned—go the fuck to hell any way they're going to."

"And, if so, what of your servant Simon Delahaye, Captain Arsen?" inquired the Englishman diffidently.

"Well, hell, man, you've got a family back in England somewhere, don't you?" demanded Arsen. "And property, too, I think you once told me."

The onetime captain of Monteleone's Horse sighed, then nodded. "Aye, 'tis true enough, Captain Arsen, though 'tis been long years since last I clapped eyes to aught of my kith or kin. Likewise, for aught I ken, my lands have been seized by others, since I bore arms and fought against the reigning king, Arthur III."

"Even so, Simon," insisted Arsen, "if the rest of us leave here and go back where we came from in the beginning, wouldn't you rather go back to England to things and folks you know, rather than live the rest of your life here, a stranger in a strange land?"

Delahaye frowned. "I . . . I cannot say of truth, Captain Arsen, I would need time to think . . . and to pray for guidance on't, for I must admit that here have I been happier than for many a long year before. Unbaptized, uncatechized heathen though they assuredly be, my two wives are both most caring and hardworking women, maintaining me in comfort and with solicitude. It would sorely pain my heart to depart from them, never to see them again.''

"You really mean to go back, then, Arsen?" asked Haigh Panoshian, Arsen's cousin. "How the hell we all gonna explain to everybody just where the hell we been all this time and all?''

Now Arsen looked troubled, very troubled. "Well," he said slowly, as if thinking even as he spoke, "as I was telling Ilsa earlier tonight, the best thing—hell, the only thing—I can figure to do is to set us all back the night before we went on that Iranian-doctor gig up north and then just not none of us go on it at all. But since the carrier says that if I do that then none of us will remember anything that happened after we were popped into that damn place in England, then I can't for the life of me figure out how we could remember to not go on that damned gig and wind up back in England in the same place and time again and do the same things over again and just keep going around in a fucking circle like for God knows how long if not forever. Shit!''

Taking a deep, deep breath, he went on, "So since it's so fucking hard to think through, I thought you all ought to know about it and *you* make the fucking decision, 'cause, boys and girls, I'm fucking thought out on it. But none of it has to be voted on tonight, mind you—just think it over and we'll meet on it again. I took one of the carriers out in that thick fog, last night, and flew down to the fucking Spanish fort area and bought us some more time, up here, before we'll have to fight anybody.''

When Sir Bass Foster, Duke of Norfolk, Markgraf von Velegrad, Earl of Rutland, Baron of Strathtyne, Lord Commander of the Royal Horse of the Kingdom of England and Wales, and presently under loan with his personal troops and ships to His Royal Highness Brian, *Ard-Righ* of Ireland, had made his formal and respectful greetings to the *Ard-Righ,* he waited in silence to learn just why he had been so peremptorily summoned to attend the burly monarch here in his fortified palace at Lagore.

Brian did not keep the great captain waiting long. With a cool smile, he inquired, "And what did our dear cousin Arthur reply to Your Grace's message dispatched to him just after you last spoke with us? We deeply envy Your Grace the incorruptibility of your retainers, you know; any other, we'd have had a copy of the message before any one else saw it. At another time and place, sometime in the future, we must sit down and discuss your grace's patent skill in securing and maintaining such a rare degree of loyalty on the parts of his subordinates."

"In other, plainer words," thought Bass, "you and your agents just found out the hard way that you can't buy or otherwise subvert Captain Farook or Walid Pasha. You're in aching need of more such shocking comeuppances, you arrogant, lying bastard.''

But aloud he said smoothly, ''Your Majesty, I felt it necessary and proper to request instructions of my own monarch before I consider agreement to take my land and sea forces so far away from his realm, lest he have need of them and they be not easily or quickly available. His Majesty's reply was that I should use my own best judgment in the matter, bearing in mind, however, that Great Ireland, for all its misleading name, is in no way any part of the Ireland of High Kings, but is rather an oversea colony—and a completely illegal one, according to the dictates of Rome—of the reigning King of Connachta, with which kingdom Your Majesty was, when last he had word of the matter, at war. His Majesty would prefer that I and my troops be employed for the original purpose for which he sent us to Ireland: to help Your Majesty in combating forces of Rome and consolidating the other small kingdoms under the suzerainty of Tara. He would be most wroth to see my men and ships frittered away in trying to take control of a distant colony which cannot in any way or form even be uncontestably claimed by its present holder, much less Your Majesty, should we succeed in conquering it for your royal arms.''

The *Ard-Righ* repressed a bestial snarl of frustrated rage with difficulty, and his big, hairy, calloused hands tightened their grip on the arms of his cathedra until the scarred knuckles shone as white as new-fallen snow. He took a deep breath, then another, then, finally, said in a tight, controlled voice, ''We bear you, personally, no slightest ill will, Your Grace. You are, above all else, a vassal of proven loyalty to your royal overlord, and such men as you cannot but be admired by other monarchs. Moreover, you have ever done no less than your best for us whilst serving us; though circumstances have conspired against our interests and goals, these were matters over which you owned and own very little if any control, and we realize that truth.

"However, we feel strongly that our dear cousin of England presumes too much and too far, for powerful as he has become in recent years he still is in no way *our* overlord, and thus he owns no right to attempt to dictate to us the uses of any of our forces, the original provenance of any of those forces being completely immaterial to the issue.

"King Arthur's entangling web of alliances has frustrated my arms and aims enough as it is, Your Grace. The completely Irish kingdoms of Ulaid and Airgialla—both of them rightfully clients of Tara— are become feoffs of a foreigner, the Regulus of the Isles, a thrice-damned Scot, and damn-all we can do to rectify this sorry mess of stinking offal. And why? Because this selfsame Regulus is, at one and the same time, vassal and overlord of King James of Scotland, who is now friend and close ally of Cousin Arthur, and should we attack the scheming Regulus to regain our own, then our dear cousin would be treaty-bound to mount attack upon us in support of his ally's suzerain-vassal.

"As if that alone were not enough to sicken a Waterford sow, Your Grace—and this may be a something of which you are not yet aware, unless your overlord mentioned it in his reply to you—that conniving, treacherous byblow of a poxy Italian mongrel, that *Duce* di Bolgia, who is King of Muma in all save only the title, has engineered a pact of mutual assistance with not only his accursed brother's new overlord, the Regulus, but with that murdering, land-grabbing, mercenary bastard who now is King of Connachta. This means that do we move against any of them—Muma, Connachta, Airgialla, or eke Ulaid—even with provocation, mind you, we stand in peril of attack from Muma in the south, from Connachta in the west, from Ulaid and Airgialla in the north, and from the fleet of the Regulus in the east. How are we to unite all *Eireann* under us are we bogged at every turn by such stinking political quagmires? Why can't those dog-vomit di Bolgias hie them back to their sun-blasted acres in Italy and take their sly, conspiratorial ways with them? We were well on the way to fulfilling our dream of fully uniting all *Eireann* and all Irishmen in peace under one king before those two came to disrupt everything so abominably.''

Bass Foster sighed silently while the *Ard-Righ* awaited an answer. At length, speaking slowly as he thought carefully to choose just the right words to lay before the mercurial and sometimes ill-controlled man, ''Look at it in this way, Your Majesty: Although Airgialla is now lost to you, you still have both Mide and Lagan, which you held before, and Breiffne and the holdings of the Northern Ui Neills, which you did not, and that is more land than your royal sire or any other *Ard-Righ* has held in centuries. Cannot this be considered at least progress? Some goals are just too much, often, for one man to achieve in one lifetime.''

The *Ard-Righ*'s growl then sounded so feral as to set the hairs of Bass's nape to rising and twitching. ''Oh, aye,'' he said bitterly, ''we still hold Mide . . . but we perforce have had to relinquish some of the most productive of the western baronies to Connachta in order to secure peace, and a humiliating peace, at that. *Righ* Roberto of Ulaid, acting in his capacity as regent for the infant *Righ* Ringeann of Airgialla, has led troops in seizing no less than two more baronies ceded to us by the late *Righ* Ronan, saying that *Righ* Ringeann cannot be bound by the mistakes of his predecessors, not even those of his own shamefully murdered sire. Moreover, a new ambassador has come to us bearing letters from *Righ* Flann Mac Corc Ui Fingen of Muma, though that piece of backbiting filth di Bolgia might as well have signed them, since his devious, Italianate hand is clear in all of them; these letters demand—*demand, God curse him!*—that we immediately cede to Muma some of the richest, most fruitful baronies we own, baronies won by our sire long years ago, promising to take them by force of arms do we not cede them peaceably. That damned di Bolgia knows that we dare not but bow to his hellish will, for do we stand in arms to defend our holdings or march against Corcaigh to take it by storm and burn it down around his hairy arse—which was our first impulse upon the reading—then the provisions of that Satan-spawn treaty he and his brother and the rest signed would be brought to bear, and we well know that we could not long stand against so many foes attacking us from every side.

"And it gets worse, Your Grace, far worse. Now *Righ* Eammon III of Lagan, whose dynasty owes its very genesis to our late sire's bounty, who is a blood cousin of us and whose late sire's intemperance in humiliating a papal legate came verily within the width of a hare's whisker of seeing all *Eireann* placed under interdict and all Irish royalty and higher nobility rendered excommunicants by papal fiat, has turned on us. It is almost more than mere flesh and blood, albeit royal, can bear, Your Grace.

"This backbiting pissant of a pocket monarch is making to turn upon his own kindred, suggesting that certain rich baronies which his plaguey sire ceded to us and Mide be returned to his ownership; otherwise, he states his intention of seeking alliance with the *Righ* of Muma and the *Righ* of Connachta. And hard on the heels of that ingratitude, that shameful degree of insolence, came the word that this son of a syphilitic sow had sent armed men to seize the Port of Wexford, cast out my garrison and officials, and declare that henceforth it and its revenues would be possessions of the *Righ* of Lagan.

"We must admit to a mistake on our part, Your Grace. At one time, for a while, we entertained the thought that Your Grace's coming, it was, had in some way begun to discommode us, cause us to see our fondest hopes and plans for *Eireann* dashed, not through conscious intent of Your Grace, perhaps, but through mischances which would not and could not have occurred without Your Grace's presence in *Eireann*. So irate did we become, on occasion, Your Grace, that we even seriously considered arranging Your Grace's quiet assassination."

It was all that Bass Foster could do to not shudder at those words, for he well knew that this amoral, devious, and often violent man was fully capable of any enormity, and if Brian chose to kill him or have him killed here, this day, for good reason or ill, not the force of all his men and ships and guns could save him . . . though they might exact a fearful vengeance against Brian and his own forces and lands and city. True, neither the words nor the momentary demeanor of the veteran warrior signaled one of his justly feared killing rages, but with him that all could change in a bare eyeblink of elapsed time, too. Nonetheless, he marshaled his courage and stood silent, unmoving, awaiting the next words from the *Ard-Righ*.

"But that," continued Brian, "was ere we closeted ourselves within a very private place and thought it all through, of a late night. Aye, a foreign, disruptive, and most divisive element was indeed introduced into *Eireann* to the detriment of all our erstwhile hopes and dreams and ambitions and eke our heartfelt prayers. It was not Your Grace, however, rather was it that evil condottiere thrust into Muma by agents of Rome, most likely, with the very purposes of division and disruption in their minds, and he and his brother have succeeded well in their schemes.

"His first actions here were to try to hoodwink me into raising my siege of Corcaigh, and when I saw through that scheme and did not cooperate with him, he and his pack did coldly murder his supposed patron, *Righ* Tàmhas Fitz Gerald of Muma, and see one Sean Fitz Robert sanctified in the place of our assassinated cousin. Then, when the scandalized Fitz Geralds rose up, slew the usurper he had forced upon them, and made to slay di Bolgia himself, he and his pack of cold-blooded mercenaries butchered every last man of that ancient house, killed until the very streets of Corcaigh ran red with noble blood. After that, with no male member of that noted Norman house still living and old enough to be sanctified as befits a *righ*, he proceeded to hunt around Muma and finally find a poor, humble, simple-minded peasant who happens to be a very, very distant descendant of the last native-Irish King of Muma and see him crowned *Righ* Flann . . . although even a blind idiot could see where the true power really lies in Muma, of course."

As the *Ard-Righ* continued to aggrievedly catalogue the many and heinous injustices committed against him and his plans for the conquering of the entire island, Bass thought that he most likely was completely right that di Bolgia had been the factor the introduction of which into Ireland had begun to dismantle the schemes of Brian the Burly. Faced only by other Irishmen—the majority of whom rigidly adhered to archaic forms and methods of waging war as the only "honorable" ways of so doing—Brian and his large and partially modernized field army had been winning rather consistently for years. Had Brian been left completely to his own devices—which devices included not just military actions but also the wiles of treaties he never intended to keep, purchase of treachery, extortion of compliance on all levels, theft, lying, betrayals, and murders—he just might have accomplished his goal of subduing all of Ireland within his lifetime, for being somewhat xenophobic, your average Irish *righ*, no matter how severely pressed or threatened, would not have so much as dreamed of arranging for aid from some foreign monarch, all of them recalling the frightful consequences of just such a step which long ago had resulted in the establishment of the Normans in Ireland.

But the di Bolgias had come to Ireland, and when once Ser Roberto di Bolgia had so miraculously become a *righ* in Ulaid,* with his elder brother, Ser Timoteo, *il Duce* di Bolgia, holding Muma with his condotta for its *righ*, they had both realized that there existed no way that their two small principalities could hope to stop or even slow for long the inexorable advance of the *Ard-Righ*'s strong forces whenever he got around to moving against them. Therefore, *Righ* Roberto had sailed across the sea to Islay, seat of the Lord or Regulus of the Western Isles, old Sir Aonghas Mac Dhomhnuill. To the immensely powerful Regulus, he had given over his pocket kingdom, then accepted it back as a feoff, thus becoming the willing vassal of the old man, but gaining for himself and his kingdom the protection of Sir Aonghas's large fleet of galleys and sailing ships, his thousands of justly feared Hebridean axemen, and, if necessary, the additional aid of yet another of Sir Aonghas's vassals, James, King of Scotland.

Realist that he seemed to be, not bearing the basically useless burdens of antique usages and customs as did most of the Irish or the almost-mediaeval

*See *Of Quests and Kings*, Signet Books, 1986.

concept of pure honor that hobbled the bulk of the Norman-Irish, but still probably bearing in mind that he could move only so far and so fast were he to continue to enjoy the full support and the faith of the somewhat backward, unmodern, barely civilized people he was trying to help, *Righ* Roberto's elder brother had most likely moved through him to establish contact with old Sir Aonghas. The condottiere had undoubtedly known that no matter how much *Righ* Flann of Muma owed him, no matter how much that new-made monarch depended upon him and his forces and counsel, he still could not and would not even consider such action as *Righ* Roberto of Ulaid had undertaken to protect himself, his people, and his lands from the rapacious, unscrupulous *Ard-Righ* Brian, and so the idea for a treaty of mutual assistance was born.

Actually, the treaty was a better plan than that earlier carried out by *Righ* Roberto, to Bass's way of thinking. While enjoying just about as much real protection through the threat of Sir Aonghas's not inconsiderable forces of sea and land, Muma still retained its freedom, not being in vassalage to any foreign power, which was more than Ulaid could say, these days.

As for the Connachta element, Bass happened to know more about that than he thought it presently wise to reveal to Brian the Burly for some time yet to come. After his several meetings with the various lesser kings of the principalities on the unhappy island, he was coming to the conclusion that almost any one of them would make Ireland a better *Ard-Righ* than was Brian.

"I wonder," he thought, "just what Arthur's reaction would be if his Lord Commander of the Royal Horse should be instrumental in replacing his cousin, Brian, with a less closely related but more efficient High King? I'd like to sound out Archbishop Hal on this subject, but I won't do it unless I can talk to him face to face and in privacy, for with Brian's spies and Arthur's spies and Rome's spies and God alone knows who else's flitting about all over the place, bribing messengers and intercepting correspondence, it would be my life to put such volatile musings onto paper or vellum in any language I know. Time was when he and I could actually talk in complete privacy by letter using twentieth-century American English, which was utterly foolproof code, unreadable by anyone then living in this world, but until somebody finds out exactly what happened to that Armenian-American dance band, learns who snatched the lot of them and where they were taken, there's no longer any guarantee that some power—Rome, for instance—doesn't currently hold one or more persons who can be hurt or terrorized into reading, translating whatever Hal and I might write to each other.''

''And so, your grace,''—the *Ard-Righ* paused long enough to drain a pint goblet of Rhenish wine, then went on, but now with something other than his litany of the abusive wrongs done him so recently and with so little cause,—''with no one left in all *Eireann* against whom I any longer dare hurl you and your justly vaunted forces, I first toyed with the thought of just sending you and yours back to Cousin Arthur with sincere thanks for the loan of you all, then I thought me of the Great *Eireann* venture, and I still may ask that you go there with enough ships and men to make it mine, but first I must know if that grim, dangerous old man on Islay considers Great *Eireann,* too, to be under this damned, hellish, illegal, and immoral treaty he has signed and sealed with that onetime mercenary, sometime jackanapes, scurvy bastard who now styles himself *Righ* of Connachta, holds the Jewel of Connachta, withholding it from me, his *Ard-Righ,* despite my many and most courteous requests for it that it may be safely held here for Connachta and him as I now hold the Magical Jewels of Mide, Lagan, Breiffne, the Northern Ui Neills, and Airgialla. This self-styled *Righ* of Connachta, since he claims and holds Great *Eireann,* must also be holding the Magical Jewel of that land, which likewise should rightly and properly be held by the *Ard-Righ,* by us." Abruptly, in mid-paragraph, the High King switched back to the regal plural. "But we doubt us that even old Aonghas longs to stretch his forces so thinly as to try to defend with them lands thousands of leagues distant and from which he draws no substance, in any case. However, he is not a man wisely taken for granted, therefore we *must* know his devious mind on the matter, ere we launch you and yours upon a course that might spell disaster for us all.

"Now, we had entertained the idea at the first of sending us a formal herald to Islay to ask the question forthrightly, one royal personage to another, but then we thought that had Aonghas not previously considered the matter at all, and knowing of old just how ill he regards us, we might by so doing give him the thought of extending his protection to Great *Eireann* simply to spite us and hinder our plans.

"Next, we thought us of sending Ser Ugo D'Orsini as a special—a very special—emissary to the court of the Regulus, he to be sent with both a public mission and a second, very private one. Italians, Moors, and Spaniards all are most adept at the proper execution of anything smacking of deceit, chicanery, dishonor, dissemblance, or the sub rosa, in general. But, alas, he bides still in England upon some papal mission.

"So, now, we have determined that the best course will be to send you and a sizable entourage to Islay aboard one of your ships. If you decide to accept this mission, Your Grace, you will be entrusted with a quantity of gold, which, if your primary mission succeeds—though we truly doubt us that it will, all truths taken into account and considered, but still it, the offer, gives you a good, believable excuse to beard the old bastard in his very den—will serve as the initial payment and *bona fides* of the transaction.

"You are to announce my intent to buy from the Regulus the lands that *Righ* Roberto of Ulaid holds in feoff from him. Drive as dear a bargain as you can, Your Grace, but know you also that *if* he *will* even consider selling us Ulaid, we will pay almost anything for that land, for with that infernal linchpin out, there would be little in it for him to justify the horrendous expenses of entering into open warfare with us and so this Christ-damned treaty would fall apart and all *Eireann* would again be ours for the mere plucking, so to speak.

"Of course, all that is a fair, fine dream which, as we have said, will almost certainly never come to pass, but we still can dream it . . . and Your Grace should still watch and listen closely, lest he miss any hint of opportunity to actually achieve it. But naturally, your real mission to Islay is that of drawing the Lord of Islay out in conversation, using the offer of feoff-purchase as the opening wedge, as it were. Feel him out as regards Great *Eireann,* but do so without mentioning the land or Connachta's supposed ownership of it or certainly not our designs upon it. Do you understand us, Your Grace?"

Bass Foster nodded. "I do, Your Majesty," he said aloud, while thinking, "Yes, I do, and far better than I think you think, you conniving, untruthful old bastard. Even while you damn anyone who opposes you and your schemes with every epithet and blasphemous insult you can dredge out of your sewer of a memory, you yourself are as much if not far more of a Byzantine, unscrupulous dissembler . . . but before this hand is played out, you old fucker, I may just break it off in you, give you exactly what you've deserved for a very long time. Nor will you be missed by any save only your creatures and sycophants; half the noblemen on this island would serve Ireland as a better High King than a greedy, lying, unstable, treacherous, murdering bastard such as you. For that matter . . . ? Well, why not? He's a Gael, too, and God knows he owns the respect of most every nobleman or soldier hereabouts.''

The old capital having been severely damaged by the cruel pounding of the big ship's guns landed on the shores of Lough Loig from the Duke of Norfolk's ship, *Revenge,* hauled up the cliffs, then laboriously dragged over to the siege site, *Righ* Roberto had decided soon after his surprising ascension to the throne that rather than undertake the certain sky-high expense of rebuilding the place he would establish a new capital city, one less close to and less exposed to the lands of the always-acquisitive Ui Neills—of either north or south.

Exploring his new realm, he had much liked the appearance of the lands surrounding Lough Cuan, mostly due to the narrow, constricted passage from the sea, which passage could be very easily defended by very few against almost any number of attackers. But his local advisers had discouraged such a choice, pointing out that only continual and expensive efforts would keep that same narrow passage passable at all to large ships, and that, enjoying as the Kingdom of Ulaid now did thanks to his majesty's sagacity the protection of the galleys and ships of the Regulus's fleet, there was scant need if any to fear of serious seaborne invaders. Considering their words and taking them to heart, therefore, *Righ* Roberto had chosen a favored site at the very head of the more northerly Lough Loig and, using as nucleus an ancient defensive structure said to have first been

erected by the old Dál Fiatach kings to defend against
the incursions of Viking and Gael, he saw initiated
the construction of a modern-design fortress even as
he saw teams of lowing oxen pull the plows that fur-
rowed out tracings in the soil where city walls would
be erected. He also envisioned another fortress on
the southern cliffs, opposite the ongoing one, but
was realist enough to admit that even with aid from
his overlord, the Regulus, he could not afford to undertake more at this time. True enough, he was getting most of the stone free from quarries in his client
state of Airgialla, to the south, but it still had to be
either hauled by land or barged in good weather up
to the building sites, then manhandled into place and
finished, and all of these tasks took men from the
land or the sea who might otherwise be laboring to
produce food of various sorts for feeding his people
or producing income for the kingdom, said realm
still a long way from being recovered from the rebellion which had led to the overthrow of the previous usurping renegade who had for so long
misruled and openly robbed Ulaid.

Sir Aonghas, the Lord of the Isles, was a kind
man and most generous to those who pleased him as
much as had *Righ* Roberto. In dim, past ages, it was
said that the then Kings of the Isles had also been
kings of not only Ulaid but wider reaches of Ireland,
and Sir Aonghas had been overjoyed to again become master of lands that he felt really should have
been a part of his birthright, anyway. Therefore,
upon receiving the fealty of Sir Roberto di Bolgia,
the magnate had not only given him back Ulaid in
feoff as pre-agreed, but had absolved him and Ulaid
in advance of all taxes for five years and half of the
taxes for five more years, remarking while so doing
that, badly as he always needed income, he still had
rather see the lands held for him by his vassals and
clients rich, safe from external foes, productive, and

enjoying the internal peace that only comes of well-fed commoners than be having to run his armies and fleet ragged helping to put down the constant rebellions of starving, desperate people hither and yon, such as too many shortsighted and greedy monarchs had done, were doing, and would do.

Further, he had pressed upon his newest vassal king a small casket of golden onzas, which he made clear to the stunned recipient was a gift of love, not a loan, along with a very fine sword, a seal of gilded silver to be henceforth used in correspondence between vassal and lord, a sleek new galley crewed by axemen of Lewes who would henceforth serve him as his bodyguard, and more than a few other small, valuable gifts.

The large, inestimably valuable gift, of course, was Aonghas's grim-smiling promise to soundly and most joyously trounce *Ard-Righ* Brian and any forces he might be so unwise as to send against *Righ* Roberto for whatever reason. And Roberto, having seen both armies and fleets, thought to himself that while it might become a close match, the Regulus could probably do it with his own force alone and could certainly do so if he called on his strongest vassal, King James of Scotland.

For all its appearance from afar, close examination had revealed the old clifftop defensive structure to be not only useless for any sort of defensive purposes but dangerous to occupy or even to be close around, much less enter. One tower had fallen in completely, and the other—with those timber supports not burnt out in ancient days and forgotten wars having long since rotted away to dust—looked to him to be held together and erect by nothing more than the weight of years, the thick mat of vines grown up over the stones, and, perhaps, prayer. Also, it loomed closer to the edges of the crumbly cliffside than he liked, so he ordered it and the ruins totally demolished, the stones to be stacked and saved for incorporation in the new fortress.

Meanwhile, in order to give at least a bare measure of protection, he had had a thick rampart of earth and timber thrown up at a likely spot along the cliffs and set thereon bombards and more modern pieces dragged over from the former capital city on the northern shore of Lough Neagh.

During the years of misreign by the late and unlamented *Righ* Conan Mac Dallain Ui Neill, all of the preceeding royal family and most of the ancient nobility had been eradicated or had wisely left the realm, and precious few had as yet chanced a return. Some of the new ''nobility''—creatures of *Righ* Conan, all—had tried in the beginning to attach themselves to Roberto's fledgling court and entourage, but he was not so naive as they obviously believed, and he recognized shameless, honorless, faithless opportunists when and where he encountered them and saw them receive exactly what they deserved.

Thus generally lacking a native nobility from whom to choose an advisory royal council, he leaned heavily upon the counsel of Father Mochtae Ui Connor, formerly a simple, common-born parish priest who had felt at last impelled to take up arms and arouse his people to resist the usurper in the rebellion which had, with the aid of the condotta of the Duke of Norfolk, succeeded in not only toppling the man but in killing him at the end. Despite his humble birth and decided lack of polish, Mochtae Ui Connor knew the kingdom and its various peoples and history every bit as well as any *filid;* moreover, he was more than simply wise, and his discernment with regard to people and their hidden motives and desires was often so accurate as to be disconcerting, for he always spoke what he thought at the time and place he thought it.

For a while, in the early months of his reign, Mochtae and a sagacious, elderly Hebridean nobleman, Sir Iain Mac Neill—a cadet of the Mac Neills of Barra, like all his ilk a distant relative of the northerly-dwelling Ui Neills and himself having fought in Ireland and numerous other places during his thirty-odd years as a mercenary officer of Outer Hebridean axemen, those fearsome warriors known in Irish lands as *galloglaiches*—had been Roberto's entire council, but as a bare trickle of the old nobility had returned from exile and as Roberto had elevated others to fill the vacancies left on the land by the ousters or deaths of those who had filled and plundered them under *Righ* Conan, he began to acquire a council worthy of that name.

Since all of them, king and council alike, had as their first and most important goal the protection of Ulaid from the designs of any of the grasping Ui Neills and an accelerated return of the lands to their onetime prosperity under this new, God-sent king, there was precious little disagreement between the members of the council and him they were set in place to advise . . . until the day that *Righ* Roberto announced during a formal meeting with them his intention of completely demolishing the ancient place atop the cliffs over the northern shore of Lough Loig, thus freeing the stones of structures, ruins, and foundations for use in the new fortress to rise there.

Owning, like his brother, a keen mind and a rare ability to easily and quickly master spoken languages and dialects—a gift of exceeding value to one who had until so recently made his living as a mercenary soldier, a sword-for-hire—Roberto had mastered a fair vocabulary in the version of Gaelic spoken in his new realm, but the mutterings he heard then from up and down the council table were not

clear to his ear, and he said as much to Father Mochtae.

"What the hell did I do or say wrong this time,
priest? Can *you* understand them, Sir Iain? What's
upsetting about knocking down and digging up some
old, now-useless stones that they might be put to real
use after so long? Is the spot a shrine of some kind,
or what? By the well-crisped pecker of Saint Law-
rence, I . . ."

The burly cleric looked pained, admonishing.
"Please, Your Majesty, blasphemy on your royal part
sets not a good example for those subjects who hear
it, nor is it salubrious to the well-being of your royal
soul.

"Your Majesty's council is alarmed, fearful that
disturbance of the underpinnings of the old castle
there might release the vengeful spirits of the ancients, the *Cruithni,* whose holy place it was long
centuries before the first men of *Erainn* came from
out the south with their chariots and their swords
and axes of iron. Right many of us *Fír-Ulad* of
today are, despite our patronymics, direct descendants of the old *Cruithni* and, through them, from
the *Pritani* and, for all any save God Almighty now
know, from the flint-men the *Pritani* themselves
displaced or slew for the possession of the land. In
those dark days of so long ago, before any knew of
the truth of God and His Word, there were mighty
wizards abroad amongst those who lived here before us, and many feel that it is always better to
allow old, heathen things to lie in peace rather than
to chance setting pagan evils afoot in the world once
more."

Roberto di Bolgia snorted his disgust at such
primitive and silly superstition, but rather than say
the scathing things that were pressing toward his lips,
he said, "Look, you, Father Mochtae, gentlemen, if
anyone of archaic times lies buried up there under

those ruins, then he or they are your ancestors, no? The stones they set in place are not being taken away, they are only going to be rearranged, so that they once more will stand in a way to serve as protection for you who are descended of these *cru* . . . whatevers. In such case, why should the shades of your distant ancestors feel or show malice toward you, eh?

"Besides, I know of hundreds—and have actually taken part in or at least witnessed a score or more— of uncoverings of things from ancient times all over Italy and Sicily. Indeed, in parts of Tuscany, the farmers can hardly plow their fields, much less dig a new well or cesspit, without uncovering old ruins, tombs, statues, and what-have-you from the antique Romans and, eke, the people who owned the lands before them. Those old ones practiced things which if not real magic at least will serve as such until the real thing comes along—some of the tombs which had not been opened or even known of in countless centuries have been found to still be lit by lamps, and they somehow produced some metal that seems to be simply bronze but is as strong as the most modern steel; indeed, my elder brother, Ser Timoteo, *il Duce* di Bolgia, owns an open-faced helm from out just such a tomb and more than one steel blade has been dulled or shattered on it in battle. Now, surely, were there any tiniest grain of truth in these tales of the spirits of disinterred pagans taking horrible vengeances on those who disturb their bones or rob their tombs, then some awful doom would long since have befallen my brother.

"But, in deference to those who came before you all, if for no other reason, I promise that if the workmen up on the cliffs should uncover anything that looks like it might possibly need blessing, then Father Mochtae will be sent for straight away. Will that be a satisfactory arrangement, Father, gentlemen?

Have ever any of you seen or heard of any demon—
pagan or otherwise—who could for long prevail
against the True Faith and the application of holy
water, silver blessed by a priest, or cold iron?''

"The child is delivered to us, big-boned and lusty, with the Bull bright upon his right palm," Regulus Aonghas wrote in his own fair hand to his younger brother, just then in England on church business. "It was as well that you were not here, however, for big and broad as the midwives could tell him to be and small as is our dear Eibhlin, especially, as it was to be her first birthing, they all warned that it might well go hard with her. Therefore, I sent to Gighas in Uist and he sent me back a true *dubhsidh*. You may upbraid me all you wish when next we two meet, my brother, but I am convinced that without the good offices of that wise old man, neither our precious Eibhlin nor this more than merely precious boy-child might have survived to give us all hope. How much better a world we might have in which to live if you and all other churchmen would set yourselves to seek out such as the *dubhsidh* in true peace and brotherhood and learn from them, rather than hunting them like wild beasts and burning any you can catch, branding them Imps of Satan.

"But the best news is that I have received word by galley from Ulaid that none other than the bairn's sire—Sir Sebastian Foster, Duke of Norfolk—is making a ship of his fleet ready to sail to Islay on the business of that hog's byblow who styles himself

the *Ard-Righ* of *Eireann*. Therefore, dear brother
mine, I pray you learn quickly all that you can of the
present whereabouts and condition of this *Sassenach*'s
mad wife, for my agents have been completely unable to recontact those who had agreed to undertake
the task for which they had been partially paid in
advance and although my agents are reasonably certain that a number of deaths occurred suddenly in
the house of a certain nursing order in Yorkshire,
they write me that they have reason to believe the
mad duchess was borne away from out that house
very shortly prior to those regrettable demises. I
know full well that you approve not of my actions in
this regard, my brother, but now we must think of
the good of our ilk before and above other considerations. Remember, I will not live forever and there
must be no blot upon or possibility of obstacle to a
quick and an orderly succession of chief and lord,
here, for our foes are many and crouch always with
talons bared awaiting the slightest chance of a stum-
ble or a misstep or fall to pounce.''

The stocky, muscular man heaved a deep sigh and
then paused to take a good pull on his jack of wine
before shaking his head and starting to reply, ''It's a
tempting offer, Your Majes—''
The man with the greying-red hair seated across
the table from him slapped a horny palm onto that
table with enough force to make the sturdy thing to
creak as well as to set everything on it to dancing.
''Now, by the ill-aimed load of old Onan, Timoteo,
I have to sit still for enough and more than enough
of titles and stilted, third-person speech from everyone else, anymore, but I'll be dipped in boiling camel's piss before I take it from an old comrade like
you. Man, I told you, when we two be alone like
this, we are but a brace of old hired soldiers, nothing
more, Timoteo di Bolgia and Daveog Mac Diugnan.

Will it be needful for me to grave it in Roman upon some tenderer portion of your hairy torso before you'll be able to get it and keep it in your thick Umbrian head?''

When, in earnest of his question, the speaker drew the big knife from out its lodgment in the crusty loaf of bread and began to thumb its edge, the other man grinned and replied, ''Try it, you mare-raping bastard, and you'll be one old *condottiere* with his own little prick in his mouth and the length of that knife lodged in his shitty arse-crack, bodyguard outside or no bodyguard outside!''

Grinning, not at all offended, *Righ* Daveog of Connachta jammed the point of the plain, sturdy knife back into the two-pound loaf and grinned so widely as to show every yellowed tooth his jaws still boasted. ''Those words, now, smack of the profane, plainspoken Timoteo I recall of happy years agone in lands far from *Eireann* and the burdens of sovgnty. You've no doubt heard the old saw that God's punishment of men is often to completely answer their prayers, to give unto them that which they think they want? Well, believe you me, old comrade, it's true, nothing ever said was truer. I know! For long, bitter years, I worked and schemed and fought and bled and prayed most mightily that I might one day ere I died reattain to my murdered sire's rightful place; the Lord heard my prayers, worse luck, and vouchsafed unto me that office and rank, and I now could but wish that I still were merely Count Ros Comain, squatting in the fern and raiding the usurper when not hiding from his hirelings.

''Not long since it was that I could saddle my own horse, arm, gather to me a few, trusty fighters, and ride off where I wished, when I wished, to do aught that I wished, without asking the leave of any man. But no more, my friend, no more. Supposedly, the most puissant man in all of Connachta I am, and it's all that which fills the lower bowels of a cow, Timoteo. Why, man, it seems that every other man in all these lands miscalled mine is my master in one way or another, anymore, since I was invested their *righ*. I *am* allowed to wipe my own arse, but that's about the extent of my freedom these days. Had I suspected any of this, imagined for even a moment that kingship is but a life sentence of incarceration in a samite-lined prison, I had thrown that cursed chunk of amber and the desiccated remains of a little beast it entombs into the sea and returned to the free life of a warrior amongst warriors in the fern, the greenwood, and the mountain caves . . . or, better yet, I had stayed in Hungary with my old condotta.

"Comrade, you would not believe, could not believe all that it took or the elapsed time that was required to see me here, eating and drinking with you, this day. Please heed you the well-meant advice of an old friend who learned the worst too late to help himself, Timoteo: Never, ever allow anyone or any set of circumstances to see a regnal crown pressed upon your head. Almost any conceivable fate is better by far than such slavery. That's one of the reasons I'd like to take you with me when I go on my voyage to visit my lands beyond the seas, you know; I much fear me that in my absence from *Eireann*, your officers and the royal councillors will prevail upon you to assume the actual kingship of Muma, letting poor, sad Flann go back to the cows he so mourns after and pines for, and I'd not be happy to see you, too, bogged in this stinking, hateful quagmire that attends regnal title, duties, and responsibilities, Timoteo. So, please agree, say you'll make the journey with me. It will be made—did I tell you this already?—in that big, beautiful, almost-new warship that I pried out of *Ard-Righ* Brian as part of his reparations to Connachta for war damages wreaked by his army, so the enjoying of her accommodations should be the sweeter, the way.''

"It's as I started to say before I was so rudely interrupted,'' replied di Bolgia. ''While I long have desired to at least see some of those new lands oversea, ere I'm too old and infirm to so do—and always providing a swordswipe or some stray chunk of lead or iron does not get into my way in the near future—still, I dare not, not now, not at this time and place. And there are good, compelling reasons, too, Daveog.

"Look you, our *righ,* our cowherd king, Flann Mac Còrc, despite your low opinion of him, is good and daily becoming better, but like the most of your singular race, he is too a little mad, too much influenced by religion and thoroughly ridden with superstitious nonsense. In short he, and the Irishmen amongst his councillors, are right often in need of a realist to keep their addled heads from up their arses.

"As, for instance, in this silly business of the Magical Jewel—so called—of Munster or Muma. Now Brian presently holds the real one, that one in the palace at Corcaigh being, while intrinsically valuable enough—real stones, good ones, and solid, heavy gold—is a jeweler's copy, though only I and a very few others know of this. Unfortunately, one of those in the know is *Righ* Flann, and it pains him mightily, for all that I have assured him over and over again that so long as he holds the lands and the loyalty of the people, with the kingdom rendered at long last completely safe from any invasion of the *Ard-Righ*'s forces through dint of our treaty of mutual assistance with you, Roberto, and the Regulus, he should not care a rotten fig if Brian diddles himself with that bauble he had stolen for him. But oh no, not our Flann. Every so often that damned Brian sends down yet another messenger bearing still another letter which always obliquely threatens to dis-

close to all in Munster that the Star of Munster there
is a forgery of the real thing unless Flann journey
up to Tara, give his kingdom to Brian, and *possibly*
receive it back as feoff, and at such times it is right
often all that I and the rational members of council
can do to prevent the *Righ* and the rest of the council
from doing just so.''

Daveog frowned and pinched his lower lip. ''Your
officers can't handle Flann, influence him, then?''

Di Bolgia sighed gustily. ''In some matters of
lesser importance, yes; in this particular matter and
certain others, no, he'll listen only to me, at the end.
So, you see, I'm as much a prisoner as you, even
without the title. I dare not leave Munster so long as
that turd of an *Ard-Righ* remain aboveground and in
power. And, dammit, your offer is one I'd dearly
love to accept, too, old friend.''

''If Brian is such a sore affliction to you, Timoteo,'' said the *Righ* of Connachta in a lower, almost
whispering voice, as he leaned across the table to be
better heard, ''then I can but wonder that your fine
Italian mind has not thought on a . . . ahem, *final*
solution to the problem he presents.''

The dark-bearded man shrugged. ''Put him down?
That's been tried, numerous times, as I'm sure you
know, Daveog. Those damned Rus-Goths of his are
brutally efficient watchdogs—my spies at his court
say that the sinewy bastards have cut down at least
two suspected assassins in just the last moon or so.
And if you can somehow get a man past them, there
are still his brace of Kalmyks with whom to reckon.
Nor is the man himself a physical coward or inexpert
with sword, axe, or other weapons.''

''Then, perhaps, a . . . ahh, quieter, less noticeable, a nonconfrontational method?'' mused the *Righ*
of Connachta.

Di Bolgia shook his head disgustedly. ''Comrade,
the man owns a charmed life, apparently, for we two

are far from his only foes, nor are we the only foes of his with access to gold. I'm told that his tasters die like flies, yet the man lives on. No, I'm about come to the conclusion that the one and only way to put this royal creature down for good and all is going to be to marshal enough of a force to meet him in battle and decisively defeat him and, does he not fall in battle, arrange for him a fatal accident.''

Regarding his companion from beneath bushy red eyebrows, *Righ* Daveog asked slyly, with feigned innocence of tone, ''Such, mayhap, as that regrettable accident that befell the late *Righ* Tàmhas Fitz Gerald of Muma, comrade mine?''

If he had expected some heated response, he was disappointed, for di Bolgia only frowned, sighed once more, and slowly shook his head, saying, ''I doubt me, Daveog, that any will ever cease to question the real manner of that old bastard's demise. For all that his was not the only death that resulted from that chaotic tumble of a group of drink-sodden, unsteady men down those treacherous stone stairs, no one I know of ever has seemed to doubt the facts of any death save only his—not Baron Fermoy's, not Sir Liam Fitz John's.''

''Hmph.'' Daveog's eyebrows arched. ''I'd not even heard of any other deaths, that night. Fermoy and this knight, then, they were killed outright, on the spot, Timoteo?''

''No,'' replied the Italian, ''after the rest of us and the servants had gotten the pile of drunken farts sorted out, it was clear to all that Sir Liam—one of *Righ* Tàmhas's Fitz Gerald's guards, mounted bodyguards, all gentlemen and most of them relatives of his in one or another degree—had a broken leg, but like the *Righ*, the Baron showed no injuries other than stone-scrapes and some bruises. But on the next morning, with the palace all aware that the *Righ* had died in the night, old Fermoy, who had been wheez-

ing and had seemed—or so his retainers later at-
tested—to be having trouble and some pain in
breathing since arising from his bed, suddenly began
to cough up quantities of frothy blood, and ere a
summoned leech could reach his rooms, his heart
ceased to beat. Following his examination, that leech
and his mates declared that an imbalance of humours
resulting from Fermoy's habitual insistence on having a window open in the rooms wherein he slept of
nights, thus fatally exposing himself to the known-
poisonous night vapors, had at last killed him, the
fall having had nothing to do with it, supposedly.
For myself, I'd say that the effect of that tumble and
nothing else is what killed the old bastard, just as it
killed his master.''

Righ Daveog nodded decisively. ''Few leeches have
any real knowledge of the true workings of men's
bodies. At best, the creatures are bumbling fools, at
worst, they're charlatans, and all of them greedy as
sin, but the chirurgeons are worse and even greedier,
I trow. No, I, too, can guess precisely what killed
Baron Fermoy. Like you, I've seen enough soldiers
die in just that way; broken ribs piercing the lungs,
that's what killed him. If night air were poisonous,
then I for one were returned to dust years agone. And
the knight died of his broken leg?''

Di Bolgia shrugged. ''In a manner of speaking,
he did; the flesh was not rent, so some of us old
soldiers set the leg on the spot and splinted it with
boards, but within a week, he developed the cursed
black-rot. The royal chirurgeon himself took the leg
off—and a very quick, craftsmanlike job he did, too,
I watched it all, having an interest in such things—
but the knight still died. I was a bit surprised at his
death, strong, strapping, lusty fellow that he was.
But, then, who amongst us ever can guess at the will
of God, eh?''

Both men signed themselves piously.

* * *

Don Guillermo, through a stroke of good fortune, was not compelled to construct timber rafts to hold his prized guns after all. On a day, a Guarda Costa sloop came beating upriver from the sea, leading a smallish galleon which was, itself, towing a sizable but shallow-draft barge—a solidly built piece of work it was, even being fitted with frames to hold tarps over the cargo area and two enclosed cabins fore and aft to give relatively comfortable housing to barge crew.

The large banner wrought of rich fabric, with devices embroidered of even richer threadings, was unfamiliar to either Don Guillermo or Don Abdullah, however, and it was not until the ship had dropped her hooks out in the channel—she drawing too deeply to risk coming any closer to the riverbanks—that they learned the provenances of both ship and banner.

Seated in the cool reception hall of the fort, with wine, salty bits, and comfits, Don Guillermo said, "Don Rogallach, this banner borne by your ship, it is not that of *Irlande Grande*."

The bald, red-bearded, hefty knight nodded, his greenish eyes twinkling, as he replied in flawless Morro-español, the unofficial language of much of the Spanish peninsula, "Ah, man-dear, but it is . . . now. The old *Righ—rey,* you would call the title—is dead, he and all his sons helped into the next world by their successor, *Righ* Daveog Mac Diugnan, the former Count Ros Comain and the son of him who was killed and supplanted by that now-nameless personage who was *righ* before *Righ* Daveog."

"God, but you people change kings fast and furiously, Don Rogallach," commented Don Abdullah. "How many is this, since you became viceroy of *Irlande Grande?*"

The bald man shook his head ruefully. *"Righ*

Daveog's grandsire was *righ* when I was born. His son—*Righ* Daveog's late sire—it was first sent me over here as one of the viceroy's lieutenants, and when he lost his life, his successor summoned the viceroy back to Connachta and his execution, then for reasons of his own named me—a man he had never met and, probably, never even seen—to replace the departed viceroy. What my fate will be under the sway of this newest *righ,* I know not . . . and it does indeed weigh heavily upon me."

"Well, look you, man," spoke up Don Guillermo, "there's no need to just sit up there and await a summons to your own execution, none at all."

The Irishman raised one thick eyebrow in silent question, absently toying with his silver winecup.

"Not in the least," agreed Don Abdullah. "My friend, there are never many Europeans of gentle birth and trained to arms in Cuba or any of the rest of our great, sprawling dominions, here. And a man such as yourself could expect true preferment from the vice regal authorities in Cuba or anywhere else of the lands ruled jointly by King and Caliph. You already speak the language far and away better than the most of our damned *criollos,* you're a belted knight come of a noble house, you have mastered the requisite skills not only to properly fight a ship but to navigate it, as well. Such things are enough to make your quick fortune . . . do you elect to serve grateful masters." He lifted the ewer and proffered it, "More wine, Don Rogallach?"

When he had tasted and savored of the dark contents of the refilled cup, the Irishman nodded slowly. "Thank you, gentle friends, it is always reassuring to know that one has a bolthole in the event one may need such suddenly. I will keep this conversation well in mind for myself, my family, and my retainers. I've the feeling that I quickly could develop a real fondness for strong, sweet wine such as this fine Spanish vintage.''

"There is this, also, and much more important, too,'' put in Don Guillermo solemnly. "You and all your folk are presently excommunicants, but if you confess your sins, do penance, and then serve those to whom God in His wisdom gave these lands, then no longer need you to fear for your immortal soul.''

Don Abdullah frowned, but quickly straightened his face. There was, he thought, such a thing as overselling, be it of product or idea. Besides which, it was in his mind that proclamations of any of the three papacies were not and never had been necessarily the indisputable will of God. Oh, yes, this particular one was a very useful thing in that it gave the forces of King and Caliph an excellent legal and moral reason for driving out or trying to drive out any interlopers on their royal and rewarding possessions, but even so, a modern, realistic man such as himself still had to admit in his own soul that it all was a matter of nationalistic politics and human greed bearing a tissue-thin gilding of religion.

As unquestionably hard a fighter, shrewd a soldier and politician, calculating a businessman as he was, Abdullah often had thought and thought so again now that Guillermo's fervent—sometimes almost rabid—piety should have seen him a priest or monk, not trader, soldier, and military governor.

"Much as I'd like to, I'll not be able to stay down here for the campaign against whoever you're going to be facing,'' said the bald man sadly. "I must soon be back in New Galway, for reasons of my duty, but I have brought you some troops—all of them properly armed, equipped, and provisioned for a lengthy campaign, mind you.

"A young fellow, hight Sir Cathal Mac Conn Fionn Ui Fallamhain, will command in my absence. He is a son out of the loins of my late predecessor, though his dam was a Pamunkey concubine; he was but a wee lad when his sire was executed and I took him into my own household and reared him like a gentleman. He's fought against the French to the north of us on several occasions and against various tribes and clans of the French-influenced redmen many's the time. I knighted him for his help in driving off those French pirate raiders who were troubling the coasts a while back.

"The troops he'll be of commanding consist of a baker's dozen veteran gun captains—fit for either bombards or cannons—enough trained half-breeds to make them all up full guncrews, and a full three-score of my own Pagan Swords. There will be the one knight and two hundred others, all told. I'd be happiest getting all the men, the barge, and the six oar-boats now loaded on it back in one piece, of course, but war isn't always considerate of a man's wishes or hopes or plans, it seems."

"These Pagan Swords, Don Rogallach," inquired Don Abdullah with patent interest, "I've heard of them, of course, here and there. The thrice-damned French have not one good word to say of them . . . which led Don Guillermo and me to the belief that the dung-eating bastards are afraid of them. Exactly what sort of indios went to make them up? How are they trained and armed, pray tell?"

The bald man laughed grimly. "The pig-fuckers have good reason to dislike my boys, good and more than sufficient reason to both hate and fear them, too. It was the French, you know, started it all, them and the damned Norse, up north, arming and training their pagans along European lines and with everything except firearms. But I, haha, I stole a march on them.

"Your red pagan is rather conservative, comes to fighting. He likes his traditional weapons much better than anything we use . . . save only for the things we will not let him use: firearms and cannon. So both the French and the Norse had a continuing problem with their own units of trained pagans, in that if not watched over very closely by their white officers, the pikemen were as likely as not to shorten their pikestaves to spear length or throw them away altogether and go at it with light axes, long dirks, or warclubs; moreover, on any campaign, they tended to 'lose' vast quantities of metal helmets and armor and jackboots.

"When first I realized that were I to adequately protect my settlements from our various foemen, it would be necessary to set up my own legion of trained pagans, I resolved me to utilize the lessons taught to those who would see them by the mistakes of both the French and the Norse. To approach a foe in great, easily visible, clanking, clumping, ordered, and relatively slow ranks is not the war way of the red pagans, who are inclined to attack swiftly, suddenly, unexpectedly from hiding, closing immediately and killing or downing as many as possible before fading away to strike the same way again, later. For this kind of fighting mode, the pike or the poleax or eke the long-hafted spear are near-useless weapons and noisy metal armor and clumsy jackboots could easily betray an ambush or cost a man his life.

"Therefore, I allowed my pagans to dress as suited them. Yes, they are trained in sleeveless jacks of thick, riveted leather and helmets of *cour bouilli* and pikemen's gauntlets, but none of them are *required* to use these in war or raids; in practice, very few of them do, and the items that do see use generally do so only during the coldest of weather, especially so the gauntlets.

"To their traditional weapons—light axe, warclub, short spear, and knife (both of these latter having largely been replaced, by the pagans' desires, with long dirks) and their short bows, I also saw them armed with and drilled and trained in the basket-hilted backsword and the targe, such as is still in use in *Eireann* and Alba.

"It proved to be one of my better ideas. A goodly proportion of my redmen are become exceeding adept at uses of backsword and targe—ox-strong in the slash, serpent-fast in the thrust of point, agile of foot and adept at consummate targe-work, quite dangerous and deadly, all in all. Were it left to the most of them, indeed, they would carry no other arms than backsword, targe, and a couple of knives, but I always have their leaders make certain that each warrior also bears along a dirk and either a light axe or a warclub, in addition to the bows and arrows."

"Bows and arrows?" asked Don Guillermo dubiously, "Oh, I see, for use against other indios or unarmored men, eh?"

The bald Irish man chuckled. "As you and yours will shortly see, my friends, these are no common, redman pagan bows . . . or arrows. No, these bows are capable of projecting an arrow with enough force to penetrate all grades of mail and, at close range, punch through some grades of plate."

"Oh, really?" said Don Abdullah with a shake of his head and clear doubt in his tone. "A good crossbow can do that, or the extra-long bows of the Welsh and the English, but none other I've ever seen. Did you then equip and train them to crossbows? Long, hard years of training and endless practice are required to master the longer bows, and they are clumsy to manage in tight places, too."

"Ah, but there is at least one other kind of long-range, armor-piercing bow, my good gentles," the Irish knight assured them, then enjoyed a long draft of wine before continuing. "Long years agone, a half brother of my late sire came back to *Eireann* lacking half of one leg and his right hand, covered with scars and glory and rich with the loot of his years as a hired sword in service of the Holy Roman Empire.

"Now this half uncle of mine had served right much of his years on the eastern frontier, serving alongside the warriors of some khans while fighting other clans of Kalmyks and their ilk, as well as Suomi, Rus-Goths, Wild Turks, Uzbekhs, and full many another singular people of those endless flat plains and icy marshlands. He took a liking to me, just a mere little lad, then, and spun me many's the fine, exciting tale of his adventures and all the passing strange things he had learned in his campaignings and travels. Thank God that I own a very good memory, for one of those bits of knowledge from away back then has helped me and my Pagan Swords and Great *Eireann* mightily, lo, these many years later in this foreign land.

"While the Kalmyks who are armed by and fight for the Empire—most of the time, at least—have been converted to the use of the light, one-hand crossbow, their wilder brethren and certain other of those eastern tribes and peoples still use a short bow of amazing strength of cast. These bows are basically wood, yet they can loose arrows half the length of those cloth-yard shafts needed for the longbows farther and more powerfully than any hand weapon other than crossbows or calivers."

"How can this be so, Don Rogallach?" demanded Don Guillermo. "Are you certain that you recall the tale aright? And that it was not just merely a fantastical tale of imaginary wonders spun to amuse a small boy? Old men have been known to so behave."

"Maybe not, Guillermo," said Abdullah slowly, "I tell you, now that my memory is prodded, I seem to recall something that a man I knew in Ifriqa once said about his own mercenary days of long, long

ago, when he served as a junior mercenary officer of
an army raised by the Comnenus of the Greeks on
some campaign to the north of the Pontus Euxinus.
He, too, as I now recall, spoke in passing of short,
stout bows that warriors could loose quickly from
the backs of galloping ponies in armor-piercing hails.
So, say on, Don Rogallach. Here, please allow me
to refresh your winecup.''

Don Abdullah just hoped that Guillermo would
hold his peace for a little while, this time. A way
in which to improve the effectiveness and power of
the bows of their own hired-on indios could prove
most useful to their arms and aims. They'd hear the
overvoluble Irish knight out, learn all they could of
the process from him, and then, once he was well
on his way back to *Irlande Grande,* they'd query
these Pagan Swords warriors in detail and, finally,
take one of these newfangled bows apart, then see
if they could do the same on the bows of their own
indios. And someday soon, the Irish trespassers just
might find themselves under attack by Spaniards and
indios armed with short, armor-piercing bows and
arrows. Of course, it would not be until after the
combined Irish-Moorish-Spanish-Portuguese force
had scotched thoroughly the French and their fi-
rearmed indios.

"So," the red-bearded man went on, willingly,
"I personally took a few bows and experimented
with them and the requisite materials until I determined the best ways of bonding the one to the others. I also set my smiths to fashioning arrowheads
of bits of steel and wrought iron, for as you know,
the stone heads shatter on armor, while the rare copper ones just bend.

"At some length, I discovered that a glue that the
pagans themselves used in securing the seams of their
bark boats was the best for the purpose I had in
mind. When once some of the leaders of the pagans

had witnessed for themselves the length of cast and multiplied power of the refurbished bows, every one of them was eager to learn how to fashion for himself so deadly a bow.

"It is amazingly simple, really, gentles; it involves merely the reinforcement of back and belly of the wooden bow with sinew and thin strips of horn."

Don Guillermo's face had gone white as curds under his tan. He shook his head slowly and said in hushed tones, "God preserve us all, Don Rogallach, what have you done? Think on it, man, teaching *indios* how to fashion so incipiently dangerous a weapon, one that can let go arrows with enough force to pierce armor—why, this is equipping these pagan savages with something even more threatening to us all than giving them calivers and arquebuses; at least they cannot make more firearms with materials readily available to them, familiar to them. Who can now tell just how many a brave soldier or hardworking settler will die as result of this, your folly?"

Even while the senior officers were drinking and talking within the fort, El Castillo de San Diego de Boca Osa, seamen and soldiers had towed the laden barge into the riverbank anchorage and warped it hard against the floating dock. Then the seamen rapidly took apart enough of the overhead framework to make it possible to lift out and float the fine whaleboats alongside, but as darkness was almost upon them, it was decided by Don Felipe that the other supplies and equipment which had been shipped aboard the barge would be left where they sat until morning gave them good light by which to work. Soggy-looking clouds rolling toward them from the west led him to order the frames quickly reassembled and the tarps all spread and tied down. Then he sent the seamen back to their ships and, after having the sergeants form up the soldiers, marched

them back to the fort, they being closely observed
all the way by half-drunken and very amused indios—their own from the south and the newer ones
armed with basket-hilted swords and small, round
shields who had arrived with the trespassing *Ir-
landeses*.

It was as well that he had broken up the working
party when he had, for soggy and water-laden as the
clouds were, they moved very fast indeed. Hardly
had the sunset *pasar lista* been completed on the
parade ground just outside the castillo walls, orders
read, and those assembled dismissed to duties, bar-
racks, or homes in the town than cold rain began to
descend in seemingly solid sheets, while thunder
rolled like unto a cannonade and bright-white lightning crackled all about.

Teniente Don Felipe knew that the farmers and
ranchers inland would doubtless be grateful for the
rain, for there had been little enough of it so far this
year, but he was soaked, chilled, and most appre-
ciative of the cup of warm mulled wine proffered
him by Don Abdullah's squire when he went up to
render his report.

"Alejandro," the Captain ordered his squire,
"strike you fire to the hearth, there. It is growing
chilly." Then, turning back to Don Felipe with a
smile, he asked, "So, how much work and material
will have to be put into that barge to make us a
decent gun platform of it, my boy? Has the thing
any decking at all in the waist?"

"*Capitán,*" replied the younger man, "it is with
exceeding pleasure that I report that that fine, sturdy
barge is full-decked over a hold which extends from
stem to stern and is all of fifteen hands high at its
center though only some cubit or less closer to the
sides. Though clearly not of European antecedents,
it was well built by a master of solid oak, elm, hick-

ory, and pine, mostly secured by trunnels, but with good-quality wrought-iron hardware, as well.

"The sides will have to be pierced, of course, and reinforced where the recoil ropes will be fastened. As for the deck . . . well, as it now is laid and supported, it would likely be safe to mount thereon a battery, so long as they were of no heavier a weight than *saqres*."

Don Abdullah frowned. "I had thought me more in terms of demicannon, anyway, or at least full culverins. I don't intend to just deface their stonework, dammit, I want to damage it enough to make a significant breach or three. A mere little *saqre* battery could burn powder and hurl little pecking-strength balls until hell freezes over solid without doing more than making ungodly amounts of noise and smoke. Will we be able to contrive to render that barge that strong? Or would we be better off using it for transport of men, powder, and victuals and constructing a log raft for the gun platform as we'd originally planned?"

"Oh, it can be done, *Capitán*," the young knight assured him. "First, another thickness of decking boards must be laid over the existing ones, and a good deal of the space in that hold will needs must be taken up by additional support timbers, while the sides of the barge, in addition to being pierced, will have to be strengthened too. Of course, all of this additional lumber and hardware, plus the weights of the guns, their trucks, powder, shot, equipment for them, the men to man them, and the barge with necessary supplies for them, all of these, sir, will unquestionably increase vastly both the draught and the towing weight of the barge."

"Hmmm." Abdullah frowned and pinched at his lower lip above his oiled and curly chinbeard, his black eyes slitted. "Towing weight is and will be no problem, for not only can the guncrews row, but we will have fourscore more strong, sturdy indios to man the oars on the trip upriver, but the increased draught, that is another and a far stickier question. Up that far, the Río Oso is of no consistent depth except in the main channel, and as you and I well know, the both of us, a severe storm flood can shift the location *and* the depth of that damned channel overnight. Remember that time that our pinnace grounded on its way back up to our slaving base on the isle?

"Even so, though, I like far more the idea of a real barge on which to mount the guns than I do that of some jerry-rigged, decked-over raft of green timber on which to risk a baron's ransom worth of fine French guns. Therefore, we'll proceed with work on the Irish barge, I think, and if it become obvious that the mounting of demicannon will dangerously deepen the draught, well . . . maybe we'll arm it with those brace of culverin-*reales,* then fill out the rest of the battery with full culverins. That would cut the weight down.''

"Dear Ms. Foster,

"Bass Foster has earned a protracted and painful death for what he has done to you. To see you now, no one could believe you to be the beautiful, charming young professional woman whom first I saw so few, short years ago. I came back here to Whyffler Hall in hopes of making an opportunity to kill him for my own personal reasons, and, discovering that he had departed bare days prior to my arrival, I have remained to await his certain eventual return and my chance to even both my score and yours.

"All here say that you are mad, insane, but that I do not believe, for that is what they said also of me, and I know it to be entirely false. You see, Arthur—ungrateful, backbiting young poseur that he is, I discovered too late—feared me and what I might do were I to reach Edinburgh and the ear of the cardinal there. Therefore he arranged to have me taken and imprisoned by a group of vile savages in the Scottish Lowlands. In their brutal hands, I was forced to watch the demise of all of my gentlemen, watch them slowly murdered in drawn-out ways too despicable and nauseating to here detail to you. Aside from casual beatings, near-starvation, and immurement in an underground cell under revolting conditions, I was unharmed until it was firmly established that I would

not be ransomed by either Arthur or Sir Francis
Whyffler; not even that mealymouthed Harold,
Archbishop of York, would dispatch the rather modest amount that would have delivered me from the
foul clutches of those barbarians.

"Once they were convinced that I would gain them
no gold or silver, they commenced to take out their
frustration and spite upon my helpless body. Although I am, of course, aware of your medical back-
ground, I still cannot bring myself to tell you exact
details of the appalling, hideously agonizing things
that those beasts did to me over the months that they
held me, things which caused me to scream for the
mercy of death, to piteously beg in vain, to pray,
even, that whatever power there may be grant me
the boon of death, of final surcease from the endless
rounds of tortures, maimings, disfigurements, and
mutilations. When it had borne its natural limit and
much more, my mind retreated from the horror
and pain that was become my waking and sleeping
living nightmare of life, so that I was unaware of
anything around me when a strong band of knights
and their retainers attacked and conquered the verminous hold of my cruel captors, intending to free
another nobleman who had already made good his
escape from out their clutches.

"It was not until almost half a year later that I
came back into my senses, and by that time I had
been named a madman and was straitly confined to
a tiny, cramped, vermin-ridden stone hut in a nursing-
order monastery east of Edinburgh, where I was
fed slops and kept naked and unwashed or shorn,
seldom seeing more than mere chinks of light, lacking even the most primitive sanitary arrangements,
forced to lick frost from off the walls to allay some-
what my constant thirst, with nothing to shield my
body from the cold save a stone trough filled with
damp, moldy straw. Nothing I said or did was taken

into any account by the monks and lay brothers; actually, I could communicate only with those few who spoke Latin, after a fashion, for no one of them could understand any dialect of English. Forced to exist so abominably, caged like some wild beast, fed and cared for with less solicitude than any good husbandman of even this cold, callous, primitive world would render an ox, my mind took to retreating into itself again for periods of indeterminate length in sheer self-protection, its only means of self-defense against true insanity, I think you will agree.

"I remained so for years. Then, one stormy night, lightning set one or more of the buildings of the monastery aflame, and, fearful that the wind-driven fires would light the thatch of the huts, I suppose, one of the monks came down and began to open the barred doors of the hutches in which I and my fellow sufferers lay imprisoned. Understandably desperate to escape, I lured the monk into my hut and there strangled him into unconsciousness, took his warm, woolen hooded habit and his rough brogues, and, amid the chaos of the fires, fled the environs of the monastery.

"When my escape was discovered, armed men were sent to hunt me down like some wild beast. After they and their hounds had driven me to bay, I was bound with ropes and chains, beaten into a coma, and borne back to the monastery hung over the back of a mule. There arrived, they stripped me of my warm robe and threw me naked back into the same fetid kennel.

"Because of the losses of nursing brothers and buildings in the fires, it was decided to bear me to another monastery of the order, one much more distant from the border, located on an island off the western coast of Scotland. I was transported, still naked and with only straw and the filth encrusting my body to shield me from the weather, in a wheeled cage formerly used to hold a bear.

"Somewhere a bit northeast of Glascow, I think, I once more escaped. While all the party slept, I moved silently about the night camp, stealing a tartan plaid, shirt, brogues, weapons, and a riding mule. I found by starlight a narrow track that looked to bear southwest and moved as fast as I could along it for the rest of that night. But then, on the next day, my mule came up lame, and thenceforth I was afoot.

"Because I still did not speak or even understand the guttural, ill-structured language of the Lowlands at all well, I avoided any contact with people, hiding in brushy ditches and woods whenever I saw or heard other travelers approaching from either direction, always more or less in fear of being again hunted down and taken back to my unjust captivity. Little brooks, rills, and springs are numerous in the area I traversed, so I seldom did thirst, but I very nearly starved before I chanced to catch a wandering chicken whose stringy flesh I was compelled to eat raw because I feared to build a fire; that fowl, a few mushrooms, and a fish of about five pounds' weight I cornered in the shallows of a brook and managed to fling ashore barehanded composed my only sustenance for the most of that long trip. But at least I felt I was free."

"Free," breathed the haggard, greying, old-looking woman. She paused in her reading of the letter, which had been written on sheets of lined yellow paper—real *paper,* legal-pad-sized paper, so nostagically familiar, so reminiscent of home. *Home!* Oh, God, *home!* Oh, God, if you really are there, if you really exist, please, oh, please, I pray you humbly, please send me back home, out of this rude, crude, hateful, comfortless world, before I die or become as truly disordered of the mind as all these barbarians think I am. You delivered your chosen people from the long captivity in Egypt; can't you deliver just this one . . . and Joe, little Joe, my son? Why do they keep Joe away from me? It's important that he start to be taught his Hebrew, he'll soon be six . . . or is it seven? . . . years old, after all. It's most likely that that lying motherfucker shithead of a so-called Archbishop, that dirty bastard Harold Kenmore, who now calls himself Harold of York, is just a goddam no-good anti-Semite, that's it. All these cocksuckers are bound to be anti-Semites, because if they aren't, how come there are no Jews anywhere in England I've heard of, huh?

"There's only me . . . all alone . . . so all alone. No one to talk to most of the time except those two thickheaded, musclebound, stupid, stinking nuns, or sometimes those even stupider common sluts who claim to be my maids. All of them always stink so bad, reek of old sweat and unwashed bodies and with breath that would gag a fucking maggot. If I wasn't so goddam filthy myself, I don't think I could stand even being in the same fucking room with them. At home, nobody'd . . .

"Oh, God, God, goddam you, God! Oh, please, please, please let me go back home. At home I can have a long, hot shower, a shower with real soap, shampoo, perfumed oil, bath gel even, I won't have to be smelling myself all the goddam time. My hair's grown back in, at least, but now my damn teeth are falling out and ache all the goddam time. And half or more of the new growth of hair is grey—white, let's face it, it would be white if it were ever really clean—and I'm not yet forty . . . I don't think; how the hell am I supposed to keep track of time here when there're no calendars, no fucking body seems to know or even care what year it is, and the damned months are called stupid things like Snow Moon, Wolf Moon, and shit like that? And I don't even menstruate anymore . . . .

"Oh, I used to lose track of time, forget the exact date, even, when I was in med school, but even then there were always television and newspapers and . . . Oh, God, *newspapers, books* . . . the only two books in this whole place, I think, are owned by those two strongarm nuns, and they're both in Church Latin and nothing but a mishmash of damn superstitious, Christian religious shit, anyway, and they're so hard to read—not printed, written in weird letters . . . .

"Letter? Written? Oh, God, I think . . . it looks exactly like pen, ball-point pen . . . ballpoint pen, *home.* . . .

On the next sheet of legal pad, the letter continued. "Eventually, the track on which I had been proceeding forked—one fork going due west and the other roughly southwest, I thought at the time. However, that night when I saw the positions of the stars, I knew that I was headed almost due south. This track, I soon discovered, had seen few if any other travelers in years and was much overgrown, but then I was just as pleased, since I had been losing time on each occasion I had had to conceal myself from such persons along the way.

"After two days more, I fetched up at a ruined hamlet beside a broad, swift river. There was no recent trace of man in the place, I quickly discovered, the crumbling, wattle-and-daub habitations by then giving lair only to small vermin, all the area long since stripped clean of anything of use or value. However, I found some tiny garden patches which had survived, reseeding themselves without the aid of man, over the years, and from these I was able to gather enough greens and root vegetables to truly fill my shrunken belly for the first time in years, that night. I established myself in the least dilapidated of the still-standing shanties, one in which the field-stone hearth still would draw properly and which even retained part of a roof of moldy, overgrown thatch.

"After so long a time of unceasing privation, suffering, and damp, aching cold, that tiny hovel seemed nirvana to me. I ever was accurate with cast stones, and this talent served me well, depleting the ranks of hares, squirrels, and the larger wood rats. I slew a viper with my sword and dined on his tender white flesh, and on another day I chased an otter away from a fish he had brought out onto the riverbank and gorged on fat, rich salmon that night, before I rolled myself into my warm tartan and slept full-bellied and free and contented on my bed of springy conifer tips bathed in the dry warmth radiated by the coals of my fire.

"But that blissful idyll could not long last, of course. The available plant foods were limited in quantity and the small beasts either departed the area or became so chary that my stones more frequently missed them than not. It at length became obvious that were I not to starve, I must find habitations of men, wherein I might trade for food or, if I was driven to such, take it by force. I might have followed the bank of the river, but I instead elected to cross it, thus to still be bound southward.

"But there was no bridge, of course, not even a ford, and the water was deep and wide and the current swift. Although the rotted, atilt piles of a dock of some sort still stood in the shallows, there was no trace of any boat, so I built a makeshift raft on which to carry my sword and baldric, targe, wallet, brogues, and bonnet, hampered in this effort by lack of any sort of real rope or thongs with which to secure the odd bits of warped lumber and green saplings which were my only available materials. Finally, I stripped bark from some of the larger trees and twisted it into a very inferior sort of twine, hoping that it would suffice.

"Alas, it did not. The raft came apart in mid-stream, and although I was able to grab my wallet and bonnet, all else not fastened to my swimming body was lost to me. The current in the main channel was much fiercer than I had guessed, and so I finally fetched up so far downstream that it took me more than two days to work my way through the trackless waste back up to the spot just opposite my original point of entry. There were piles in the shallows there, too, and a good-sized rowboat was drawn up half out of the river, but it was so rotted that the wood crumbled at the touch.

"A tiny ruined and deserted hamlet was clustered up the bank from this landing, too, just as on the opposite bank, and I stayed in it until I had exhausted the food resources, then set out along a weedy, overgrown track that meandered southeast—barefoot, with only a dirk, a small knife, a brass razor, a torn shirt, a faded tartan with its belt, wallet, and bonnet to my name, plus a stout staff which had recently been a sapling. Better for me, alas, had I been mother-naked.

"The brutal people who inhabit that portion of the Kingdom of Scotland, I discovered to my pain and sorrow, despise and abominate all those of the Highlands and Islands; my attire was that of just those areas, of course, the sett of the tartan identifying the wearer as come of one of the most hated ilks, Mac Ghillie Eoin, a sept of the Mac Leans of the Western Isles, such as had raided and ravaged parts of the Lowlands from time immemorial.

"I knew myself to be in the Lowlands, of course, but I had no knowledge at all of my precise location, and it was not until much later that I even realized that the river I had swum had been the River Clyde. A few days farther along the winding track, which had clearly seen little if any use in years, I came into yet another deserted hamlet, this one a bit larger than had been those back beside the river. Here the houses were mostly not so ruined and the small gardens had volunteered more vegetables, thus attracting more small game beasts, and so I was able to stop there for some weeks.

"Just the same as the previous two in which I had halted, this one seemed to be utterly devoid of artifacts, those not missing altogether having rotted into uselessness. However, on one occasion, while I was rooting among the sagging thatch of a roof in search of still-dry material to use for freshening my bed, what should come tumbling out but a tiny basket of wicker containing a rotted bag of rawhide and, inside it, a dozen or so copper coins and three small, well-clipped ones of silver. Oh, would that I never had found that cursed money, Ms. Foster."

With the Italian–Northern European Faction solidly mounted in the saddle, the reins firmly in hand, with the Spanish-Moorish Faction broken, shattered of any real power, all of their armed forces either become dust or having fled as fugitives the peninsula of Italy and the island of Sicily, Holy Roman Emperor Egon and his victorious hosts began to slowly, gradually withdraw from the ravaged, war-torn, but now unthreatened papal and allied states, bound for the Alpine passes which the melting snows had once more opened for passage.

Despite the fact that a large minority of the Imperial Army had consisted of mercenaries hired from all over Europe, and had marched and fought the length and width of the Italian peninsula—besieging, overawing, defeating field forces, subduing principalities of many and varying sizes, and, at last, pursuing, hunting, harrying, hounding the scattered remnants of the might of the Spanish-Moorish Faction and their allies and mercenaries into the sea or unto death—Emperor Egon and his noble officers had

seen to it that it had been for the time and the place
a relatively clean, minimally destructive war.

Himself a young, vital man, though a veteran of
many a hard-fought battle and long, grueling campaign as an officer of mercenary horse under the
command of his justly famous uncle, *Reichsherzog*
Wolfgang, who was widely reknowned as a great
captain in the classic mold, the Emperor had laid
down firm law to his mercenaries and vassals at the
very outset, whilst still his huge, conglomerate army
was camped in the southerly foothills of the Alps, in
the lands of his client state, Savoy.

"Gentlemen, captains, we are come south to right
wrongs, not to wreak more woe upon those not our
enemies. We, personally, would much liefer be biding back at our Eagle Palace with our Empress and
children than riding long, dusty, weary miles every
day, then laying our sore, tired body down in the
discomfort and reeking, foetid noisomeness of a
military camp every night. But are we to not see our
papacy pass irrevocably under the evil control of men
whose concepts are not those of true religion but of
grasping for more and more temporal power to the
detriment of emperor, kings, archdukes, dukes,
marquises, counts, barons, and even simple *frei-
herren*, we suppose, then a firm stroke must be made
and we are the only available power to strike that
blow.

"Nonetheless, you all and all your men, down to
the very lowliest muleteer, must understand: We are
not come with this host of ours to Italy as conquerers
or would-be conquerers of all the lands, cities, castles, and peoples. No, we are come rather to purge
out the elements inimical to the well-being of our
Church, her properties and cities and loyal allies.
For years already now, they have been ravaged and
looted and intimidated and abused by the armed
might of those who are their foes and ours and we

will not see our own force add to their woes by commission of similar outrages. Let that be abundantly clear to all who march under our banner.

"Casual looting, murder, and rape along the line-of-march will not be tolerated under any circumstances, for our baggage trains are long and complete and contain all the necessities, including plenty of strong rope for hanging transgressors against our stated wishes. If any come up with a new horse, fat pigs or fowls, fancy clothing or jewelry, he had better have a bill of sale or witnesses—a goodly number of them and all unimpeachable, too—or, noble, gentle, or common, he may well find himself dancing a jig upon the tightrope. Nor will it be advisable for any to make to gull us, for we have been long a soldier and in command of soldiers in foreign lands, we know well and of old every hoary trick and stratagem, and any who might think he has chanced upon a new one with which to hoodwink us might recall before so doing that although death is invariably quick, the approach to it can be made exceeding long and hideously unpleasant; we are certain that our Kalmyk bodyguards could show some rare skill in prolonging an execution if given their head in the matter.

"With regard to intakings, now: Every walled place, public or private, will be invited to yield, to contribute at least a token force to our numbers and cause as indication of goodwill. Those who do so are thenceforth our friends and there will be no depredations of any of their possessions or vassals. Those who do not . . . well, that is a horse of an entirely different color. Defiers will be invested then and there; our siege train is large, complete, and well supplied, and we have hired on some of the most accomplished sappers in all of Europe, so we doubt us that any city, any castle, will long stand against our might. All treating of any nature, however, must always be done prior to investment. Once any place has been invested, even if it then freely surrenders, it will be considered to have been taken by storm and will suffer accordingly.

"But ordained sacks must still be done according to our standards. There is to be no arson, and fires started by accident or prior bombardment must be immediately extinguished. Unless defended by armed might, residences are not to be slighted or unduly damaged to no account. Churches, church properties, churchmen and -women are inviolable under any conditions and the right of sanctuary will be assiduously honored on pain of death. Otherwise,"—he showed his strong, white teeth in a wolfish grin,— "it can be a normal sack, with all which that implies. As all of you know, or should know, to be especially cruel, brutal, in the first few such things on a campaign projected to be a long one will, if some of the sacked are allowed to escape into the countryside, either terrify the foe still to be met or harden him to meet us in the field rather than exposing his family to such. This will benefit us, for we are certain that there presently exists no armed force in all of Italy which could stand against our might and emerge the victor.

"There is one thing to be point out, however. You all are most certainly aware that at least three big-name slave buyers are come already to follow our arms into Italy, and more are certain to gather. There will be absolutely no kidnappings of peasants for sale to them by anyone. However, there is no such protection afforded the common, nonransomable inhabitants of places which chance to fall by storm, so you would be well advised to caution your fighters that the throat they cut for sport in a sack might, if left whole, have added a bit of weight to their purses, even if poor as a churchmouse; and before they merrily bash in the heads of the brats of the women they are enjoying, they might check to see how much the slave dealers are paying for them . . . the women, too, for that matter.''

The young Emperor's assessment of the qualities of the forces opposing him had been accurate; his well-organized, well-balanced army had never been defeated in any major battle. Also, after some notable, well-publicized intakings of walled places held by the Spanish-Moorish Faction or their supporters, no other cities or towns and precious few castle-fortresses had defied him; many had, indeed, sent delegations spurring hard to meet his vanguard as far as possible from environs of their walls to offer him conditional surrender and so escape siege, bombardment, slaughter, rape, pillage, torture, and slavery.

The efforts of King Giovanni IX of Naples, who had assembled a small but tough army and pushed up from the south to take the much beleaguered Spanish-Moorish Faction's reduced host in the rear, had been sincerely appreciated by Egon, but not at all necessary. The three significant meetings of real armies in the field had all taken place at or near rivers and were remembered by the names of those waterways—Tiber, Ofanto, Agri. All three were great, crashing battles in the grand tradition, and in them, Emperor Egon showed all the world that despite his relatively young age, he had learned well from his uncle and other military mentors.

The only encounter which might have been a close contest ceased to be such when the strong vanguard of the Neapolitan Army smote the Spanish-Moorish Army and its mercenaries in the rear, burned their wagon-laager, looted their camp, captured their baggage and siege train, then drove on to strike the rear of the already hotly engaged battle line itself. What might have been a decided defeat for the Spanish-Moorish Faction was thus transformed into an utter rout of their largest, best-equipped army and opened

the way for Egon to Rome. The pursuit of the van-
guished was long, vicious, merciless, and unremit-
ting. Nonetheless, enough escaped to form with their
more southerly-ranging counterparts a second army.

This one was brought to open battle one stifling
August day near to the banks of the Ofanto River.
Egon cleverly tricked them into leaving a well-drawn
and well-placed line of battle to attack an apparently
confused and ill-placed enemy, then butchered them
in detail. The murderous crossfire of cunningly concealed light cannon decimated the attack while still
it was far from the now-firm lines, his arquebu-
siers—employing the new, multishot weapons developed in England during the calamitious attempts to
subdue that land by the late and unlamented Pope
Abdul—poured fourteen volleys of thumb-thick
leaden balls into the attackers, and then, when they
had retired behind the ranks of pikemen, ranks
parted all along the battle line to reveal the grinning
mouths of larger field guns, all loaded to almost the
muzzlebands with grape and langrage and carcasses
filled with arquebus and caliver balls.

King Giovanni, by choice in command of the horse
for this battle, had been nibbling at the flanks and
rear of the attackers with his light horse, his heavy
horse being in the midst of their own running battle
against their opposite numbers of the foe. Hard on
the heels of the incredibly sanguineous impact of the
heavy-gun volley, he sent his reserve horse hard
against the right flank of the shaken line of attackers,
even as the Imperial foot countercharged with pike,
sword, axe, and pole weapons their battered and bemused enemy. Most of the survivors of this engage-
ment were those who had been so wise or so
cowardly as to flee prior to the worst of the carnage.

The battle on the Agri had been little more than
the valiant but vain attempt of a scratch force of the
Spanish-Moorish Faction to hold back the advance

of the Imperial Army and its now-legion force of new allies long enough for the bulk of the remaining faction to escape across the strait to Messina, through a gantlet of Genoan, Imperial, and other Italian Faction warships and galleys. These men fought hard, fought well, from carefully prepared and skillfully selected positions, and for the first time in an open battle of this campaign, the young Emperor had the blood banner uncased and borne the length of the lines, where all could see it and understand its grim message: *no quarter*, kill them all to the last man, succor no wounded, take no prisoners. No single man of any rank had lived of that defensive force when at last their vastly superior enemies had passed over the deathly-silent earthworks and moved on toward Calabria (which Moorish-held duchy King Giovanni long had coveted, restrained from taking it only by the awesome power of Rome).

However, due to a number of factors, mistakes and miscalculations on the parts of many, a significant enough number of the forces and leading men of the Spanish-Moorish Faction found their way out of Italy and into Sicily that the Archbishop of Palermo—Cardinal D'Este, one of the foremost of the Italian Faction—had the recently elevated Pope Sicola prevail upon the Emperor, the Savior of Rome and of all Italy, to land a significant force in Sicily and cleanse it, too, of the Spanish-Moorish foulnesses.

At that time, Egon and his army had already been on the march to or in Italy for more than two years, and he was anxious to return to his own lands and family soon, thereby curtailing the hideous expense of keeping his forces together, fed, fit, and fighting, for there had been—by his own commands—little enough loot or income from slave sales to help ease his financial burden. But neither did he like the idea of a possible regrouping of his foes on an island

which would, due to location and length of coast-
lines, be absurdly easy to reman, resupply, and re-
arm from either Ifriqa or any of the Spanish
kingdoms or caliphates; to do so might well see him
having to do it all over again in the near future.

He did send some troops—these mostly vassals,
landholders and their retainers—back north to cross
the Alps before winter closed the passes to them.
Most of the force, therefore, that he took into Sicily
were mercenaries or Italian allies. There was no
shortage of seaborne transport of any and every class
and no opposition to be expected on the sea, for the
Genoans and others had driven home to the Moors
the point that the waters around Italy, Sicily, Sar-
dinia, and Corsica were now most unhealthy for their
ships in any kind of weather.

The Count of Messina, after a protracted interdic-
tion of his trade by sea and several long-drawn-out
and very destructive cannonadings of his harbor defenses by the allied fleets, had raised his vassals and
thrown out the Spanish-Moorish officials and garrison, then declared Messina open to the forces of
Pope Sicola and His Holiness's supporters; he also
had prayed help of a military nature to prevent the
retaking of his city-port by the recently ousted enemy. He got it. Egon landed the bulk of his expe-
ditionary force there, ferrying them over from
Calabria, that duchy now held by King Giovanni of
Naples, held now with the blessing of Pope Sicola.

Prior to that landing, Egon had never before seen
or visited the island so loved by his distant ancestor
the Emperor Friedrich II Hohenstauffen, but after
the protracted and bloody and hellishly costly campaign he eventually won there, he entertained no
fond memories of the place. Indeed, he often after-
wards stated that he would be happiest if he never
again saw or heard of the place. He could be glad of
only one thing: that the casualties, the very stiff price

inflicted in the desperate battles of doomed men who fought with the savagry of cornered rats, had fallen upon his Italian allies and hired swords, rather than his own vassals. In the full year that had been required to stamp out the last remnants of the forces of the Spanish-Moorish Faction and their Sicilian abettors, the blood banner had been displayed more often than not, and the intakings had been many and exceedingly grim, especially so in the south and southwest of the island, those areas wherein the general population was ethnically of a mostly moorish cast.

Of the mercenaries he had brought down from the north, some had fallen dead or wounded in Italy, far more had fallen in Sicily, and most of those who remained had, with his assent, been speedily hired on by various of his Italian allies, this in preparation for the soon-to-be-commenced battle royal for chunks of Sicily. Egon himself, recognizing a good market when he saw one, also got good prices for cannon, other firearms, polearms, siege trains, supplies of all sorts, armor, draught beasts, wheeled transport, horses and mules, and almost anything else of his dissolving forces that would bring him a profit.

After the great public fetes, receptions, acclamations, and parades which marked his return to Rome, when he and his nobles all had been heaped with honors and blessings, thanked and praised to the very skies by everyone except the prisoners in the dungeons, sat in attendance at torturings, maimings, burnings, impalements, and more inventive or novel executions of more prominent officers of the defeated faction, then he saw his few remaining thousands mounted and began the march back north, moving as fast as he could without unnecessarily tiring marching men or horses and without giving needless offense to those along the way set upon expressing their gratitude of his aid against and final victories over the oppressors.

As it developed, he and his force and trains did get through the passes ahead of the snows . . . but only barely. They progressed from higher mountains down to lower mountains, from lower mountains down to the foothills, they passed from out the fiercely republican cantons of the Switzers onto Empire lands, marching directly into a new war.

The Elder met with two Younger Ones on a tiny pinpoint of rock set in the midst of the raging sea between Scotland and Ireland, a rocky islet that was visited only by seabirds and the occasional seal. Three of the silvery carriers, their lids open, reposed a few inches above the rocks, guano, and shards of old birdshell, their bulks and protective fields giving the men some measure of ease from the lashing winds and the spray, their soft, greenish glow affording the only light on the dark, stormy night.

Addressing one of the Younger ones, the Elder said, "Now that you once more have a carrier and its gear, you should depart York and return to your station to await orders. Before you ask, I will say that I have journeyed to our place in the east and they have not yet been able to trace any of the three missing carriers; if they still are on this world, then they are either exceedingly well hidden and not in use or they are in some place so far out of the way that it has been thought needless to search it, ere this."

The other Younger, he not being addressed, said diffidently, "Your pardon, Elder One, but perhaps some of these beings who were projected here by the primitive meddlers or some of the meddlers themselves stole away my carrier and the third one. If it was the meddlers, then they might well have taken the carriers back to their own world and time."

Gently, but with clear admonishment, the Elder replied, "Younger One, seek you wisdom or you will remain a Younger One for much longer than you might wish. Those more elder than I have been conducting the search. Think you that they have not scanned the entire area of the meddlers? Of course they have . . . and found no identifiable vibrations of a carrier-brain. As for those poor persons their primitive, ill-designed equipment threw here from out their own milieus, it is my opinion that none of them are possessed of the mental and emotional sophistication to learn to use one of even these simple carriers properly; even the best of them, alas, are little more advanced than the native peoples here resident. The one you serve and observe, Younger One, the old man in York, now, he is of the milieu of the meddlers, and one such as he just might possess the requirements to understand and eventually to even master one of our simple carriers and its capabilities, but those earlier, more backward men and women, no. The thought is ridiculous.

"No, I mean not to frighten or alarm you, but merely to bid extreme caution for an indeterminate time. The eastern elders are become of the impression that the carriers may have been seized for whatever occult purpose by the Others, because on two different sweeps, now, the sensors detected indications of one of Them, fleeting impressions both of them, but nonetheless unmistakable."

"Why?" asked the other Younger, a bit plaintively. "Elder One, why can't They, why don't They, let us alone here? We are hurting this world and its people in no way; we have been very careful to introduce no single anachronism of our time and world into this one. We have sent out many of our own people round and about this world to observe and listen and be certain that nothing of us gets to any race or group of the natives. We are only taking minerals from out-of-the-way, unpopulated, almost un-inhabitable places here and there, in deserts, mountains, and swamps. It would be so much easier for us if only They would go back to their own time and world and leave us alone here.''

"You, too, must learn wisdom, are you to ever advance, Younger One,'' was the Elder One's patient reply. ''There is simply no fathoming of the minds or the motives of Them, for They are as far above us as we are above the meddlers, or even farther. We can only be assured that They have Their reasons and that we must abide and obey Them, for They could crush us with as little effort as this.'' He picked a bit of weathered eggshell from near his foot and powdered it between his horny, sinewy fingers.

Kogh Ademian was seated at the workbench in his basement shop patiently crimping, one after the other, the skeet shells he had just as patiently reloaded when his eldest son, Arsen, came through the door, closing it behind him. With a smile, the older man said, "Oh, hello, son. Be with you shortly." Then he finished the work, wiped his hands on a dingy towel, and swiveled around to face his visitor, by then seated on a battered footlocker.

"Papa," asked Arsen, "how much did Ademian net last year?"

Kogh frowned, scratched the shiny scalp under his thinning hair with a work-blackened fingernail, and replied, "Hell, son, I don't know those figures . . . not exactly, anyway. I'm just the fucking chairman of the board. But the comptroller would know. Want me to call Greenberg? It's late, sure, but . . ."

Arsen shook his head and chuckled, "No, no, Papa, it's not that important, but then tell me this: How much did you, personally, knock down last year, huh?"

The older man just shrugged. "For that I'd have to call my accountants, Arsen. I don't know, I've never had a need to know in years; I let Byrd, Bradley and Baum handle everything, that's what they get paid for, you know. But look, son, you need cash or anything, you just tell me how much and I guarantee you I can get it . . . here, tonight, even, if that's what it takes. It's more than just one fucking safe over at the complex, you know, and . . .''

The younger man nodded. ''We'll get back to that in a minute, Papa, but what I was getting at is this: With as much money as you have, not to mention the billions on billions of rounds of small-arms ammo in the various Ademian warehouses *or* the ammunition manufacturing plant Ademian owns in . . . where is it, Papa?''

''It's four plants, Arsen,'' Kogh answered, ''but only one in the States . . . and we don't own it, only part of it. What about it?''

''What about it? This, Papa: Why the hell do you have to reload your old shotgun shells?'' demanded Arsen. ''Shitfire, you could shoot off brand-spanking-new factory loads until hell froze over or your barrel curled down and never notice it, so why waste your evening and weekend free time doing this shit, like some poor middle-class slob trying to save enough money to buy a new hunting hat?''

Ademian Senior picked up a leather cigar case from where it lay on the work bench, fished a small knife from out a pocket, opened it, took a hand-rolled, illegal Cuban cigar from the case and began to lick down the wrappings and otherwise prepare it for the lighting while he spoke. ''Why, Arsen? Because I want to, that's why. If that ain't a good enough fucking reason, Mr. Smartass, it's because doing things like this relaxes me, gets my mind off all the shit that's all the time going down every day at the complex.

''Besides, factory loads just don't shoot the same as the ones I do myself, don't pattern right a whole lot of the fucking time, even the custom jobs I used to get done for me. If you want something like thishere done right, do it your fucking self. Your grandpapa used to say that same thing about black-smithing work, too, Arsen, but not''—he grinned a little sheepishly—''necessarily in those exact words.''

After a brief, visual check to be certain that no gunpowder or primer containers lay open or uncovered, Kogh took the thick cigar gently between his lips, ignited a wooden kitchen match with a thumbnail, waited until it ceased to flare, then entered into the long, painstaking ceremony of evenly lighting the smoke. After he had dropped the butt of the match into a water-filled butt can and had taken a long, luxurious puff on the mild, very odorous cigar, he nodded. ''Now, what can I do for you, Arsen? Or did you just come to smart off and ride my ass, huh? Listen, your Uncle Boghos and Aunt Mariya do mor'n enough of that fucking shit already. Listen, was it up to them two health freaks, I wouldn't be smoking nothing or drinking anything 'cept mineral water and carrot juice and living on raw veg'tables and broiled fish and chicken breasts with no skin and not even any fucking salt, f'r crap's sake. They want me to start up double-timing like a fucking boot ever morning, like Boghos does, that and lifting weights like those musclebound faggots you can see at the fucking Y.

''You know what a good cook your Aunt Mariya used to be, son? Well, she ain't no more, hell no! Those two, they live on fucking cow-chow, mostly, anymore, and they've both gone and got skinnier even than the pictures you used to see of the poor fuckers the Krauts and the Nips had in their prison camps in World War Two. My sister, she use to be a damn good-looking woman, but she looks like one them scarecrow Noo Yawk models now, anymore—no tits a man can see easy and hipbones you could hang your fucking hat on sticking out both sides of her. If old Boghos is still shagging her, I don't know how come he ain't flat ruptured himself on all those bones, boy!''

He luxuriated in another long puff, then grinned evilly. ''And with all his fucking fitness shit and all, Kogh Ademian is sitting here tonight enjoying himself after a good dinner, smoking a damn fine cigar, and the smartass fucking Dr. Boghos Panoshian is laying in a bed in Henrico Doctors' Hospital with a concussion, a face that looks like he took on a pro boxer or three, one arm in a cast, and strapped-up ribs. *Heheheheh!''*

Knowing his father's rare but dangerous rages of old, and well, Arsen began, ''Papa . . . ? Look, you know Uncle Boghos and Aunt Mariya mean well, want the best for you, and . . . look, I know they get to you sometimes, they used to get to me, too, and to their own kids, too. But . . . but, Papa . . . you didn't beat up on Uncle Boghos . . . ? Did you?''

This time, Kogh Ademian really laughed, laughed until tears were pouring down his cheeks, laughed until he was forced to lean back against the work bench for support, laughed until he had dropped his loved cigar unheeded and was holding his aching sides with both of his hands, gasping for air.

At length, when he once more could breath normally, when he had wiped the tears and perspiration from his face (at the same time, streaking it with black dirt from the towel), when he had picked up the cigar and puffed it back to life, he told his son the story, now and then unable to repress a chuckle.

''That fucking know-it-all, my esteemed brother-in-law, Dr. Boghos Panoshian, who really looks anymore like a *real* starvin' Armenian, for all that he's worth almost as much as Fort Knox is and the damn AMA has given him a fucking lifetime license to steal and mint money, that fucker that can't stand to think somebody somewhere might be eating good, drinking good, and smoking a good smoke, he took to double-timing—'jogging,' he calls it. Okay, fine, he wants to run his skinny ass off when he ain't seeing how much pig iron he can lift up or in his fucking Olympic-size swimming pool that's heated or batting a tennis ball around on his private courts with my sister, no fucking body should ought to object. Right? Right. He owns enough land out there to run himself to death on, if that's what he wants to do. But that ain't what the fruitcake wants to do, Arsen. Hell, no, it ain't.

"He owns as many or more cars as I do, but the crazy fucker, he took to *running* the six miles to and from his West End office, ever day. Come rain or mud, come shit or blood, here was that fucking lunatic asshole in a vest shirt and swimming trunks and basketball shoes, suntanned as dark as a high-yeller nigger, running on River Road and Cary Street Road and College Road and Patterson Avenue."

"During rush hours, Papa? As narrow as the roads are?" asked Arsen, unbelieving. "Is he suicidal?"

Kogh shook his head slowly. "You know, when I found out what he was doing, I asked him that, too. He come back at me with thishere pure Grade-A shit about how he paid taxes and road fees, too, so the roads was as much his as anybody's, and since pedestrians have the right-of-way in Virginia, the cars would all just have to slow down until they could pass him and maybe some of them would fin'ly take to leaving their cars at home and running with him. Arsen, he use to be a all right guy, years ago, but he's a looney tune, anymore; anymore, he hates cars as much as he hates red meat and booze and tobacco and anybody else having a good time 'cept by his rules, his nutty rules. Honest, Arsen, I think my sister is married to a real, lockupable crazy man. He's wrote long letters to Washington and the governor and the fucking newspaper saying that cars and trucks and airplanes and any kind of guns should ought to be made illegal for anybody to own or use 'cept of the army and the police and ambulances, maybe. He thinks everbody else should oughta be made to go everwhere by running or riding bicycles. He thinks the gover'ment should oughta be throwing people in jail for selling red meat or liquor or tobacco, just like they do for selling dope, f'r crissakes! You ever hear shit like that laid down before?''

"Whew!" commented Arsen, feelingly. "He really is off his nut, Papa. But what happened to him to put him in the hospital and all? A car hit him?''

Kogh guffawed again. "Better'n that, son, better'n that. Okay, here he was running along right at the edge of the blacktop on River Road outside of Richmond city limits, where it curves all the time and it's all them little hills and all. The road is two-lane and narrow as hell, to boot, and the poor, fucking drivers is all blowing their horns at him and cussing him, prob'ly, and taking godawful chances to get past him so they can get to work on time.

''Then, somewhere away back down the road behind of him, comes the sound of a sireen, getting closer ever second. Okay, now he's a fucking doctor, so he might've thought it might be a meat wagon, right, and got off of the road and up on the shoulder there, so the cars could get out of the way faster, or at least pull far enough over to make a lane in the middle of the road. Oh, no, not Boghos. He allowed later he had built up his 'pace' and didn't want to stop, and, besides, the shoulder was muddy. He just kept right on double-timing, happy as a hog rolling in shit, breathing the way his kind of crazies breathe when they're getting their rocks off that way, with the cars passing him by the skin of their teeth.

''Then along comes thishere dump truck with a load of shale, with a Goochland County Rescue Squad meat wagon right on his tail. He says he blowed his horn, nearly blowed the guts out of the fucker at Boghos, but for all he could see it done Boghos might've been doped up or deaf. So just then the driver seen a opening in the cars coming the other way and he pulled to the left and floorboarded it. But the leading edge of the bed fetched Boghos in the shoulder and knocked him ass-over-biscuit into the ditch, and along right there, the ditch was concrete-lined and the slabs weren't even account of the winters and he landed mostly on his face and chest.

"Of course, the meat wagon stopped and loaded him in, too, and took the both of them on to the fucking hospital. I'm just hoping and praying that now they got him in a place can a whole lot of doctors look at him and talk to him and listen to him, they'll some of them find out how nutty he is and put him someplace and get him and his crazy shit the fuck out of my hair while I still got any hair left, is all."

Arsen sighed. "Don't count on it, Papa, and don't try holding your breath till they lock Uncle Boghos up, either. Medical folks don't do any kind of a decent job policing their own ranks, you know—that's why there're so damn many shitty, half-ass, inept or alcoholic or dope-addict doctors still crippling or killing their trusting patients. Besides, I heard the new thing is to just let nuts out of institutions, anyway, turn them all loose to be as nutty as they want to be with nobody to control them or take care of them. Don't ask me why, and don't ask the psychiatrists why, either—the reasons they all give make you wonder why they aren't locked up themselves.

"But, Papa, back to what I came for tonight. How much will about twenty-eight pounds of silver, about nine ounces of platinum, and maybe twice that much titanium cost, do you think? There's some other stuff I'll need, too, but I think most of it if not all of it is in your big lab at the complex."

"Hell, Arsen," declared Kogh, "I don't know anything about stuff like that. Last I heard, silver—bulk silver—was selling for five, six dollars a ounce, but it's going up with all this Ayrab-oil shit going on. I think platinum is a little more than gold a ounce, but I don't know and I doubt I could get firm figures before Monday morning, either. Titanium I don't know shit about. Why?"

"I need to make something else in your lab, Papa," replied Arsen. "The carrier has told me how to make it and what I'll be needing to make it and how much of what it'll take to make it. The gold I've got, but the rest of it you'll have to get for me, here.

"Look, you see if you can get the stuff for me. I'll write out a list and leave it with you. Then I'll take to projecting the carrier directly into your private office at the complex every night until I find you there with the stuff. Okay? But Papa, I need to get that stuff and build the device soon—the sooner the better. A whole lot of things for a whole hell of a lot of folks depends on getting it finished and operative, *soon*. You couldn't begin to imagine just how much is riding on it. And not just in this world, either."

ABOUT THE AUTHOR

Robert Adams lives in Seminole County, Florida. Like the characters in his books, he is partial to fencing and fancy swordplay, hunting and riding, good food and drink. At one time Robert could be found slaving over a hot forge, making a new sword or busily reconstructing a historically accurate military costume, but, unfortunately, he no longer has time for this as he's far too busy writing.

For more information about Robert Adams and his books, contact the National Horseclans Society, P.O. Box 1770, Apopka, FL 32704-1770

Ⓞ **SIGNET SCIENCE FICTION** (0451)

FROM A TIME OUT OF LEGEND . . .

comes Robert Adams' *Horseclans* Series.

☐ **A WOMAN OF THE HORSECLANS (Horseclans #12).** The frightened girl who Tim Krooguh had rescued from certain death was destined to become a living legend among the Kindred, a fighter whose courage would rouse the clans against a foul and dangerous foe . . . (133676—$2.95)

☐ **HORSES OF THE NORTH (Horseclans #13).** "Kindred must not fight Kindred!" So said the ancient and unbroken law. But now, clans Linsee and Skaht were on the brink of a bloodfeud that could spread like prairie fire throughout the Horseclans. Could even Milo smother the sparks of hatred before they blazed up to destroy all of the Horseclans . . . ?

(136268—$3.50)

☐ **A MAN CALLED MILO MORAI (Horseclans #14).** In an effort to heal the rift between the feuding clans of Linsee and Skaht, Milo must take the assembled sons and daughters on a journey of the mind to a strange and distant place . . . back to the twentieth century! (141288—$2.95)

☐ **THE MEMORIES OF MILO MORAI (Horseclans #15).** Ancient treasure and sudden danger await Milo and the Horseclans in the heart of a long-dead city, where the heirs to a legacy of violence lie waiting to claim the men and women of the Horseclans as the final victims in a war that should have ended hundreds of years ago. . . . (145488—$2.95)

☐ **TRUMPETS OF WAR (Horseclans #16).** Now that chaos reigns there, can the undying allies of the High Lord's Confederation reconquer their war-torn lands? Or will traitors betray Milo's warriors to a terrible doom? (147154—$3.50)

☐ **FRIENDS OF THE HORSECLANS edited by Robert Adams and Pamela Crippen Adams.** For over ten years, Robert Adams has been weaving his magnificent tales of the *Horseclans*. Now he has opened his world to such top authors as Joel Rosenberg, Andre Norton, John Steakley and others hwo join him in chronicling twelve unforgettable new tales of Milo Morai and his band of followers. (147898—$3.50)

Prices slightly higher in Canada

Buy them at your local bookstore or use this convenient coupon for ordering.

NEW AMERICAN LIBRARY
P.O. Box 999, Bergenfield, New Jersey 07621

Please send me the books I have checked above. I am enclosing $_____
(please add $1.00 to this order to cover postage and handling). Send check or money order—no cash or C.O.D.'s. Prices and numbers are subject to change without notice.

Name_____

Address_____

City _____ State _____ Zip Code _____

Allow 4-6 weeks for delivery.
This offer is subject to withdrawal without notice.